The Aerial Valley

IN THE SAME SERIES

The Aerial Valley
and Other French Utopian Fantasies

translated, annotated and introduced by
Brian Stableford

A Black Coat Press Book

ISBN 978-1-61227-435-5. First Printing. October 2015. Published by Black Coat Press, an imprint of Hollywood Comics.com, LLC, P.O. Box 17270, Encino, CA 91416.
Printed in the United States of America.

TABLE OF CONTENTS

Introduction

Le Vallon aérien ou Relation du voyage d'un aéronaute dans un pays inconnu jusqu'à présent; suivie de l'histoire de ses habitants et de la description de leurs mœurs, signed "J. Mosneron, ex-Législateur," here translated as "The Aerial Valley," was originally published in 1810 by J. Chaumerot.

The author, whose full name was Jean-Baptiste Mosneron, Baron de Launay, was born in 1738 in Nantes, the son of a ship-owner who made his money in the slave trade. After studying law in Paris he returned to Nantes to practice, and did a good deal of work for the family firm, while pursuing his literary interests as a sideline, albeit with a considerable degree of interest and intensity. His early work was mostly done for the theater, and remains unpublished, but he also published a French translation of *Paradise Lost*, a biography of John Milton and several other items of non-fiction, plus two novels.

Following the French revolution, Mosneron was appointed as a delegate to the new Legislative Assembly in 1791 and was sent to Paris with a specific mandate to defend the slave trade against possible prohibition by a government ostensibly committed to the rights of man. The artful speech that he made in that cause—probably not without a certain amount of risk— became his most notorious work; it was published in a number of places and can now be read on-line. He sat on the right of the Chambre and opposed the execution of Louis XVI, in spite of the fact that his Protestant family had absolutely nothing for which to thank the Bourbons; that was certainly not without risk. He was arrested and imprisoned during the Terror, but he escaped execution and was released when Robespierre fell. He came back to the legislative assembly after Bonaparte's coup overturned the Directoire but did not remain there for long.

7

Mosneron's combative tendencies are displayed in both of his novels, the first of which, *Memnon, ou le Jeune Israélite* (1806), was the first of numerous French fictional accounts of the life of Jesus, carefully stripped of any miracle-working—a project calculated to cause offense to devout believers, but carried out with the author's typical care and craft; the other writers who repeated the project subsequently included Alexandre Dumas and Félicien Champsaur. *Le Vallon aérien* might be reckoned a trifle mild by comparison, and also somewhat disjointed—its numerous chronological inconsistencies might well stem from an attempt to stitch together several different fragments into a more-or-less unified whole—but it is nevertheless notable within the rich history of French utopian fiction as one of the most readable, as well as one of the most conscientiously self-doubting works of that kind. Although it follows a relatively orthodox basic line in suggesting that a utopian society can only maintain stability if it is carefully technologically limited and sternly isolated from outside influences, and must at all costs resist the disruptive effects of technological progress, it examines that proposition with an even-handed approach that scrupulously gives consideration both sides of its principal arguments—as only a lawyer accustomed to considering both sides of a case might be expected to do.

The patchwork account of the "aerial valley" and its inhabitants is awkwardly-structured, involving a number of different narrators as well as a hypothetical "editor," who adds his own quibbling footnotes to those supplied by the account of the aeronaut who rediscovers the valley after more than a century of near-total isolation, but the eccentric product is nevertheless successful in building up a mosaic account of the circumstances that led the founders of the fugitive society to flee from France, the evolution of the society and its politics, and the reasons for its commitment to continued isolation. The balance of that detailed and multi-sided consideration is sufficiently dutiful to introduce an interesting thought-experiment into the story, in the form of the importation into the rigidly

stable and naïve society of a well-meaning but subtly dangerous outsider, whose endeavors serve to test both the resilience
and the justice of the story's fundamental assumptions. That
inclusion also helps to make the plot of the story more enter-
prising and more robust than is commonly the case in utopian
fiction.

As a modest anti-progressive utopia *Le Vallon aérien*
cannot be reckoned, with the aid of hindsight, to be in the
mainstream of the development of French utopian thought, but
it is interesting as one of the more eloquent arguments for the
"anti-euchronian" case, and one of the most sensitive chal-
lenges to the philosophy of progress as an instrument of perfectibility.

L'An deux mil huit cent, ou Le Rêve d'un solitaire, first
published as a pamphlet in Tours in 1829, and here translated
as "The Year 2800" is, by contrast, a euchronian work in the
tradition of Louis-Sébastien Mercier's pioneering *L'An deux
mille quatre cent quarante* (1770; tr. as *Memoirs of the Year
Two Thousand Five Hundred*), but it serves to illustrate the
fact that the nascent genre remained only marginally influ-
enced by the notion that technological progress would be an
essential component of social progress for some considerable
time, basing its anticipations of future improvement almost
entirely on social reforms.

The booklet is listed by the Bibliothèque Nationale as an
anonymous work, although it bears the signature "Turrault de
Rochecorbon" at the end of the text. That signature also appears on one other text of the period, similarly published in
Tours, the three-act comedy *L'Épreuve de l'amour* [The Proof
of Love] (1827), and Turrault appears to be a moderately
common name in the département of the Indre-et-Loire, in
which the commune if Rochecorbon is located. The work's
utopian scheme is unremarkable, but it is interesting as one of
the few works of that kind published between the fall of Napoléon I and the July Revolution of 1830 which created a consti-
tutional monarchy; it imagines its reforms firmly within the

9

context of what might be described, if the term were not oxy-moronic, as a modified absolute monarchy.

Paris en songe: essai sur les logements à bon marché, le bien-être des masses, la protection due aux femmes, les splendeurs de Paris et divers progrès moraux tels que chambres de transactions, justice à trois degrés, tribunaux d'indulgence et pardon, honorariat du commerce, parlement de paix by Jacques Fabien, here translated as "Paris in Dream" was first published as a small book in Paris by Dentu in 1863. The signature is surely a pseudonym, but there does not seem to be any published indication as to who the person behind it might have been; it might well have been one of Dentu's regular authors, as it would have been an odd book for that publisher to issue while the Second Empire was still going strong, and its censors were still active, even though the text employs a conspicuously soft pedal in its treatment of government. It is also a relatively lively and well-written work, which suggests that the author was no novice.

As with Turrault's work, Fabien's fits solidly into a euchronian tradition that had achieved a degree of dominance by the 1860s, especially with regard to specific examinations of the future of Paris, greatly encouraged by the ongoing endeavors of Baron Haussmann, who was busy remodeling the city in accordance with a utopian design. That exploit inevitably occasioned a great deal of discussion as to what the consequences of the remodeling might be, and how the scheme might be carried forward beyond Haussmann's particular plans. Fabien's version is one of the most elaborate, although the author restricts himself to the kind of modifications that Haussmann might have embarked upon had he had the inclination and the support of the relevant political will.

Although it is not anti-technological in the way that the hypothetical inhabitants of the Aerial Valley decide to be, and nor is it oblivious to technological change, as Turrault de Rochecorbon seems to be, Fabien's utopian dream is rather remarkable in its particular skepticism regarding the potential social value of electricity, in the contemporary applications of which it suspects a lurking catastrophe. For that reason, it differs significantly from most of the other visions of future Paris produced during the Second Empire.

The succinct account of "L'Avenir" by Victor Hugo, here translated as "The Future," is much more typical of the general run of future-Paris texts of the period. It was the first chapter of the great man's introduction to a guide-book produced for visitors to the Exposition Universelle of 1867, although most surviving copies of the text date from 1869, when the guide was reprinted as a book for sale to the general public. It was published while the author was still living in exile in the Channel Islands, having refused to return to Paris—in spite of the offer of an amnesty—while Napoléon III was still in power.

The invitation to the exile to write the preface to a guide book to one of the principal showpieces of the emperor's reign might be reckoned a trifle unusual, but Hugo was universally recognized as the greatest writer in France, and by far the most appropriate individual to sing the praises of an Exposition Universelle staged in Paris. In any case, the futuristic vision is not unduly revolutionary in its suggestions, and it seems unlikely that the political censors saw any occasion to interfere with it, especially in view of its nationalistic fervor, which anticipate Paris being elevated in the twentieth century to the capital of a unified Europe.

That same suggestion is reiterated in *L'Amour en mille ans d'ici* by Gustave Marx, a humorist better known under the pseudonym A. Vémar, and here translated as "Love a Thousand Years Hence." The item in question was published in several parts in a reprint periodical called *L'Omnibus* 1889, but must have appeared previously in another periodical, almost certainly in 1873, which is the date of composition implied by the text, and corresponds more closely to the period when the author was in the most productive phase of his career.

The misleadingly-titled story is a satire of the glut of utopian accounts of future Paris, perhaps penned with both

"Jacques Fabien" and Victor Hugo in mind, as well as earlier high-profile contributors to the subgenre such as Théophile Gautier and Joseph Méry; it is written with tongue firmly in cheek, although not all the commentators on the recent ArchéoSF reprint of the text seems to have noticed the fact that it is a deliberate farce.

As is normal with satires, the deliberate exaggeration goes far beyond the standard routine of possibilities featured in the earnest utopias of the period, although not all of the supposedly ludicrous possibilities still seem as absurd today as they would have done in 1873, and several seem distinctively conservative, especially in the matter of their chronology. The satirical wit also helps, of course, to make the story more readable than many of the works that it is parodying, and the narrative is conspicuously buoyant by the standards of the futuristic fiction of the period.

Marx's account of the future is remarkable in several ways, perhaps most particularly for its charmingly absurd account of the exploration of the solar system by travelers unreeling long metal cables behind them in order that all the planets—except, for some unstated reason, Mars—can enter into communication with one another by telegraphy. As a utopian fantasy it stands in exceedingly sharp contrast to *Le Vallon aérien*, although the intermediate texts in the present anthology offer an approximate series of stepping-stones illustrating the process of literary development that connects the two texts, adding an intermediary patchwork to the internal collages of the two parenthetical texts, and thus enabling the whole of the present volume to be a trifle more than the sum of its parts

The translation of *Le Vallon aérien* was made from the copy of the edition reproduced on the Bibliothèque Nationale's *gallica* website. The translation of *L'An deux mil huit cent, ou Le Rêve d'un solitaire* was made from the copy of the Goisbault-Belebreton edition of 1829 reproduced on *gallica*. The translation of *Paris en songe* was made from the copy of the Dentu edition reproduced on *gallica*. The translation of "L'Avenir" was made from the version reprinted in the Kindle edition of Philippe Ethuin's ArchéoSF anthology *Paris Futurs* (2014). The translation of *L'Amour en mille ans d'ici* was made from the Kindle edition of the 2012 ArchéoSF reprint.

Brian Stableford

Baron Jean-Baptiste Mosneron de Launay: *The Aerial Valley*

(1810)

Editor's Preface

The discovery by Monsieur de Montgolfier, the most extraordinary of the discoveries of the eighteenth century, has not had any useful result. The research of scientists and the expectation of the public have been equally disappointed; aerostatics, which ought to have procured enlightenment regarding the higher regions of the atmosphere, assistance to commerce and services to military art has only offered an astonishing spectacle, and the ascension of a balloon only seems appropriate henceforth to figure in fêtes, as a very singular, very curious but utterly sterile showpiece.

Such, at least, has been the general opinion of balloons for some time. The scientists, despairing of extracting veritable fruit from their endeavors, have renounced their use, and Monsieur Blanchard, parading his spectacle from one capital to another, enjoys his glory with regard to the public purse without competition.[1] In the depths of Gascony, however, living in the greatest obscurity, there is a skillful aeronaut who had found perhaps the only means of rendering his ascensions useful. Monsieur de Montagnac floated in a balloon over the Pyrenean chain, making a map of the mountains, sometimes stopping on summits inaccessible to Ramond, Humboldt and

---

[1] The pioneering aeronaut Jean-Pierre Blanchard was killed in March 1809, so Mosneron's text was presumably written prior to that date.

Saussure,[2] and made profound observations relative to geology, mineralogy and botany.

He studied the gradations of temperature of the atmosphere, relative to altitude, and had even recognized regular air currents and periodic monsoons. But that modest man and veritable scientist did not want to make the public party to his discoveries until he was perfectly certain of their reliability. Departing from Perpignan and heading toward Bayonne, he had only traveled over half the chain in the space of eight years, because he repeated the same observations several times and was often obliged to wait a long time for the light air current favorable to his direction.

When he had completed his excursions and Aerial studies over the Pyrenees, he planned to repeat them over the Alps; it was at the end of those difficult endeavors that the public was to collect their fruit. The work that would have resulted from them would doubtless have been epoch-making in the history of nineteenth-century discovery, but death took that estimable scientist by surprise in the little village of Saumède in the middle of the Pyrenees, where he had come down after a third ascension over Maladetta.

I was then on holiday in those mountains, and had made the acquaintance of Monsieur de Montagnac there. The conformity of our tastes for the same study, which is the most powerful as well as the most agreeable of bonds, had brought us together from our very first meeting. The extreme amiability of his society had tightened our friendship, and if the death of that man of genius is an irreparable loss for the sciences, it will be a subject of eternal regret for my heart. He bequeathed me all his papers, giving me the freedom to dispose of them as I thought appropriate, but he recommended to me particularly the account of his voyage to the Aerial Valley. That voyage continually came back to his memory; it was the object of his

---

[2] The references are to the Pyrenean explorers Louis Ramond de Carbonnières (1755-1827), Wilhelm von Humboldt (1767-1835) and Horace-Bénédict de Saussure (1740-1799).

most tender affections. I am, therefore, merely acquitting a sacred debt in publishing this account. I have left out everything pertaining to mineralogy and botany, because the scientific endeavor of which those studies are a part will form the subject matter of a separate work, which I hope to publish after this one.

Relation of my voyage to the Aerial Valley

I had perceived in one of my recent ascensions a group of mountains arranged in a circle, in the middle of which I suspected the existence of a plain of considerable extent. Before rising up over that part of the Pyrenean chain, I wanted to know the name that had been given to the place, and whether it was inhabited. I therefore went to the foot of the mountains and sought enlightenment from the shepherds who came to establish themselves there in the summer with their flocks.

They told me that the interior of the enclosure was as deep as the mountains were high, that nobody had ever been able to penetrate it, because all around the exterior there was a perpendicular rampart, as smooth as ice, but that everyone knew that the enclosure was the dwelling of a company of sorcerers who, if they were not true devils, at least had a close relationship with Hell. It had been observed that every time that hail fell, a frost or some other baneful accident, some of those sorcerers were seen laughing uproariously on the ramparts of the enclosure, which made it evident that they had sent the scourge.

That was the only information that I could get out of those poor herdsmen. It would have been pointless to try to disabuse them: "Man is ice to verity, but fire to lies."[3] Those lines have a universal application, and it seems, given the interest that such fictions inspire in all classes of society, that they are necessary to the human mind; it often by invention alone that it can prove its thought, and the greater part of the human race would be reduced to the state of imbecility if truth were the only source from which he could extract his ideas.

I concluded from the opinion of my shepherds, shared by all the inhabitants of the region, that the interior of that group

---

[3] The quotation comes from Jean de La Fontaine's fable "Le Statuaire et la statue de Jupiter" (tr. as "The Sculptor and the Statue of Jupiter").

of mountains merited examination. On the tenth of July I took advantage of an almost absolute calm to rise up to their height. Floating at a height of several hundred toises[4] above that basin, it was easy for me to see humans with the naked eye, but as soon as they saw me they fled and disappeared—which would have been quite sufficient, had I had any doubt in that regard, to persuade me that those people had no relationship with the infernal empire. However, when I descended to the ground after having opened the valve to let a part of the gas out of my balloon, I armed myself against any eventuality before emerging from my nacelle, with two pistols and my saber.

All the objects surrounding me presented the image of civilization; at my feet were cultivated fields planted with various species of grains; on the hillsides there were herds of various animals, bushes, followers and a garden. Toward the middle there was an aggregation of cabins aligned in a regular order. Amid that apparent population, however, there was the most profound solitude; even the pastors guarding the flocks had disappeared, and nothing remained in the fields under cultivation but a few agricultural implements that attested the presence of humans.

Following the path that led toward the cabins, I felt gripped by a violent anxiety. Who were the inhabitants of this place, unknown to the rest of the world? Brigands, perhaps, or murderers, who had only been able to find that refuge in order to hide from the law. What was going to become of me in the midst of them, alone, without help or protection? Those peaceful flocks, however, and those innocent crops announced mild mores. Agricultural peoples are sociable and good; only those bloodthirsty men who live by hunting and carnage are ferocious.

---

[4] Prior to 1812, a toise was six feet; it as redefined at two meters when France adopt the metric system, but that was after the publication of the present text.

Meditating these various thoughts, I arrived in the village. All the doors were closed and I could not hear the slightest sound. Among the cabins I distinguished one that was larger and more ornate than the others. I thought that if there was any humanity in the place, it might be found preferentially in the home of the individual who seemed to have the most wealth, and consequently the most enlightenment. I therefore went to knock on that door, which, like all the others, was only closed by a simple wooden latch.

It opened, and I felt penetrated by confidence and veneration at the sight of a tall and handsome man wearing a long beard, who said to me, with an affectionate smile: "My brother, you have run a great danger, and we were very fearful ourselves of that huge monstrous animal that held you in its claws. It is doubtless dead, since you are alive."

After these words, and without waiting for a reply, the patriarch took me by the arm and drew me outside the house. His wife and two children followed him.

When he was to the steps in front of his dwelling he sounded a horn, which was suspended by his side, three times. At that signal, all the inhabitants emerged from their cabins and arranged themselves in a semicircle around the perron. Meanwhile, they often turned their heads to look in the direction of the balloon, showing evident signs of fear.

"Speak now," said my guide, who appeared to be the chief of the people. "Tell your friends whether you are quite certain of having killed the monster that carried you hear, and whether there is anything more to fear from it."

I tried to make them understand that my balloon was only an insensible machine, absolutely incapable of doing any harm to anyone, but, perceiving that a great deal of anxiety still remained, I implored them to follow me in order to reassure themselves with their own eyes.

When I had returned to the machine and I had touched it and had the boldest among them touch it on all sides, they passed from an excess of fear to an excess of license. They all strove competitively to get inside in order to trample it. I hastened to prevent the consequences of such bravado, by making the chief understand how important it was to me that the machine should not be damaged.

Then he described a great circle around it, at a distance of three paces, and forbade everyone to step over it, instructing the mothers to keep watch on their children.

When all subject of fear and disquiet had disappeared on either side, I devoted myself to an examination of my new hosts. All the men seemed to resemble Apollo and all the women Venus, by virtue of their beautiful form and noble stature; but the bounty painted on the faces of the former replaced the pride of the serpent-vanquishing god, and all the features of the latter expressed innocence and candor, instead of the cunning and coquetry of the goddess who was the lover of Mars.

That external beauty, so general among the two sexes, had to have a common cause, and the aftermath of my observations convinced me that it was principally the result of internal perfection. Others have remarked, as I have, that good families distinguished by a long filiation of hereditary virtues are mostly characterized by a beautiful face, and at the very least by a benevolent face. If there are exceptions to the rule, they only relate to a few individuals, and not to the races that conserve, so long as the marked influence of the moral over the physical, the harmony between the soul and the body, does not degenerate.

The population I had before me was redolent of something ancient and patriarchal. I seemed to be looking at the first descendants of Adam grouped around their chief, before the fall, before Cain had troubled the innocence and peace of the earth.

They only comprise a single family; they call one another by the affectionate names of "brother" and "sister," as in the earliest times. The chief has the authority of virtue over them, which, only deployed for the happiness of the people who are submissive to it, draws so much strength from the love that it inspires. He is, in consequence, their common father; all his decisions are sacred laws, because he never wants anything except to make them happy.

The power of the chief is sanctioned by God himself. He is His representative on earth; it is in the name of the Supreme Being that he announces his decisions. Thus, it is from God himself that all laws emanate; He is present in all thoughts and all actions. In a word, it is theocratic government, but very different from that of Moses, for it commands neither the sacrifice of animals nor the massacre of humans, and is as gentle as the other was terrible.

One thing even more astonishing than the purity of morals in that corner of the Pyrenees is the education: the accuracy of intelligence and the correction of the language common to all the inhabitants. What an incredible phenomenon! In the middle of a country that seems to be three centuries behind the civilization of the rest of France, where men who are still savage only speak a coarse patois limited, like their ideas, solely to the expression of physical needs;[5] in the most rustic region

---

[5] Author's note: "The inhabitants of the Pyrenees, very different from the Swiss, the Auvergnats and the Savoyards, are constantly attached to their ingrate mountains. One does not see them, like other mountain folk, emigrating at certain times of year to procure a more abundant substance. Accustomed to a meager and hard life, they prefer the deprivation of poverty to the ease that they might obtain by excursions outside their territory. Whence comes that character peculiar to the inhabitant of the Pyrenees? It seems to me that it is the result of its isolation. For eight months of the year, the greater part of the mountains is devoid of communication with Spain for want of practicable roads, and with no other relation to France that that which its mineral waters can procure, so that the mountain folk are almost perpetually separated from the whole world. The means of putting the region in society with France would be to give birth to a branch of commerce, and I think a rich one might be found in the establishment of a few factories. Running water falls everywhere, and several mountainsides

of the country, which one would have thought on seeing its enclosure to be only appropriate to serve as a refuge for eagles and bears, people exist who are mild, virtuous and amiable, to an extent that none similar is any longer found on earth.

In order to form an idea of them it is necessary to have recourse to what is most marvelous in history and fable. Imagine a select society from the beautiful century of Louis XIV, having escaped the contagion of the following century, in which mature reason has replaced the politeness of the lips with that of the heart, and flashes of wit with the ever-even light of common sense. Such is the people of the Aerial Valley.

Although it is difficult to avoid a hint of enthusiasm in making the description of such a people, it is nevertheless faithfully traced from nature. The imagination might well seek

---

contain mines of different metals that were once exploited successfully. Recently, the Germans have established at Bagnères de Luchon a cobalt factory that might have become very precious; it was directed by the Comte de Beust, now ambassador to a German court. The Revolution wrecked that establishment, but it would be all the easier to reactivate it because some of the necessary buildings still survive. Communication with Spain would be practical all year round if a few of the gaps in the mountains that serve as limits to France, which are usually closed by snow and ice for eight or nine months, were flattened. The construction of a few roads in that part of our frontier might be obtained without it costing the public treasury a sou. It would only require the income from the mountain forests and mineral water to be applied to it for a few years, and the taxation of the privilege of gaming casinos that are established during the watering season, if the Government sees fit to let those sources of corruption and death subsist near the salutary springs of the Pyrenees. The use that would be made of them would then serve as an antidote to the poison of gaming." The cobalt mine to which the author refers was established in 1784.

to embellish a few strokes of a painting when one copies it, but none have been added here that are not in the model. I cannot be accused of exaggeration when I am restricting myself to the literal expression of what I have seen, and that is what I am doing, religiously, and I will consent to the application of *mentiris impudentissime*, if my colleagues, the aeronauts who make the same voyage, do not confirm this account.

After what I have just said about the degree of civilization of that people, it is not a great marvel that every individual knows how to read and write. If I were writing a romance I would add that there is a paper factory in the country, a printing press and authors, but, as a faithful voice of the simple truth, I will say that for want of paper, of which they make no use, given that they do not manufacture it, they make use of parchment to write, and that the entire library of the country is composed of a hundred volumes printed in Paris between a hundred and thirty and a hundred and fifty years ago, that none of those of the eighteenth century[6] are known, and that the only new books are manuscripts that have been composed in the place.

Those books are a political and moral catechism of which there are as many examples as inhabitants over the age of twenty, for everyone is obliged to make a copy as soon as he has reached the age of reason. That catechism contains rules of conduct for everyone, which, not being inspired by nature, relate to the conventions and proprieties of the society. Thus the reciprocal obligations between fathers and children are not included therein, because they emanate from sentiment and it would be to misunderstand sentiment to make it a duty.

Religion furnishes the text of the first and principal chapter of that catechism. That religion is, as I have said, essential-

---

[6] Author's note: "It is quite probable that after the threat issued by the chief of the colony, which will be found at the end of this account, no other aeronaut will expose himself to the risk of a voyage into the Aerial Valley."

ly theocratic. The chief, being the representative of God, combines the two powers, temporal and spiritual. He it is who, every morning, intones the canticle of praise and homage to the Supreme Being, which all the people repeat after him. He then prescribes the different tasks to which each one must devote himself in the course of the day.

In every place that a man might be, and whatever his thoughts and actions might be, he is continually under the gaze of God. The chief may, when he pleases, sound the horn that he alone has the right to bear; at that signal, all the people, without exception, quit their tasks and addressing their homage to Heaven in common. That homage is renewed before the commencement and after the end of every meal, and after the end of the working day. Sundays, the annual feasts instituted for different causes, birth, marriages and funerals are all celebrated by hymns, religious songs analogous to the subject of the ceremony.

That is the only worship, the only external action of the religion of the people; and I would add that none more pious has ever appeared on earth. The Roman Church has no saints purer, and their virtues seem, like their abode, to be situated between heaven and earth placing them while still alive at the rank of the angels.

Such is the summary of the first chapter.

The second chapter deals with the authority of the chief, the obedience of the people and the reciprocal obligations of each to the other.

In the other chapters, the mode of elevation to the rank of chief is fixed. It is hereditary for men alone, and by order of primogeniture.

There is a council of elders, which assembles twice a week, and without which the chief can order noting new or deviate from the habitual rule. The same council is responsible for making an examination of the life of an individual who has just died and of drafting, in conformity with that examination, the inscription that is engraved on his tomb. It is the council that, conjointly with the chief, fixes every year the extent of the lands to be cultivated and the kinds of grain to be sown there, for there is no distinct property; everything is common, with the sole exception of persons, lodgings and clothing.

But the people are not the only ones whose conduct is regulated; a strict law also applied to that of the chief. Since the archangel Satan abused his power, everything demonstrates that there is no creature, however perfect it might be, that is not able to exceed the measure of its power, if that power does not have limits and overseers who can make them respected. All instances of usurpation of authority and despotism are foreseen in the catechism, and reprehension thereof is confided to the council of elders.

Furthermore, one can say of that people, with much more reason than Tacitus said of the Germans, that mores take the place of laws there. The isolation of that fortunate refuge of virtue guarantees it against the contagion of vice, and if a few faults have slipped in there inseparable from humanity, slight corrections suffice to repress them.[7]

---

[7] Author's note: "I doubt that there has ever been a time when humans existed in isolation, wandering the earth without family, domicile of fatherland. A celebrated Writer has made the history or romance of the human species in the first period of its creation; he found many virtues therein that were really only the absence of vices, and said: 'Man is good, only men are wicked,' As no monument exists that establishes that humans such as he conceives them ever existed, one can neither affirm not deny that presumed bounty; but that men are wicked, that passions, vices and crimes are born in the bosom of societies, nothing is more certain; and I also think, like J.-J., that those passions and vices become more energetic as societies become more civilized. An admirable problem, therefore, would be to find a social organization such that humans enjoy the advantages of a perfectly civilized society without experiencing its inconveniences. Now, it is that problem that I find completely resolved in *The Aerial Valley*. The great passion that kills the societies of the world, ambition, is not found in

I am limiting myself to this summary because I have brought away a copy of that singular catechism, which I shall have printed separately in its entirety, if that is desired.[8]

The other book, also in manuscript, contains the annals of that people from the origin of its establishment to the present day. That one is not as widespread as the first; the chief and the members of the council are the only ones who have a copy of it. They were kind enough to give me one, which I shall transcribe after this relation.[9]

I shall resume the description of my new discovery.

That canton of the Pyrenees was once known by the name of the Valley of Mambre; it is now the Aerial Valley. The population that inhabits it has almost doubled in the hundred and thirty years since it settled there and has been living there entirely unknown to the rest of the world. Men wear full length beards; their hair, similarly long, is gathered and attached behind. Their clothing consists of a straw bonnet or hat, gaiters, culottes and a waistcoat, and in winter an overcoat. Those garments are in wool woven in the valley. The clothing of women consists of a skirt, a corset and a mantilla in winter.

---

that one. All the individuals are perfectly equal and have no motive to aspire to any distinction, for there are no riches, no honors and no powers to distribute. All are equal and always will be, whatever the difference in personal merit might be; the governor is the only one who enjoys any authority. Consequent to J.'J.'s principle, all men here, like his man *par excellence*, are good and excellent. [Note by M. de Montagnac]"
"J.-J." is Jean-Jacques Rousseau.

[8] Author's note: "That work would certainly be very curious to know, but Monsieur de Montagnac must be mistaken, for it was not found among his papers. [Note by the Editor]"

[9] Author's note: "These annals are printed here in the order that Monsieur de Montagnac designed, but only in fragments. A few notes will explain why the work has not been printed in its entirety. I have divided it into chapters in order to render the reading easier. [Note by the Editor]"

Their long hair is plaited into braids beneath a straw hat similar to that of the men. The shoes of both sexes are rope sandals like those worn on all high mountains.

They have two meals a day, one at eleven o'clock in the morning and the other at seven o'clock in the evening. For aliments they have excellent bread, very well baked, trout, eggs, vegetables and meat only twice a week, but their favorite food, of which they make their principal nourishment, is the dairy produce that is so delicious in the mountains. Their beverage of choice is water, or a small beer that they succeed in making very good. Raspberries and strawberries, so perfumed in the Pyrenees, grow abundantly in the valley, but our other fruits do not do as well there, including the grape, which I only saw in small quantity, either because they were unable to or did not want to multiply the production of vines sufficiently to make wine their habitual beverage.

They take their meals together, in groups of about a dozen, without distinction between relatives and others. A similar confusion was commonplace among the Spartans in their public tables, but the objective was not the same. Lycurgus wanted by that means to weaken the love of fathers for their children and children for their fathers, in order to harden the hearts of both and render them impassive, and consequently more appropriate to the harsh métier of war. The legislator of the Aerial Valley proposed, on the contrary, to extend to the whole population the attachment of family members to one another, in such a fashion as really to make a single great family; and, if one judges by appearances, he has succeeded perfectly, for it seemed to me that all the inhabitants were brothers and sisters in sentiment as they were by name.

All those mountain folk appeared to me to combine with their beautiful forms a healthy and robust constitution. I saw several octogenarians in a condition to support the fatigues of agriculture every day. The only malady that I judged liable to make considerable ravages in the new colony is smallpox. The majority of faces were scarred by it, and I learned that there had been periods of malignity when the scourge had harvested a quarter of the population.

I then informed the governor about the recent discovery of vaccine;[10] I explained the numerous advantages to him, and as I always carried fresh vaccine with me, I offered to employ it on a few children of the colony, informing them at the same time of the means of multiplying the remedy and extending it to all the young. I tried in vain, however, to persuade him of the bounty of that preservative; I would not have been able obtain permission to make any application of it if several fathers who had lost some of their children to smallpox, still fearing for those that remained, had not strongly supported my request.

I am far from criticizing the obstinacy of the governor in rejecting the vaccine, when I think about the long difficulties that inoculation experienced in becoming established in Europe. The first impulse of nature is to reject a certain evil, whatever hope there might be that the evil might procure good. Only experience can educate in that regard, but it requires a thousand facts to destroy an accredited prejudice. The remedy that I introduced will soon become known; its good effects will be too evident not to ensure its triumph, and I enjoy in advance the deep satisfaction of having extirpated the principal scourge of that beautiful abode.

Although my curiosity was very pressing, and I asked a host of questions, the good mountain folk did not appear importuned; they replied with a great deal of mildness and clarity—but to my great astonishment, that curiosity was not reciprocal. Not only, contrary to my expectation, were they quite insouciant regarding the country from which I came, but they even avoided talking about it.

I attributed that indifference to the inferior world, which sometimes went as far as aversion, to the memory of the mis-

---

[10] The smallpox vaccine was developed by Edward Jenner in 1798; the discovery was publicized throughout Europe by 1800 but remained controversial for some years thereafter.

fortunes that their ancestors had suffered. There were still several individuals in the Aerial Valley whose fathers had lived in that world. They had painted it in colors so black that they had made it into a kind of Hell. Such was the tradition of the Valley, which will become even stronger as it grows old, with the result that, in a century or two, the entire world will be inhabited, according to them, but nothing but devils. The Valley will be the sole refuge preserved from the infernal flames, where a few elect can live peacefully while awaiting their passage to the immortal life of the celestial empire.

All the intellectual faculties, raised to the high degree of elevation that I observed among the people, however, supposed a great depth of curiosity, for science can only be born of a desire to know; but what would have been difficult for me to define is that the principal object of the curiosity of the Valley's inhabitants was the knowledge of the stars. Indifferent to everything that was happening on earth, they were avid to read what happens in the sky; they knew its map quite well; they distinguished the planets; they followed their movements; they had calculated with the greatest precision the apparent revolution of the sun, and their year corresponded exactly with ours.

The same study was common to those ancient nomadic people, such as the Chaldeans, who, living in peace with the entire earth, only sought to make conquests in the vast field of the stars.

One can also remark that all the great astronomers have had the same peace and quietude: Copernicus, Galileo, Newton and our Lalande. The latter, in spite of his opinion of creation, surely very immoral, was the best of men.

The telescope that they used for observation was very imperfect. Since the time of its construction optics had made great progress. I offered them an excellent telescope that I carried with me on all my Aerial voyages. They accepted it with great pleasure; they were amazed by the new astronomical discoveries to which I introduced them.

They were also occupied with the study of agriculture, and the part of botany that has for its object the knowledge of plants salutary in different maladies. That branch of medical knowledge, the only one that nature has indicated to the animals, and which suffices for them to ward off or cure their ills, also suffices for those people, who live a simple and frugal life exempt from any species of passion, only subject to maladies common to all beings that receive existence, and the seed of death therewith.

Only the arts might have been capable of reconciling the inhabitants of the Aerial Valley with the earth. The kinds of art that had been transmitted to them by their ancestors were mostly as in the time of their invention. A few others had been discovered since. The improvement of the former and the invention of others excited their admiration.

They showed me the watches of the founders of the colony, which had stopped a hundred and forty years ago,[11] entirely broken down and without movement, and asked me whether we now had anything better. By way of reply I showed them the two that I carried; one of them was a Berthoud marine watch, the other a Breguet, a repeater indicating the day of the month, fitted with a second hand, etc.[12]

The governor could not contain his joy at the sight of those precious effects; he immediately took them from my hands and suspended them in his room. He also appropriated my barometer, my thermometer, my compass and a few other instruments useful to my voyages. In acting thus he was only following the received custom of the Aerial Valley, where everything, in general, is common and no distinct property is recognized. However, my gaze, fixed with astonishment on

---

[11] We subsequently learn that the valley was settled after the revocation of the Edict of Nantes in 1685, so this figure of 140 years is clearly mistaken. The chronology of the story contains several other significant anomalies.

[12] Although both names are misrendered in the original the intended references are obviously to the watchmakers Ferdinand Berthoud (1727-1807) and Abraham-Louis Breguet (1747-1823).

his, recalled to his mind that our customs were very different from his; then he wanted to return everything to me, a little confused by his action, but I hastened to restore his tranquility by making him a present of them.

The time for the evening meal having arrived, I sat down at table with the governor, his family and a few inhabitants of the Valley, who were all invited successively in their turn, unless some fault excluded them for a time from the chief's table—and that punishment was the most sensible that could be inflicted.

Fish, vegetables, dairy products and strawberries composed the supper. The dishes and other utensils of that kind were made of a clay very convenient for that usage, found in a gorge in one of the mountains. The beverage was a rather agreeable small beer. I had a few liqueurs in my nacelle but I carefully refrained from offering them; that is the sole wealth of our world that would have been a misfortune for that one. If their reason would not have been troubled by it for the moment, the privation of that tender beverage would at least have prepared for them a future of impotent regrets.

Some time after the end of the supper, the air was filled with the most beautiful concert that I had ever heard in my life. It was the evening canticle, sung in chorus by all the inhabitants gathered together. A celestial modulation married the voices of the mountain men, naturally strong and harmonious, with the soft and fresh voices of their wives. An accident augmented the solemnity of the religious song even further; the evening had been stormy and the thunder rumbling in the distance came closer by degrees; it seemed to be the voice of the Divinity, applauding the homage of His beloved children.

Nothing disposes one better to peaceful sleep than beautiful music. Before separating in order to enjoy it, we entertained ourselves for some time with the majestic storm that had provided such a beautiful bass to their concert. I told them that, thanks to new discoveries, that meteor was no longer redoubtable on our earth. They heard with a great deal of interest the history of the celebrated Franklin's lightning conductors. That instrument would have been absolutely useless in their Valley, for it was unknown for lightning ever to cause the slightest damage there. All the phenomena of electricity, or galvanism, in general, and of physics, that I recounted to them captured their imagination and admiration no less vividly.

My bed had been prepared in a room next to that of the governor. Music and songs appropriate to the birth of the day, as those of the evening were to its end, terminated my slumber agreeably. After having saluted the governor, I proposed a walk to him. The purity of the air, the calm of the sky and the perfume of the mountains inspired a mild serenity in all the senses. It seemed to me that I had been transported to the creation of the world, and into that place of delights where the course of time is only marked by the variety of pleasures.

"Ah!" I exclaimed. "This is paradise!"

"You're right, my friend," said the governor, "but the difference between our paradise and Adam's is that vanity caused the first man to leave his, and it is to the wickedness of your forefathers that we owe the fortune encounter with ours. Here, our species has raised itself up again from its original fall. Here, it has recovered the advantages that it had lost, and of which you are deprived. We are in the first rank of beings for our happiness as well as our intelligence, while in your degenerate world you are only above the animals by your knowledge; they are less intelligent, but they are happier than you. A strange reversal produced by your passions! The noblest of creatures is the most unfortunate."

"Yes, that's a certain fact. Our world has remained under the effect of the curse. The faculty of recalling the past and seeing into the future, which augments the happiness of the virtuous man, is the torture of the guilty. It would be better for him if he were limited, like an animal, to the enjoyment of the present. I thought once that the progress of civilization and enlightenment would contribute to the amelioration as well as the improvement of the human race. Experience and reflection have disillusioned me."

"My friend," said the governor, "your opinion was just and you were wrong to change it. Enlightenment raises humans up and ignorance degrades them, but it is necessary for that effect that the enlightenment should be permanent and that the entire mass is penetrated by it. The inconstancy of your governments does not permit that stability. Today you have a king who protects literature and the sciences; he is replaced by another, who only has a passion for conquests; a third succeeds him, devoid of character, taste and ideas.

"From that continual change a superficiality of mind results, incapable of piercing the truth. One takes instead of it a few seductive illusions, a few deceptive lights, which one follows and goes astray. Better the ignorance that remains in the same place—but let study be constantly followed, and let the torch of science always shine with the same light, and you will see the human species march with a slow but steady pace toward perfectibility. It is to that sole advantage that we owe what astonishes you.

"All the intellectual faculties with which we are endowed have been constantly directed toward our happiness. It is to that sole objective that they ought to tend; such is the intention of nature in according them to us—and it is to render oneself unworthy of her favors to occupy one's time with speculative studies that produce no useful fruit, even if one is assured of having the greatest success therein."

Everything that I saw announced to me that, indeed, the happiness of that people was not like ours, a rapid flash of lightning that shines and is almost immediately extinguished in the midst of dense and long darkness. There, it begins with life and only finishes with it. Work, far from interrupting it, is a new pleasure.

That work, intermingled with smiles, agreeable speech and joyful songs, is a living image of that which occupied our first forefathers in their magnificent garden, according to the beautiful description of Milton. It contributes similarly to savoring the voluptuousness of repose and the delights of a salubrious meal.

Throughout the summer that meal is taken in the open air, on a carpet of flowers on the bank of a stream, in the shade of an avenue of linden trees that snakes alongside it across the meadow, and forms a bed of verdure parallel to that of the waters.

The elders, tottering under the weight of the years, are carried by their children to the rustic banqueting-hall. They arrive in triumph, and everyone rises to their feet as they approach. The small quantity of wine that is harvested in the Valley is reserved for that last period of life, when the chilled blood has need of auxiliary warmth. The worthy elders rediscover in the beneficent liquor a few memories of their youth; they recall the old song that accompanied the dance of their time.

When the meal is finished, other pleasures succeed that of the feast. All the people deliver themselves to the amusements that are most to their taste; some form dances whose steps are marked out by joy; others play various games, either of exercise or skill. In all those frolics, a decency reigns without study and without art. Virtues are so natural among the people that it would cost them more to detach themselves from it than it costs a corrupt people to practice it.

It is thus that all the days of the inhabitants of the Aerial Valley go by. Enjoying a labor devoid of fatigue and a repose devoid of idleness, their felicity is far superior to that of the celebrated valley of Tempé, whose pastoral monotony must conceal many moments of ennui.

I have said that all that good people lack is a knowledge of the sciences and arts of Europe. When the conversation turned to that subject, the governor observed to me that any novelty of that kind could only be communicated to his brothers after being submitted to examination and obtaining the approval of the council. In perusing the annals that he communicated to me, I saw that the law in question had been motivated by the extreme danger that the society had run in receiving into its midst a stranger named Renou and adopting some of his opinions.

The governor was only animated by the desire to make his brethren happy, but, rendered circumspect by the example of the past, he asked me to tell him frankly what I thought myself about the result of our learned acquisitions.

"Have your scientists," he said to me, "improved any of the five human senses? Have they discovered and new enjoyment? In brief, have their endeavors augmented the portion of happiness measured for our species?"

"Alas," I replied, "of the three great discoveries made in the last two thousand years or so—to wit, the compass, gunpowder and printing—the first two have only served to depopulate the earth; only the third has enlightened it.

"All the science of our astronomers has only, as yet, succeeded in making a good almanac; that of our physicists of knowing the relative weights of substances; that of our chemists of decomposing them. Beyond that, all is doubt and uncertainty.

"Thus, the arts and sciences that are so vaunted attest to a very high degree of intelligence, but have been, in general, more harmful than useful. It is not the same in literature. Beautiful eloquence, sublime poetry, faithful depictions of history, touching reveries of the imagination, the great thoughts of philosophy, at least console our evils, if they do not prevent them. Our life is most often a path between two precipices; instead of wasting time filing in the abysses, is it not better to hide them from view by extending carpets of flowers to either side?"

"In all times and all countries," the governor said, "the culture of the sciences has preceded that of literature. Things go before words, and it is only after having thought that one can improve the art of explaining thought. It would appear to me quite astonishing, therefore, if the century following that of Louis XIV had not produced great litterateurs. I would be charmed to know them."

"The century of Louis XIV," I replied, "has been followed not by the century of Louis XV but by the eighteenth century; for it is only great kings who give their name to their century, and that century will, in fact, be eternally celebrated by its litterateurs. Those who have principally honored it are four in number: Voltaire, Buffon, Montesquieu and J.-J. Rousseau.

"The first was a tragic and epic poet, a historian, a moralist and a writer of romances; in brief he exercised all the strings of the lyre, and all in an original and interesting manner. However, he only appears in the second rank of epic poets when he is compared to Homer, Tasso or Milton; in tragedy when compared to Racine; in history if one reads him after Robertson;[13] among moralists when one recalls Montaigne or La Bruyère; and he only occupies the first rank when it is a matter of ordering those of frivolous poets. But one thing that will always win him a large number of votes is his talent as an observer, in depicting mores, in grasping the consequences of historical events, and distributing therein an amiable and instructive philosophy. In all his writings, including the most frivolous, he interests by the art of furnishing a text with the chatter of men of the world and the meditations of thinkers. He seems by virtue of that the author of all Ages and all tastes.

"Another writer has enriched with the most brilliant style the history he had made of all organic creatures. Humankind is the first link in the chain of those beings. The historian of nature covers all the species; he grasps with a sure hand, in the physiology of each one, the features that are common and those that are particular to them. What an admirable enchainment from the most intelligent animal to the one that seems only akin to an insensible pant! The genius of the great naturalist is deployed, above all, in the high station from which he contemplates nature. It is from there soaring above creation, that he unfurls the magnificent tableau before our eyes. Thus, the savant geographer, in raising his thought above the terres-

---

[13] The Scottish historian William Robertson (1721-1793).

trial globe, ceases to perceive the petty divisions of provinces and estates traced by the human hand, no longer seeing anything but the great masses of nature, the seas, the continents, the islands, the principal rivers, designs their lineaments and contours with exactitude, and encapsulates the entire earth in the circumference of his compass.

"What Buffon did for natural history, another author has carried out for civil history. A new Oedipus, he has divined the enigma of the obscure and barbaric laws that once governed several great peoples. What patience, to examine their codes, buried under the dust of centuries! What sagacity, to penetrate through that rubble to discover the primitive disposition of the materials and the motive that directed them, to discern the parts of the edifice that were sagely ordered and those which sinned by some hidden vice, in order to render the faults of the fathers useful to the children, to draw the lessons of experience and instruct people in the science that touches them most intimately: that of living in society in the manner most appropriate for them to be happy!

"That labor, on the principles that have governed the different nations, had been prepared by another, on those which have raised to the highest degree of elevation the sovereign people, and on the causes of its decadence. History is filled with individuals born on a throne or in the ranks of the vulgar who have made great conquests, but where can one find elsewhere than among the Romans an entire people conquering by means of a political system, constantly followed for more than ten centuries? The event is almost prodigious, and for nearly two thousand years one has only been able to admire it. Montesquieu cast a glance over that phenomenon, unique on earth; immediately, the prestige vanished; but the admiration perhaps only increased, in relating the effects to the simple and natural causes that his book has revealed. Thus, the construction of the church of St. Peter in Rome is less astonishing than the imagination of the architect who, in tracing the plan of that edifice, foresaw what it would be when it was finished.

"Alongside those masters marches a man who combines the most profound knowledge of the human heart with the greatest talent for expressing the passions. No one has equaled him in the depiction of love, of its voluptuousness, its storms, and the succession of its pains and pleasures. Endowed simultaneously with an exquisite sensibility, a strong conception and a fortunate facility in embracing several different subjects, from the smallest details of domestic life he has risen to the highest questions of politics and morality. Everything is embellished under his pen. His eloquence is seductive in itself; it sometimes draws him to sustain the most absurd paradoxes; he goes astray, without a doubt, and believes in good faith that the entire world, except him, is outside the path of truth. That prodigious magic of style won him a host of enthusiastic partisans at first, especially among women and young men, but gradually, sage people have dissipated a part of his charm. However, J.-J. Rousseau still retains a fine portion of glory. Education owes important reforms to him; and if no one was, with as much intelligence, more unhappy during his life and more castigated after his death, tender spouses and good mothers will hasten to console the ashes of their friend, and cover with flowers the tomb of the man who occupied himself with so much care to sowing them beneath the feet of their children."

"According to the picture you have given me of the great men of the eighteenth century," the governor said, "I see that they have had one great advantage over those of the seventeenth. Style was formed when they were writing. They have made use of it to ornament science and render instruction agreeable. Undoubtedly they have only had admirers among you."

"The Pradons and Cottins did not have critics more bitter.[14] A time will come when merit will be put in its place, and

---

[14] The names of Jacques (or Nicolas) Pradon (1632-1698) and Charles Cotin or Cottin (1604-1681) were frequently grouped together for the purposes of collective denigration in this plu-

when sane men will render it a dazzling homage, but at the moment, the sages are silent; it is only stupidity that makes a noise."

"What cowardice!"

"You're too severe. Remember that we have barely emerged from a revolution that had struck all the pillars of society. Everything was broken or overturned at the same time. In politics, it is anarchy that has seized empire; in morality, crime; in literature, bad taste. Since the appearance of the man of Providence, everything is gradually returning to order; a just government has replaced the absence of laws, principles of honor have distinguished the citizen; common sense will have its turn; unreason and impudence will have to return to dust."

"What are your honest men saying and doing while waiting for their day to come? What, in sum, is your public spirit?"

"There is none any longer, and that's quite natural. The inhabitants of a country in which the most violent earthquake has just burst forth, remain nonplussed, immobilized by far and terror on the edge of the abyss that has engulfed thousand of their fellow citizens, for a long time."

"I understand," said the governor. "Your nation is enfeebled; the revolution has accelerated its final phase, and now everything there is exhausted."

"Everything except for the military spirit."

"That is an admirable thing. The end of empires is generally announced by softness and cowardice. Yours, on the contrary, after twelve centuries of existence, is returning to the point from which is departed. If that is sustained, France will become a second Roman Empire; the entire world will be submissive to her. Can the sciences and literature also be regenerated in her bosom? Without that, her glory will be sad and catastrophic."

---

ral form during the 18th century, by Jean-Jacques Rousseau among many others

"Don't worry. The man who is renewing the political bases of Europe will be able to reignite the torch of genius. Already, crowns of glory are suspended in the arena, soliciting in all parts the competition of athletes; the first combats will doubtless not be signaled by a great celebrity, but soon the favorites of Mars will become those of Minerva, and literature, after long days of sadness and mourning, will reappear more brilliant than ever."

While I was speaking, the governor was observing the height of the sun. "Now," he told me, "it's time for today's council meeting. I'll leave you in order to go to it. Continue your walk; I'll come back to join you as soon as I'm free."

As I went up the hill I saw several groups of children, who appeared to be hunting for strawberries, and who ran toward me as soon as they saw me. As they came close to me, they reached out their hands in a suppliant manner.

I thought at first they were requesting alms, and, although somewhat surprised to find beggars here, I gave them a few coins, but on seeing them smile and throw the money away, I reflected that they had no idea of its value, and that, in consequence, it could not be money but sugary sweets, of which I had already taught them the value, that they were requesting from me.

All the children combined with the grace of their age a generosity that does not always accompany it. Several of them could scarcely walk, some had been taken from their cradles; the strongest took turn carrying the latter, the others being led by the hand. The most amiable benevolence animated all of that charming youth. It was the spring of a year of the Golden Age.

Baskets full of perfumed strawberries were presented to me by the boys; the girls were behind them and scarcely dared allow themselves to be seen. Gradually, their childish modesty vanished, and those timid Galateas, after hiding behind the willows, gradually became emboldened and ended up giving lessons in boldness to their little companions.

When the children had become more accustomed to me, I wanted to obtain from their ingenuity some enlightenment regarding domestic mores. No sooner had they understood me than they hastened to compete in satisfying my curiosity. The chatter, often interrupted but never disputed, passed from one mouth to another, merrily. It was unending on the love that they had for their parents, the evidences of tenderness that they received every day, their veneration for the Supreme Being that they were already beginning to perceive above them, and on their profound submission to His sage laws.

I was moved to tears by the naïve expression of those sentiments. In the middle of the touching scene the governor arrived. His face changed when he saw the children surrounding me, and in a severe tone he ordered them to go away.

Astonished by such a sudden alteration, I thought I glimpsed the reason for it, and I could not hide it.

"You've come from the council," I said. "Is my presence here beginning to cause them some anxiety?"

"Not exactly."

"They can be reassured; I'll leave today."

"I hope, Monsieur, that you won't refuse us a favor in return for the hospitality that we have accorded you."

"What is it?"

"That of not saying, when you return to your own country, that you have found us—or, at least, remaining silent as to the geographical location of our refuge."

"For fear, apparently, that we might come to conquer it. I can't help laughing at your terror."

"I warn you, in any case, that the first balloon that appears over our heads will be received with a volley of arrows."

"Would you like me to inform France of your declaration of war?"

"Whatever you please, if you are indiscreet. Observe, however, that we have no intention of attacking, but only of defending ourselves if we are attacked."

We were at the bottom of the hill when he finished that remark. I suppressed the emotion that it excited in me, thinking that Monsieur Renou's conduct justified that of the council. At first I had been received with open arms, and I would doubtless still have enjoyed the same confidence if my hosts had not recalled the lesson of experience. That lesson had been terrible, and it would have been inexcusable for them not to profit from it. However insulting to me the council's decision was, therefore, I could only approve of it, and hasten to submit to it by going to work on the preparations for my departure.

A good deal of gas still remained in the balloon; I could easily augment the volume with air rarefied by fire. While its ascension was being solicited by that procedure, I put into the nacelle the plants that I had discovered in the Valley, with the manuscripts and a few curious objects that had been give to me.

I could not take my leave of my hosts without bursting into tears. They were equally emotional, and expressed to me several times how distressed they were by the harshness of the law that experience imposed upon them.

Without that terrible lesson in misfortune, I might perhaps have settled among them. Oh, with simple and placid tastes, how would I not have cherished the only place on earth where a man has no need of a fortune to be esteemed and where all hearts, strangers to hatred, are only full of benevolence and love?

Oh, without a doubt I shall keep the secret that has been imposed upon me of the location of that last refuge of innocence. It is only to convert it to the Christian faith that its conquest would be undertaken, for it possesses only virtues, without a particle of gold or silver, but by announcing themselves to study the mores of its inhabitants, our learned missionaries would infect them with theirs; they would spread in the source of the generations of that Elysium the terrible poison that devours the population of our modern Babylons.

Those reflections accumulated in my bosom at the moment of quitting my hosts, and I shouted:

"Adieu, worthy inhabitants of a celestial land; adieu, people truly cherished by God. Persist in your sage severity, reject without pity the reckless who attempt to violate your refuge. You deliver yourselves now without fear to the desires of nature, regulated by reason; your chaste spouses know no other pleasures than their duties; your modest daughters listen to no other lover than the one who is to be their husband; you have neither masters not slaves, and you are exempt from pride as from baseness.

"Everything would be overturned if you permitted a stranger to establish himself among you, No more mores, no more innocence, no more happiness: a vain babble, a sterile display, external impostures replacing that which is most precious in the world, probity among men, honesty among women."

I rose into the air before the astonished eyes of the inhabitants of the valley. Cries of admiration mingled with wishes for a fortunate voyage, expressed in harmonious song. I had ceased to be visible to their gaze while that delightful melody was still ringing in my ears. I descended again still pursued by those celestial voices.

Everything marvelous that I had seen and heard delighted me so much than when I touched the ground I thought that I was waking up and emerging from a dream that had transported me into the heavens.

My first concern was to write down an account of it; that is what you have just read. It is very imperfect in several respects, and it would be much less so if I had had the liberty to make a second voyage to that terrestrial paradise. I confess that my love of science would not have been my principal motive for undertaking it. When the heart is fully satisfied, the mind has no desires; and there has been no moment in my life when I was as completely happy as in the Aerial Valley.

Since I cannot hope to see it again, I can at least maintain the happy memories that the enchanting sojourn has left me, by rereading the annals that I shall copy out after this record.

The Annals of the Aerial Valley

I

I am writing the annals of the Aerial Valley. These annals would be devoid of interest for the men of our former fatherland; they will not find in them any bloody wars, any violent revolution, nor any overturned throne. They would say: "What does the history of a people who made no noise upon the earth matter to us? For it is by the noise they make that people and sovereigns alike are appreciated down there. But our readers will be as peaceful as we are; they will be touched by the happiness that we shall have enjoyed, the great examples of fathers will serve as models for children, and successively, from age to age, our virtues and our felicity will be handed down to our ultimate posterity.

Ought we to hope for a posterity, though? Perhaps the rarefied air we breathe in this Valley is not appropriate to human life; perhaps the population that inhabits this place, isolated between heaven and earth, will disappear without leaving generation. But if this population is perpetuated, it is at least probable that the little knowledge it possesses will be lost for the want of means to maintain it. Enlightenment has made a tour of the world; it is now fixed in Europe within a certain latitude; but, communications having become easier than ever before, and all men being in contact mentally, the countries that are presently in darkness will perhaps be brilliant with light tomorrow. There is no hope of that here. If the seeds of knowledge that we cultivate in this Valley perish, it is forever; the soil will become rustic again, as it was before we settled here, and there will be no return.

That future of darkness and death is, however, inevitable, for the history of all peoples proves, incontrovertibly, that the sciences and the arts have a period of growth, a stationary period, and then a period of decadence; that succession is as general, and seems to be as natural, as the life and death of

45

everything that exists on earth. This writing will therefore one day, perhaps in a small number of years, be buried in the eternal abyss of forgetfulness.[15]

That is a pity, for I think it will be truly curious, in a few centuries, to know the origin of the settlement of this elevated region. But how curious, too, would that knowledge be for the earth from which we are forever separated! What an incredible romance our history would appear to all of Europe, if it succeeded in becoming known to it! The poor author would be treated as an extravagant visionary! However, I am only telling the simple truth; my brothers in this Valley, the only ones who will read this script, would not allow it a moment's existence if I permitted myself to mingle the slightest fiction in it. I shall tell that truth about things as about people, without, any more than Tacitus, being stimulated by the desire for praise or held back by fear of criticism.

I shall begin by making known the motives that led me to this Valley. That event derives from the story of my life, which will find its place elsewhere, but so long as the Aerial

---

[15] Author's note: "No one, in the situation in which the author of these annals found himself, would have thought differently. It required a discovery as marvellous as that of balloons to belie his prediction, and for the Aerial Valley, its inhabitants and their mores to be known outside its bounds. The author is equally mistaken about the duration of enlightenment in this corner of the Pyrenees; that enlightenment has spread there more generally than in his time, and if it has not made progress in the same proportion, at least it has not declined. Our conjectures regarding the ulterior future might have no more solid basis than those of the Author of the Annals. Who can assign limits to the human mind? Who can foresee to what extent a perfectly organized society will take the development of its mental faculties? The mind has a power that is presently only directed by ambition; who knows of what progress it might be capable, if it were under the jurisdiction of wisdom? [Note by M. de Montagnac]"

colony subsists and has a posterity, will that posterity under-stand me if I speak about the world I have quit and which they will never know? Will they be able to form any idea of that other world, physically or mentally? Will not the bounds of the Valley be, for them, the limits of the world? Will they un-derstand that this Valley is only one imperceptible point in the vast extent of the globe? Geographical maps only present sen-sible figures for those who are able to compare the real object with its representation; it is necessary to have traveled a little, over some distance, visited a few countries, in order to relate to the different objects on the map; and it is only then, extend-ing by analogy the positive knowledge that one has acquired, that one can succeed in understanding clearly all the parts and divisions on the earth.

Even supposing that our posterity is not stopped by that obstacle in the study of the description of the globe, the maps that we have brought, whatever care we take of them, will perish under the effects of time, along with our printed books. Then, that posterity will be like La Fontaine's Mouse; its hole will be the entire universe. But let us leave the future there, which will take care of itself; we have done our best to en-lighten it and render it happy. Our means are feeble and lim-ited, but those of Providence are omnipotent; let us hope that it will take as much care of the children as it has of the fathers.

After that digression, which will not be the last, and which my brothers will surely be disposed to forgive me, I shall come to the story of my establishment in this Valley.

I am not one of its first founders; the colony had already been commenced three years before I came to join it. This is how that came to pass.

A cruel malady had brought me to Barèges; for two years I had been spending the winter in Tarbes and the summer close to my salutary urn. The water in this corner of the Pyre-nees enjoyed great favor since the still-recent voyage made by the Duc de Maine, accompanied by Madame Scarron.[16] Fashion, more than necessity, were attracting, along with the brilliant society of the court, the rich people of the neighboring provinces. But to the same extent that Louis XIV's court was brilliant with wit, grace and elegance, the provinces were obscured by ignorance and gaucherie.[17] That line of demarcation disappeared, and another was formed by the mixture. The change was not for the better, for provincial ignorance was compensated by a good deal of frankness and simplicity. Those good qualities gave way to preciosity and affectation. Brilliant vice caused innocence to blush; people became ridiculous in trying to imitate the manners of the court, and art only succeeded in disfiguring nature.

I rarely went to the assemblies where a brilliant swarm of young courtiers made a game out of making fools of a few simpletons, cheating them at lansquenet or abducting some novice beauty from her mother or her husband. I preferred to wander in the beautiful mountains, which present, as in a painting, a variety of crops, productions and colors that is scarcely seen on the surface of the most extensive and diversified plain. What completed giving a magical aspect to the pic-

---

[16] The Duc de Maine's first visit to the Barèges spa, in the company of Madame de Maintenon and other members of Louis XIV's court, took place in 1675.

[17] Author's note: "Times have certainly changed; there are no longer any but slight differences between the Court, the Capital and the Provinces. Communications having become more frequent, the inhabitants of France have almost the same physiognomy; it would be difficult at present to distinguish a provincial from a Parisian, except for the time of dinner and a few other customs of similar importance. But the provinces will doubtless not take long to raise themselves to the level of the capital with regard to those grave matters, and it is necessary to expect that their inhabitants will soon have, like Parisians, high collars, bulging bellies, good stomachs and strong lungs. [Note by the Editor]"

ture were the light vapors that, rising continually from the valleys, enriched it with a varnish that never seemed so brilliant in the most beautiful landscapes by Poussin.

The season of the waters was approaching its end, however; already the fir-trees of the mountains were raising their somber pyramidal verdure in the midst of the yellowing foliage of the beech, the hornbeam and the birch, seeming as many blackened spikes half-consumed by the fire of the thunder. The brilliant carriages had departed; all that still remained were a few inhabitants of the locality and its surroundings, who, either because of the humidity of their valleys, the salted meats on which they nourished themselves, the dirtiness of their dwellings and garments or the habit of walking barefoot in waters as cold as the snow from which they came, were afflicted by goiters, rheumatism, paralysis and other similar maladies. Fortunately for them, nature has placed the remedy close to the evil.[18]

Before communications were cut off by the snow, and humans ceded their places to wolves and bears, the only inhabitants of Barèges during the winter, I had a strong desire to meet two hermits who, it was said, lived in the middle of the Pyrenees, on the almost-inaccessible summit of one of the

---

[18] Author's note: "I believe that the lack of renewal of air is the cause of goiters in the Pyrenees. I have always observed that the inhabitants afflicted with those excrescences have dwellings sheltered from the wind and the sun, in the depths of some mountain gorge where a humidity reigns that is never expelled and an air that is constantly calm and stagnant. I will cite, among other villages, that of St. Mamé, backed up against the north of the mountain at he very end of the valley of Luchon, of which almost all the inhabitants are goiterous, while half a league away, Bagnères de Luchon, more advanced in the plain and exposed to the rays of the rising and midday sun, is exempt from that malady. What fortifies my opinion is that all the goiterous are completely cured after a sojourn of some while on the mountain. [Note by the Editor]"

mountains. Everyone was talking about them, but no one knew where they lived, nor what road led there.

I was told that I could obtain reliable information on that subject in a little village that was rarely visited, situated three leagues from Barèges. I resolved to go and establish myself for some time in the village, in order to win that the confidence of the inhabitants more easily, and obtain by that means the information I sought. I colored my journey with the pretext of seeing some of the land that was for sale in the vicinity, and I introduced myself in the simple costume of a mountain man who enjoyed a little ease in his fortune.

That ease furnished me with the means of giving the inhabitants a few good dinners, and I was soon admitted to their familiarity. I learned then that they were all of the reformed religion, and when they knew that I professed the same faith, they no longer had any secrets from me. That of the hermits was confided to me. They were two Protestants persecuted for their beliefs who had taken refuge with their families in that unknown location. They had been established there for three years. During the first two they had maintained frequent relations with the village in order to procure the necessary means of subsistence, but as soon as the soil had assured them of a sufficient harvest and they had been provided with a few indispensable objects they had apparently renounced society entirely.

"It has been a year," one of the inhabitants of the village added, "since any of us has been to see them, and only once has their servant come to see us on their behalf. He reiterated on their behalf the offer they had already made to us to go and share their refuge, and we shall infallibly be forced to that emigration if the persecution continues. We invite you to join us when the time comes. In the meantime, we will give you a letter of recommendation to our common brethren and a guide to their dwelling."

I refused the recommendation but accepted the guide, who was indispensable to me, and we departed the following morning.

After an eight-hour march, I arrived at the foot of a long rampart of perpendicular rocks about three hundred toises high. I thought then that my guide had mistaken the route, for it seemed to me to be absolutely impossible to penetrate any further by the path we had followed thus far; but the sight of that enormous barrier, on the contrary, restored his confidence, which had begun to waver.

"I'm no longer anxious now," he exclaimed. "We're close to the Aerial Valley, there's no longer anything but this wall off rock separating us from it."

"Eh! How are we going to get over it, without the wings of those eagles soaring over its summit?"

"It won't be as easy for us as for those eagles, but we'll succeed. Let's begin by leaving our mules here, and let's each arm ourselves with one of these iron-tipped staffs I've brought."

We dismounted, and I followed my guide, who first followed the bed of a stream that emerged from the foot of the rock. That exit was masked by a thicket of bushes, and it was only by crouching almost down to the ground that we were able to advance. We proceeded thus, bowed down, for fifty paces; at the end of that distance there was a small, extremely steep path to the right, which we followed for a quarter of an hour, and we finally reached a narrow ledge that snaked along the flank of the rock. It was there that our rope footwear and our iron-tipped staffs rendered us great service. We switched them from one hand to the other, following the different direction of the ledge, in such a way that the tip was always applied to the edge of the precipice. Sometimes the ledge was interrupted and it was necessary to leap across the gap. My guide was an intrepid chamois-hunter, but when we reached the summit of the rock he confessed that he would never have attempted the route if he had known that it was so perilous.

From that summit we had a view of the Valley, which appeared to me to be about a league in diameter. It was completely surrounded by a girdle of rocks similar to the one that we had just scaled. I could make out the hermits' cabins near the center. In order to reach the Valley it was necessary to descend in almost as far as we had climbed up, but the sinuosities of that descent, by an easy path, which could be followed by eye all the way to the valley floor, was exempt from any kind of danger. As there was little daylight left, I decided to take my leave of my guide, in order that he would have time to descend along the ledge and seek shelter under an outcrop of rock before nightfall.

The sun had set, obscurity was beginning to descend, and a few stars were already scintillating in the sky when I reached the Valley. The purest serenity promised one of the brilliant nights that one only sees in all their beauty in places elevated above the grosser vapors of the atmosphere. I admired the profound silence of those deserts, only interrupted by the hum of a few insects and the melancholy babble of distant steams descending from the higher slopes.

Soon, harmonious sounds struck my ears; I thought at first that it was the effect of water falling upon some sonorous substance, but on listening attentively, O charm of arts! O supreme director of things! ravishing sounds in that bears den! celestial music under the pole! I marched with a long stride and then heard, distinctly, a woman's voice singing a ballad, accompanied by a theorb. Another voice, more masculine, reinforced at intervals the passages that lent themselves to harmony. I was alternately retained by the fear of causing alarm and excited by the desire to see the producers of such a concert in such a place. A dog, which I heard barking, decided me precipitately to advance.

The door of the cabin was open. Scarcely had I appeared before it than a young woman uttered a cry of fright, and the man came toward me abruptly. He paused momentarily, nonplussed, but, seeing that I was unarmed, with my hat in my hand and a cordial smile on my lips, he collected himself.

"Who are you, Monsieur, and how were you able to penetrate this enclosure? What are you looking for?"

While he was speaking a host of confused ideas captivated my mind; these were not foreigners, they were French people, who appeared to have been born in a distinguished class. Two men had been mentioned to me, but I only saw one. Might the young woman have disguised her sex? But why that mystery? Why...?

The gaze of the man, who armed himself with severity, recalled me to myself.

"Monsieur," I replied, "The sole desire to see you brought me to this place. I hope that you will not find my curiosity indiscreet when you know its motive. I ask you for hospitality for the night."

My response did not appear to satisfy him. He received me in his house with a cold politeness, but, my purpose being entirely innocent, I did not feel at all offended by that coldness, and I accept frankly the seat by the fire that he indicated to me with his hand. Sticks of fir-wood illuminated the cabin brightly, and I was able to consider the pretended hermits.

The man, who appeared to be about fifty years old, had one of those faces characterized by great ordeals. When the impetuosity of age is past and the struggle between passions and reason commences to die down, one then perceives, with the triumph of virtue, the scars of the heart. There remains in the features an imprint of austere melancholy, which is alarming at first glance, and it is only when one knows a man better, when one has penetrated his soul, that one becomes attached to him and loves him.

The young woman, for her face was evidently that of a virgin, was between sixteen and eighteen years of age. I had never seen so much beauty united with so much naivety. From the astonishment, emotion and curiosity that was painted in all her features it was easy to divine that I was the first civilized man who had appeared before her. Her timidity, her modesty and her grace were the work of nature alone. It seemed to me that I had been suddenly transported back to the first age of the world, and that I found myself in the bosom of the family of some ancient patriarch. The man's garment was made from a bearskin, the young woman's from the skin of a ewe.

The father—for I did not take long to learn that the young woman was his daughter—was only concerned to begin with to know who I was, where I came from and by what incomprehensible means I had scaled the wall of the valley. I read in his face that my answers satisfied him, and it was only then that I was satisfied myself. If nothing troubles the mind as much as the fear of displeasing, there is also nothing that restores free respiration that the certainty of being regarded with a kindly eye by people that one is meeting for the first time.

I could not prevent myself from asking a host of questions in my turn. These are the only enlightenments that he thought it appropriate to give me for the time being:

He had been living in the valley for three years with six other people that I would see before long. The path that had brought them here had been wider then; it had permitted them to bring a number of animals with them. They had broken the ledge themselves. They had not imagined that they could be visited by any living being except eagles and chamois. The latter animals had only hazarded to follow that perilous route when beings vigorously pursued. The return journey was impracticable for them, with the result that they found themselves imprisoned for the rest of their life.

During our conversation, Dina—that was the young woman's name—had taken up a distaff and was spinning thread, darting sly glances at me from time to time, of curiosity as much as astonishment. Both sentiments were quite natural, in view of my strange visit and my equally strange clothing.

"Ah! There they are!" she exclaimed, suddenly.

At that moment, the door opened, and I saw two men enter who seemed to me to be father and son. Both had beautiful faces in the manner of Henri IV, which respired frankness and attracted confidence. They too were clad in animal skins, and were carrying agricultural tools on their shoulders, which they went to deposit in a room adjacent to the one we were in.

Both of them, on perceiving me, uttered exclamations of surprise, but the older one resumed his ordinary cheerful expression when he had observed the tranquility of his friend.

"Monsieur," he said, "You've apparently come here on the back of some eagle. I imagine our astonishment is equal to ours, and that you were scarcely expecting to find humans so close to heaven."

While I repeated the story of my journey, supper was prepared in the next room, and it was served shortly afterwards.

I expected a frugal meal of roots, but a young woman who appeared to be a servant garnished the table with a dish of fine trout, white bread and bottles of bear made in the Valley.

"You can see," said Simeon—he was the latter of the two hermits that I had seen—"that if our desert resembles the Thebaid, we nevertheless don't live entirely like anchorites."

I agreed, and they were able to perceive by my appetite that I would have been difficult to content with a meat of roots—which was not astonishing after such a long and difficult journey.

After the supper, everyone gathered in a circle around the fire. I wanted to please my hosts, and thought that there was no better way to succeed in that than by bringing the conversation to the political news, which must be absolutely unknown to them after such a long intervals. To my great surprise, however, I was interrupted as soon as I broached the subject by Antonin, the older of the two solitaries.

"What does the news matter to us," he said, "of a house of which we are no longer tenants? What could you tell us? Burned cities, devastated fields, the blood of several thousand men spilled, and all those horror in exchange for a few leagues of terrain that will be passed on at the same price tomorrow, to their original owners or someone else? Talk to us about the sciences, literature and the arts; those are the only things whose progress interests us, because they make the happiness, or at least the consolation, of the human race."

"For myself," Simeon said, "I'm still more interested in the fate of good agriculturalists. Let the people—the laborers who make up the most numerous and the healthiest part of the people be happy—that's all I desire. The glory of the great fatigued me before; I only breathe easily with the idea of public tranquility and wellbeing."

We did not have to fear the espionage or the denunciation of the servants of Le Tellier and Louvois,[19] and we were able to speak the truth frankly. As I knew that the hermits were among the number of victims persecuted for their religion on the orders of Louis XIV, I expected violent declamations against that monarch, but I saw, on the contrary the confirmation of the saying that solitude deadens the passions, especially hatred, while fortifying reason.

"We mourn sincerely," they told me, "kings who want to do good but cannot. They are surrounded by people who are more interested in the evil that they do. It would require the penetration of God himself to distinguish a true friend of the public good among that crowd of egotists who are only occupied with themselves. And what torches can be given to the son of kings to enlighten them in the midst of the darkness that surrounds them?

"Incontrovertibly, the most difficult of all métiers is the government of a great nation, and it is the man who studies it least that fortune destines for it. What am I saying? They

---

[19] Charles Le Tellier (1603-1685) became Chancellor of France in 1677, and played a leading role in persuading Louis XIV to revoke the Edict of Nantes, which protected Protestants from persecution, but died a fortnight after putting his signature to the document. His son, the Marquis de Louvois (1641-1691), was the Secretary of State for War, and the architect of the plan made in 1681 to billet dragoons in Protestant homes, with a tacit licence to abuse them in every way possible in order to terrorize them into conversion or exile. Once the Edict was revoked these "dragonnades" became increasingly violent, and frequently murderous.

learn, on the contrary, that only evil means do that great work. How could one reproach a pupil in the art of Apelles who is merely a dauber, or a poet who can only write doggerel, if, instead of exercising a salutary censure over their faults, they were constantly credited with sublime beauties?

"In truth, considering all the obstacles they have to over-come, it is not the rarity of good kings by which it is necessary to be astonished, but the fact that there are any at all. They are phenomena, extraordinary favors of Providence, who cannot be admired or cherished too greatly.

"But let us postpone that conversation until another day; you must need repose. You'll be taken to the cabin where you can spend the night peacefully."

Then a young shepherd took a few strands of lighted pine-branches, and, walking ahead of me, guided me to a small cottage a few paces away from the one from which I emerged. I found a bed there, which, like the interior of the cottage, was of the utmost cleanliness. That cleanliness, which contrasted so remarkably with the habits of the inhabitants of the mountains, was the spectacle that had struck me immedi-ately on entering the dwelling of the hermits, and since then I had not seen it belied anywhere in what belonged to them.

II

The next morning I got up before dawn. I was impatient to explore the domain of the solitaries and the conquests that their industry had made over raw nature. The air was calm, the sky pure, the firmament spangled only by the principal stars; the rest had disappeared, eclipsed by the approach of day, which was already bleaching part of the horizon, where the great star was about to rise in all its majesty.

Soon, I was able to distinguish the contours of the Val-ley. I observed that it was uncovered to the east, and that no mountain was interposed in the direction of the sun, from which I concluded that the first rays would soon appeared in the plain situated in the same latitude. The part of the north which looked toward France, by contrast, was closed by a very high hill, which was the one by which I had descended. I judged that such a disposition, given the encasement of the valley, must soften the vivacity of the air in that high region considerably, and that even in the middle of winter, if the sun was not veiled by any cloud, there would be some place where the temperature was as mild as Hyères or Nice.

I walked, plunged in the reveries inspired in me by the beauties of the place and its worthy inhabitants. My thoughts went back to the valley of Tempé, the terrestrial paradise, the fortunate Golden Age, one of the most beautiful fictions of poetry.

I said to myself: *These people have lived in high society; everything announces that they are as distinguished by their birth as by their courage. Some great misfortune has doubtless cast them into this solitude. Well, where is the man tossed by events on to the reefs strewn in such great number in the bosom of society who, in order to escape the shipwreck, has not thought of seeking a refuge on some desert island, in some corner of the world forever separated from despotism and servitude? But one dreams of happiness and one thinks of fortune. These, perhaps, are the only men who have had the courage to render themselves free and happy in spite of opinion and prejudice.*

Meanwhile, the sun was already gilding the summits of the occidental mountains when I found myself on the edge of a lake whose crystal was as clear and transparent as the air. I saw at my feet trout skimming the sand in the deep water, and far above my head, an eagle describing vast circles in the air. A flock was heading for the mountain, preceded by adventurous goats wearing little bells around the neck, and guided by the shepherd's son, a young Orpheus who was charming the silent march of his faithful companions with an old ballad of the region.

Following the shore of the lake, I arrived at the enclosure of a kind of park, the entrance of which was closed by a gate. I met Simeon there with his son Rubens, who served as my guides in the enclosure.

If the harmony of the previous day had struck me with astonishment, what I saw as I advanced caused me no less. It was a garden of the Chinese genre, but as far above all those of that species as the great models of nature are above the paltry copies of art. Imagine the most ingenious distribution of the beauties of the region, of waters, rocks, caverns, mountains, verdure and flowers. All those things had received from the hands of a savant industry the most picturesque and fortunate combinations.

Here, a cascade rose up again in a single jet to half its height; there the water fell in a sheet disposed in such a manner as to form a superb rainbow in the sun's rays; further away, one passed under an arch of rock that served as the bed of a torrent. Emerging from there, one found oneself in the midst of enormous granite blocks, dispersed in confusion, among which snaked a narrow path, and one suddenly arrived in a meadow enameled with the most beautiful Alpine flowers.

At the far end rose an enormous rock in the base of which was a door almost entirely hidden by ivy, vines and other climbing plants. That door closed the entrance to a grotto, in the depths of which were two baths carved into the very rock, which received water from a thermal spring of the greatest virtue.

In another direction, groves of willows, acacias, sorb trees, hawthorns and lindens suspended perfumed garlands of various colors.

The stream, which had disappeared under dense foliage, returned to the daylight and formed various meanders in the distance, where its curved arms were seen to embrace a vast rock. A rustic bridge, which traversed the steam at that point, was supported at its far end on the rock, the top of which could be reached by a sequence of projections disposed all around it in the form of a spiral. One arrived thus at the summit, which was flat and covered with flowers, among which a pretty thornless rose could be distinguished. In the middle stood a beech tree, which, extending its vast branches, spread an agreeable cool shade. Seats of moss embraced the foot of the tree; the view from here embraced the full extent of the Valley.

The same stream went on to form another, more extensive, island on which a few chamois were grazing, removed from the wild state at the most tender age, and which habit had submitted to domesticity. The bed of the stream, hollowed out and broadened in that place, had extinguished any idea of liberty in them, and the most attentive cares of their masters had rendered them to amiable servitude.

Far from having sacrificed the useful to the agreeable, however, the latter had been made to contribute to the increase of the former. The trees and the rocks protected an orchard and a vegetable garden from cold winds, situated in the part of the valley exposed for the longest time to the sun's rays.

A sandy path had directed our march, and my two guides and I found ourselves back at the entrance to the park, when I thought we were still at the opposite end. Some distance from the enclosure I looked back and admired it more, on observing that it only occupied one of the less precious parts of the valley. The whole of the bottom of the valley, which received fertilizer from the mountains, was given over to culture, and only awaited a greater number of arms; the mountain-sides were meadows, and the upper slopes were crowned with woods.

One going back into the cabin, we found Antonin with his daughter Dina, who were waiting for us to have the morning meal, which consisted of milk, butter and cakes.

When it was finished, Antonin said to me: "We won't interrupt the accustomed order of our occupations; for your part, Monsieur, act with the same frankness. When you want to leave us, it will be entirely your decision; we shall facilitate your exit, but we warn you that at the same time, we shall take infallible measures to ensure that neither you nor anyone else can penetrate into this retreat in future. On the other hand, if you desire to settle here with us, we will tell you in a few days whether you are acceptable to us."

After this declaration, the two hermits went out with Rubens. I told them that I was going to finish exploring their valley, and directed my steps southwards, toward the part that faced Spain. That side was only closed by a simple hill, not very high, the top of which it was easy to reach. The purity of the air, the perfume of the plants, the variety of locations and the rich vegetation that I encountered everywhere made that little journey a delightful stroll. From the summit of the hill, the view extended over an immense horizon, but the distribution of the other side of the hill rendered access to that part of the valley even more impracticable than the other, for the entire crest, in the extent of a full semicircle, advanced externally as a protrusion, in such a manner that it was impossible to see the foot of the rock, which was more than three hundred toises below. I explored the crest in the direction of the part that looked toward France, all the way to the escarpment that it was impossible for me to scale.

It was easy for me to judge by that disposition of the encasement of the valley, entirely open to the south and closed to the north, that it must experience the mildest temperature that it elevation could permit.

A short time after my return to the cabin, dinner was served; my hosts warned me that they would follow their custom that day of only taking two meals, and by the abundance of that one I understood that supper would be combined with it.

The surprise, for those solitaries, after three years, of seeing an inhabitant of a world that one existed now in their memory, the ideas that encounter inspired in them, and the desire on my part to satisfy the curiosity of the good hermits, prolonged the meal.

I shall only report of the conversation that followed it that which is indispensable to the explanation of my establishment in the Valley.

"With Monsieur's permission," Dina's father said to me, "we shall continue the reading commenced before his arrival. Rubens, go fetch it from the library."

"A library!" I exclaimed.

And, indeed, Rubens having drawn a curtain at the back of the room, I perceived several shelves of books.

"You seem" Antonin continued, "The excellent society of our soirées. These are the only friends that have remained faithful to us, so it is from them alone that we have not separated ourselves."

Having approached the bookshelves, I noticed a few books damaged by insects. "Your friends," I said, "are resenting their solitude somewhat. In a few years they will have abandoned you like all the others, if you don't take more care of them."

"Our plan," he replied, "was certainly to enclose them in a cupboard, but after having wasted wood and time we renounced it. My dear Simeon has proved to be no more skilled than I am for that work."

"In your place, I would not have been so embarrassed."

"Monsieur is apparently a carpenter?"

"Yes, like Télémaque. That book had just appeared when my father occupied himself with my education,[20] and thanks to a little natural ability, I could compete with the best worker of that genre in Paris. You have the wood and the tools; I guarantee that within a week, your books will be sheltered from any accident."

From that moment on I was part of the little family. The three of us combined between us what was necessary, not only to found a society, but also to civilize and educate it. One was an excellent cultivator, the other a good musician and lit-

---

[20] Fénelon's *Les Aventures de Télémaque* was first published, anonymously, in 1699—a date that is far too late to be consistent with the information that the present narrator subsequently gives of his life, or with the datable events in the stories of Simeon and Antonin.

terateur, and I, in addition to the art of carpentry, possessed some knowledge of mathematics and was a passable draughtsman.

The work made rapid progress, and the body of the bookcase was in place before the time that I had promised.

That task was immediately followed by another, rendered very urgent by the rigor of the season, which was beginning to make itself felt, which was to have doors and windows that closed exactly.

The Pyrenees, in that part of architecture, and in general in relationship to the arts, and even to civilization, is about two hundred years behind the rest of France. Situated at the extremity of France and Spain, for eight months of the year it is almost devoid of communication with either of those two empires, and for the other four months only sees rich people who come to exchange their money and their vices for the local mineral waters. If any scientist or artist passes through, it is as if he were among Hottentots, incapable of appreciating his talent, much less profiting from it.

Furthermore, the inhabitant of those mountains rarely goes far from his native soil; he has neither the appetite for work nor the industry necessary to seek his fortune in others regions. His dialect, half Spanish and half French, and limited in either respect, would be sufficient to render him a foreigner anywhere else. Thus, everything collaborates to isolate the Pyrenees, and until some branch of commerce and sociability is discovered there, that part of France will languish for a long time in ignorance and the species of barbarity into which it is plunged. That matter often served as a text for our evening conversations; we combined them with reading and music.

Eventually, when I had obtained the entire confidence of my hosts, one of them revealed to me the motive for their retreat into this solitude in the following terms.

III

"I was born in Toulouse into the reformed religion. My father was one of the Lutheran counselors of the Parliament of that city. He was the best of men. Philanthropy was his only passion. Incessantly occupied with the wellbeing of his fellows, he consecrated to that honorable occupation all his time and a part of his fortune. Brought up in the Protestant religion, he was attached to it above all because it was the most tolerant, because in practicing it one could accord one's esteem to all religions that render men sensitive, compassionate, generous and bring them to love their fellow and consider him as a brother, whatever his country of origin, his religion and his birth might be.

"'The creator of the Universe,' he said, 'is the father of all human beings; he spreads his sunlight and his dew over all the continents of the earth. The man who persecutes his brother, because he does not render God the same worship as himself, is mad or wicked. What happens between the creator and his creature ought to be irrelevant to the government; its sole duty is to watch over the actions of humans in relation to one another.'

"In exercising those virtues he was constantly cherished by his family, esteemed by his colleagues and honored by the public. My education was in the first rank of his pleasures as well as his duties, and in order to complete it, he took care to guide the first sentiments of my heart toward a young woman that he judged best suited to my happiness by virtue of her personal qualities as well as those relative to public opinion. Shortly afterwards he obtained for me the succession to his responsibilities as a counselor.

"Eventually, his health having been eroded even more by work then by age, I was accorded, at his request, the faculty of exercising that responsibility, of which he only retained the honorific title. I had replaced him for ten years, as happy as it is permissible for a man to be with my worthy spouse, my son, a few friends, and the best of them all, my respectable father, when the persecutions against the reformed commenced.

"The government then had for ministers two men who, either out of ignorance or prejudice, excited the monarch to violent measures against the inhabitants of his realm who professed the Lutheran belief. At first, attempts were made to win over the leaders of the party by means of money and honors, but when it was perceived that those means only succeeded with cowardly souls devoid of credit, the opposite means was decided: that of rigor.

"Nearly five years passed in uncertainty and irresolution, which proved the ignorance of the government even m more than its weakness. Finally, the military and despotic spirit of the master prevailed over all advice and all considerations; in consequence, the Edict of Nantes was revoked, and all the favors accorded to the reformed—especially the principal one, Parliaments composed equally of Catholics and Protestants—were annulled.

"We had anticipated the blow for some time and I had rid myself of my responsibilities before the decree was published, but what was infinitely more sensible to me was the order of the council to remove the children from Protestant families in order to have them brought up in the Catholic religion. That terrible order struck a mortal blow at the two people who were most dear to me, my father and my wife.

"I was left alone with my son; overwhelmed by the grief of the losses I had just experienced I trembled that at any moment, it might be completed by the removal of my child. Well before the sale of my responsibility, I had already liquidated all my property in the region; thus being perfectly free, I did not hesitate to escape from the last and most frightful of the misfortunes that threatened me. I left my house furtively, taking my son and all my servants, who, professing the same religion as me, would have been exposed to the same persecutions, and I went to take refuge in a village in the Pyrenees, whose inhabitants, all of the reformed religion, had the greatest obligations to my father.

65

"A short time afterwards, I saw one of my oldest friends, who lived all the year on a considerable estate in the vicinity of Toulouse, arrive in the same village. He had his daughter with him, twelve years old; it was the same motive that had torn them away from their home. It was a great consolation in my misfortune to share it with such a friend; we promised never to separate; but before making an extreme decision we thought it appropriate to be precisely informed regarding the present state of affairs. We flattered ourselves with the idea that the storm had been too violent to be durable, and hoped that sane politics would have prevailed over passion and opened eyes to the disastrous consequences of a momentous error.

"In consequence, we sent an enlightened and prudent man to seek information as to the present and to sound out the future. The news that he brought us only increased our alarm. The barbaric Council of France, despairing of conversion, had resolved to suppress or annihilate; undisciplined dragoons were covering all the roads and chasing fugitive Protestants before them, like cruel tigers chasing a flock of timid ewes. All those that were caught were massacred pitilessly.

"There was no more to deliberate; it was necessary to leave France—but where could we go from the frontier to which we had been driven? Into Spain, the country of ignorance and the Inquisition? There would be nothing there but a pyre ardent to consume us. Thus, we were enclosed on all sides in these mountains. New Israelites, chased from our hearths, it was necessary for us to seek a new promised land, which, without being covered in honey and irrigated by milk, could at least provide for our needs and shelter us from Pharaoh's pursuits.

"We learned from our hosts that there was a valley on the Spanish frontier that had once belonged to that kingdom, which had been conceded to the Duc de Bellegarde In exchange for a domain in the Low Countries that the lord in question had given to the Spaniards. That valley, which was leased to shepherds, as many from Spain as from France, appeared to us, according to the description given of it, to suit our objective perfectly. We went to visit it, and found that there was, indeed, no refuge that combined as many advantages.

"We negotiated to buy it under an assumed name. The parties were soon in agreement with regard to the price. Monsieur de Bellegarde was as eager to sell a domain almost devoid of income as we were to buy it. We came to an arrangement thereafter for all the animals in the valley—sheep, cows, mules and horses—as well as the cabins and stables that had been constructed there.

"Our plan was to take with us all the inhabitants of the Protestant village where we were and to found in that isolated region a new, perfectly independent colony, but the people, almost entirely limited to physical existence, could scarcely see beyond the moment. The evils of the future only affected them like bad dreams, rarely enough to influence their conduct. Our hosts were also attached to the ground they inhabited by their properties, for the loss of which, in their eyes, no others could compensate. A few unmarried young people, reduced to the state of domestic service, were the only ones who consented to come with us. They helped us to transport a great many objects of every species, of which we were perhaps about to be deprived forever.

"Our first concern on arriving in this place was to render it inaccessible. Only one path led to it, which was the cornice that you scaled, and which was wide enough to permit the passage of animals. We succeeded, with the aid of long and assiduous labor, in narrowing it to the condition in which you have seen it. You are the first person in three years who has proved, much to our surprise, that it was not impracticable. Of all animals, only the chamois could cross it. Access being absolutely denied to the two other species of the bear and the wolf, so murderous in these mountains, we had no more to do than destroy the animals of those species that were enclosed in the valley in order to free our flocks from the fury of their enemies, as we were from ours.

"As soon as we had ensured our tranquility against any species of attack from without, we redirected our attentions to the interior. First we regulated the order of labor. We had brought sufficient supplies to get us through the bad season, but after having isolated ourselves completely in this retreat, it was necessary to find means within its bounds to provide for the needs of the future.

"Our predecessors had already made an attempt at cultivation that had succeeded perfectly, which was infallible in virgin ground fecundated for so many centuries by the rich deposits of the mountains. We had no more to do than to augment and vary that cultivation. All the plantations succeeded. We have brought in abundant harvests of wheat; you've seen the beauty of our vegetable garden; fruit trees, and even vines, so recalcitrant in the Pyrenees, gave us fortunate hopes.

"The only thing that we lack is weavers to put to work the wool of our ewes and the flax of our harvests. The study that you appear to have made of the mechanical arts will surely be useful to us in that regard, and I hope that with your help we will soon be able to renounce the garments of savages and dress like civilized people.

"It only remains for me to talk to you about the administration of the colony and the education of our children— which includes everything, the civil and the moral, for politics is henceforth an absolutely dead letter for us. But the evening is too far advanced to make a start on that matter. We shall leave it for another day, if you consent to remain with us. It is enough to say to you frankly that we desire you to do so. You have had time to reflect and we shall expect your response tomorrow morning.

"It is necessary to warn you, however," he added, in a solemn tone, "that whatever decision you make, whether to remain in this solitude or to leave, we have decided to break the remainder of the cornice that permitted your entry. Thus, either you will be fixed here for life, or you will never return."

IV

I had spent part of the night reflecting on the choice that had been put to me. The next day, I went to find my hosts; I told them that I had decided to share their solitude, but that, before accepting me as a companion, it was appropriate that they should know who I was, and I gave them a brief account of my history in these terms:

"I descend from an ancient Scots family attached at all times to the house of Stuart. My father, Lord Odgermont, occupied a distinguished place at the court of Charles I, and although faithful to the reformed religion of his ancestors, he enjoyed all the esteem of that unfortunate monarch. If he had also possessed his confidence, he would have inspired him with measures more in conformity with the mores of the English and the principles of their government, and the good but overly weak sovereign would have been able to conserve his crown and his life. His death brought the ruination of my entire family.

"My father was arrested and condemned shortly after him, and I, the sole inheritor of immense properties that were all confiscated and sold, was saved by one of our faithful servants and taken to France in the retinue of Charles II. When that prince was recalled to his fatherland in order to remount the throne of his fathers, I constantly resisted all the requests that he made for me to accompany him.[21] What would I have found in England? A brilliant servitude in a corrupt court, where cruel vengeances would need to be exercised if I hoped to recover my former heritage—a morality and principles that horrified me. With what eyes would the young favorites of a king delivered without restraint to all the impetuosity of the senses look upon a sage of their own age issuing by his conduct a daily censure of the court?

---

[21] Charles II returned to England in 1660, twenty-five years before the revocation of the Edict of Nantes, so the chronology of Odgermont's story is somewhat awry.

"It is necessary to confess to you, however, that that precocious sagacity was inspired less by virtue than by the love with which I was smitten for a young Frenchwoman in Louis XIV's court. I was rewarded in return, and, already occupying a distinguished rank in the army, I was able to hope to make my fortune promptly under a conquering king, and one day to obtain the consent of my beloved's parents. I did not take long, in fact, to make it evident that I was guided by love and honor; the campaigns I made covered me with glory and recompenses.

"Welcomed from then on with distinction by the family into which I desired to enter, I hazarded a request that was favorably received. A short while afterwards our union was decided and the contract taken to the king for signature. I was waiting for that formality, to which a great price was attached, when the edict forbidding marriages between Catholics and Protestants burst forth like a thunderclap, and closed forever entry to all positions, as many civil as military.

"I was not immediately designated for the furies of intolerance; I had no fortune susceptible of encouraging the zeal of persecutors, and I belonged, in any case, to a family accredited in a court that there was too much interest in sparing. But the sudden cooling of my beloved's parents, the insulting politeness of the ministers and the circumspect and reserved welcome of the courtiers informed me that I ought not to count on the political regard that I had, and that, sooner or later, I would swell the list of the unfortunates targeted by the furies of fanaticism.

"I did not wait for that last moment. I retired into these mountains, to which cruel maladies, the fruit of my zeal in the service of the king, had already brought me for two years in succession. Undecided as to the choice of a third fatherland to replace the one I which I was born and the one I had adopted, the retreat that you are offering me is the most fortunate I can encounter. We have all been battered by the same tempest, we are now united in the same haven. I bless my misfortunes, since they have procured me such a consolation."

A short time later I sent one of my hosts' domestics with a few letters, some to arrange my friends and the others to bid my friends an eternal adieu. On his return, the man was to bring a few effects that I had left.

In the interval, my hosts made me party to the project they had conceived in order to ensure the inviolable tranquility of our refuge. It was to mine, by means of holes hollowed out and intervals and filled with powder, the remains of the cornice that still associated the refuge with France. To each of those holes a fuse was attached, which descended from the top of the rock. Thus, by setting fire to those fuses, the perpendicular face of the rock would be flattened, in such a manner as to render it absolutely inaccessible.

The holes had already been bored for some time, it was no longer a matter of anything but filling them with powder and placing the fuses. That was what we did the following day, and, mounted on the rampart of the valley, we were waiting for the return of our messenger to set fire to the fuses when tumultuous cries suddenly rose up from the base of the rock. It was all the inhabitants of the Protestant village that had served as a refuge for the two friends, whose faces and voices they immediately recognized.

One of them having gone down and climbed up again a short time later, we learned that the unfortunates had fled, with a great deal of difficulty, the fury of dragoons while the latter were occupied in looting and burning their homes. They had brought a part of their flocks and some mules, loaded with everything they had been able to save. They implored hospitality, submitting to any conditions that might be imposed upon them.

Their request was easily granted. We immediately hastened to establish planks across the interruptions in the cornice, in order to give passage to the animals and to facilitate that of the women and children. When the entire troop had passed over and reached the summit, we climbed up after them and set fire to the fuses. They had scarcely been lit when we saw the dragoons coming, sabers in hand. A few moments later, the mines exploded.

That unexpected detonation, and the blocks of stone that it launched at the satellites of fanaticism doubtless struck them with fear and despair, for since that day we have seen a few observers measuring our inaccessible ramparts with their eyes, but none has approached with the insensate project of scaling them.

Here my story ends. I had only begun to tell it with the intention of making known to the public, on my return from the valley, the truly astonishing things that I had seen there. Now there is no more public for me. The whole earth is the valley that I inhabit, and my two hosts form the population of the entire world. It is, therefore, to them that I am giving this manuscript; they will dispose of it as they see fit.

V

After several days of interruption I am resuming this written account, no longer on my own behalf but that of the Aerial Valley.

The savage inhabitants of a few recently discovered islands, ignorant of their origin, have made up a chimerical account of it. The reports of voyagers on that matter have often given rise to scholarly dissertations. The Aerial Valley is like an island, but its situation and the fluid that surrounds it, impracticable to human industry, will doubtless hide it forever from all the research of curiosity. It is not, therefore for scholars foreign to our refuge that I am writing, but only for our descendants, fellow inhabitants of the valley.

One of the fundamental principles of our new government being not to mislead the people with lies, and, on the contrary, always to tell them the truth, it is indispensable that they should know that of their origin.

Henceforth, this account will bear the title *Annals of the Aerial Valley*. I have been given the responsibility of drafting it by the new governors. Eternally separated from the rest of the earth, praise and criticism are absolutely foreign to me, and I hope that the truth of my writings will always conform to the purity of my conscience.

10 September 16**

The inhabitants of the village of Garringue, pursued by the satellites of fanaticism, who wanted, under pain of death, to make them renounce the religion of their fathers, have run to ask us for shelter at the moment when we were about to destroy the rest of the cornice that, snaking over the perpendicular face of the French rock, still kept open a communication between our Valley and the people of the exterior. Having consented to their requests, we have facilitated their passage by placing planks over all the breaches in the cornice.

This is the number of humans and animals who have been introduced:

102 persons, as many men as women and children.
52 cows.
5 bulls.
20 mules.
10 horses.
400 sheep.
52 goats.
10 dogs.
22 cats.

Plus several plows and other agricultural implements, and tools appropriate to several métiers.

When everything had been taken up to the rampart of the Valley we said an eternal adieu to the rest of the earth, and broke the unique route of communication that we still had with it.

All those people, embarrassed with regard to nourishment and lodgings, addressed themselves to the two owners of the Valley, Antonin and Simeon, but before using the authority accorded to them, that latter wanted to it be deferred to them by ordinary means, and in consequence, for one or several chiefs to be appointed by the plurality of suffrages, invested with a superior power. After that proposal, votes were taken individually. They were all united upon Antonin and Simeon, whose names have been decorated with the particular distinction of the title of Dom. Dom Antonin and Dom Simeon have accepted the government of the Valley, but on condition that their power be limited by a constitution and laws that they will be authorized to propose.

The first care of the governors has been to take a census of what there is in the Valley of the subsistence of different species, inasmuch as the newcomers have brought with them what remains of ample harvests they had made. It was found that there was enough to nourish the whole population until the next harvest. Present needs being assured, all that remained was to provide for those of the future. They ordered, in consequence, that from the following day onwards, everyone, without distinction, would be employing in laboring and inseminating fields.

That which regards religion and mores has also been regulated by the governors. This is the substance of the various speeches that Dom Antonin made on that subject:

"A host of causes acting one upon another since the formation of empires modify them variously from one century to another, without all the science and power of humans being able either to change or anticipate the state that will succeed their present state. It is a molten metal that cannot take on any determined form because it is continuously exposed to the most ardent fire.

"Our situation is absolutely different. The people we have to govern have only just been born with virgin mores and a healthy and robust temperament. In order to conserve its mores and its health, it requires laws as simple as its aliments. Adam was governed solely by the word of God and nourished himself solely on the fruits of Eden so long as he was in the terrestrial paradise. This Valley is a second Eden, and its inhabitants are the children of Adam before his fall. Let us therefore accustom them to recognizing no other sovereign but God. Let them love him for the benefits that he lavishes every day; let them fear his justice, which punishes as it rewards.

"Above all, let nothing be interposed between the creator and the creature. One can say to people that the figures of stone, metal or wood that they venerate are nothing in themselves, and that it is to the object they represent that homage ought to be addressed, but the senses obscure intelligence; they take the place thereof and soon the idea of God vanishes, while the image alone captivates thought.

"It is principally to that cause that it is necessary to attribute the degeneration of Christianity. That religion, so benign and humane, has often only had for protectors imbecilic sovereigns who persecuted all those who, recognizing the creator of the universe, did not adore him as they did under a deceptive image. It was necessary not to have any religion except theirs, and to render homage not to the uncreated author of all things but to the one who was the work of their own hands. In brief, the Christians of those times were true atheists.

"It is thus that, in drawing away from its source, Christianity has been denatured. If one wants to consider its degeneration in all its horror, cast an eye upon Spain, on the Inquisition, on the massacre of Vaudois, that of Saint Bartholomew's Eve, and finally, on the revocation of the Edict of Nantes, of which we are the innocent and unfortunate victims.[22]

"Perhaps, I confess, the reestablishment of the primitive purity of Christianity among the nations of Europe aged in corruption would now be too feeble a brake, and too easily broken by the tempest of passions, but it is to a virgin people

---

[22] Author's note: "It is easy to perceive that the man who is speaking here is a Protestant embittered by the persecutions that forced him into exile from his homeland. It is impossible to judge things soundly when one's mind is troubled by the resentment of a violent outrage."

that I am offering it, to a nascent society as pure as the air it breathes."

The minister replied: "You are only exposing your opinion to us, Monsieur le Gouverneur, in order to submit it to our examination. You will doubtless only institute it in principle if it emerges victorious from that proof. I will therefore tell you frankly that that opinion has been devastated for a long time, not only by the doctrine of Christianity but by something even more powerful, by the experience of centuries. No people has ever existed that did not have an ostensible religion."

"That is because until now, it has been thought impossible or dangerous to teach them to do without one."

"Teach the people to do without organized religion? How can that be one, pray?"

"By enlightening them. A savage is limited to the physical; he only has half a life, since mental life is entirely void to him. It is, however, that life which is the entirety of humanity. Without intelligence, thought and sentiment, humans cannot fulfill their destination; they vegetate like brutes, like insensitive plants. How can one develop human mentality? As one develops the physique, by exercise. What the gymnastics of the ancients did for corporeal strength, a well-extended education does for intellectual strength.

"The opinion generally spread over the world, I know, is that the common people cannot and ought not to be educated, that it is necessary not to raise their intelligence above the coarse labor to which nature has condemned them. That opinion is founded on the same reasoning that caused some northern sovereign to say that it was not necessary for a peasant to have two legs. In fact, a lame people is more easily enslaved to cultivating the fields, just as a people brutalized by ignorance is more entirely dependent on its priests and its kings. It is when a people is completely blind that it can no longer do without its guides, and it is also then that all its actions are regulated by the temporal master and all its thoughts by the spiritual master. 'Do as I order you to,' is cried at it from one side, and from the other, 'Believe what I say: no examination, you are incapable of it, I alone am enlightened; obey, vile automaton.'

"That is surely the true means of making slaves and fanatics; and no one is unaware that it is from that double source, of servitude and fanaticism, that the greatest evils of the world emerge.

"But as it is not for ourselves, but for the inhabitants of this Valley that we have accepted the government, we want, not merely to conserve their reason, but also to give it all the development of which it is susceptible. The rights of our brother to intelligence will not diminish his duties toward society. He will be neither a closeted scholar what has cultivated the domain of thought nor an agriculturalist or an artisan who moves nothing but his arms, but a man who, having exercised his mind and body equally, will be able to think and work; he will be both a good laborer and a good philosopher; he will have the sentiment of his dignity, will know his place in the world; and, submissive to his chiefs without being constrained by soldiers, he will adore God without being sermonized by priests.

"It is to that last point above all that it is important to direct human enlightenment. People penetrated by the existence of a Supreme Being, the immensity of his power and his wisdom, who will be intimately persuaded that that Being sees everything and knows everything, our thoughts as well as our actions, will have no need of laws to be always just and good. It is that belief, so pure and so sublime, relegated during the reign of Mythology to the schools of a few philosophers and the temples of a few initiates, that Moses proclaimed in order to guide the people of Israel in the desert; it is the same belief—deteriorated by time, like all human institutions—that Jesus restored in its primitive purity. It is in forming the essence of Christianity that he made that religion the simplest and strongest of all religions. That beautiful institution has degenerated for a second time. Men have taken the place of God; they have lent him their vices, they have painted him with their own colors. Monstrous abuses have been substituted for the doctrine of Jesus. No one is able any longer to worship in spirit and in truth. In brief, instead of Christians there are no longer any but superstitious individuals and hypocrites.

"Will it be possible to reestablish for the third time Christianity is its primitive purity? I don't know, relative to the rest of the world. But I believe that reestablishment to be not merely possible but very easy in this Valley.

"There is a God who created the world and who conserves it, who created humankind and is present in human thought as well as human action; that is our only symbol. Let it be engraved in the heart, not by faith but by reason, in order that it should never be effaced."[23]

Such is the substance of the speeches that Dom Antonin made at various times on religion.

Since the creator of the universe is present, and interested in all the thoughts as well as all the actions of humans, he will recompense and punish the culpable, either in this life or anther that follows it. People owe to that Supreme Being a tribute of gratitude and homage, which they will render every morning and every evening; Sunday will be entirely devoted to that holy duty; they will not be distracted from it by any labor.

Independently of Sunday, two other festivals have been instituted, one for the anniversary of the first possession of the Valley by it governors, the other for the arrival of the inhabitants of the village of Garringue. Those two festivals have a character both religious and political.

The same simplicity has presided over the civil constitution. The products of all labor will be placed in common; a council of sages has been appointed for their distribution. The same council is charged with supervising mores, preventing faults and expressing those which, in spite of their direction

---

[23] Author's note: "The reader might care to observe that this reform in religion is proposed for a kind of human who is very close to the nature of angels. [Note by the Editor]"

and the good intelligence of our brothers, might escape due to human weakness.

Religious laws are only necessary to people profoundly corroded and corrupted. They are old buildings only sustained by means of stays. None are necessary for a new people, still full of innate innocence, who are just and good by sentiment, bearing, engraved in their hearts the divine precept: *You shall love God with all your soul, and your neighbor as yourself.* All morality is encapsulated within that dictum, and whoever is thoroughly penetrated by it has no need of laws to be a good citizen, a good parent and a good spouse.

Thus, the interior guide leads people surely and naturally to the accomplishment of their moral duties. But society demands other services, which, not being inspired by conscience, need to be imposed by sage government.

The primary labor of the inhabitants of the Valley has been the plowing and insemination of the ground; everyone without exception, has been employed in it. That labor, commenced on the fifteenth of October, was finished before the end of the month.

That work concluded, all strength was brought to the construction of the new cabins necessitated by the augmentation of the population. Until then, it had been lodged in barns and stables. As all houses in these mountains are built of wood, and that material is found close at hand in great abundance, the number of cabins necessary has been completed before the heavy frosts.

It was only when all those public works had been done that each individual was able to devote himself to the particular labor of his métier. There were all kinds in the colony that came to us. The blacksmith has made plowshares and other agricultural implements; the carpenters have made furniture for the cabins; and all the arms not occupied with these different tasks, including those of women and children, have been spinning wool or linen, or weaving those threads into fabrics.

The morning and evening prayers have continued regularly to be made in common, as well as the solemnization of

Sunday. The principal object of these acts of piety has always been the persuasion of the eternal presence of God in all our actions and all our thoughts, and of his justice is recompensing good works and punishing evil actions. The speeches relative to that great idea have not been a vain and monotonous formula that the habit of pronunciation had ended up depriving of all expression. Those speeches are improvised and vary every day. The success of those daily homilies is such that the whole population veritably seems to be a single family, marching continuously under the eye of its celestial father. The children brought up in that virginal innocence, entirely strangers to any other idea, promise a generation even better than that of their fathers. Thus, everything announces for the future a moral picture that will be the inverse of the one presented by Horace.

In spite of the means that the governors have established to develop and cultivate the intelligence of the colony, there remains an ineradicable line of demarcation between the individuals who have not been subjected since birth by the need for physical labor and those whom fortune has condemned to it. They are two different species, who cannot be fused together into a common society; thought, language and everything make them distinct. They would both experience a mortal ennui if they were continually united.

In consequence of that law of nature, the two governors, their two children, the old officer, the former minister of the gospel and I assemble together every evening.

On one of those evenings, the officer told us the story of his life in these terms.

VI

"I was born in the Palatinate. My father was one of the most illustrious scholars in Germany; he had made his studies at the university of Gottingen. The Elector, who loved and cultivated letters, invited him to his Estates and appointed him director of the College of Worms.

"A short while after that establishment, my father married a young woman from one of the foremost families in the land. Four children were the fruits of that union; two boys and two girls. As the eldest, I was destined in childhood to replace my father, and made in consequence al the studies relative to his profession. My natural tastes seconded by a few dispositions, enabled me to make rapid progress. Having only attained the age of twenty-two, I was teaching literature in the college, of which I had already been named as heir to the directorship.

"A young Frenchwoman, passing through our city by chance with her mother, was curious to hear me. I had the misfortune to please her, to get to know her, to love him and be loved by her. Birth, education, tastes and fortune all seemed to unite us; only the difference of fatherland erected an insurmountable barrier between us. My father was one of those patriots who, like those of the early days of ancient Rome, adored his country and detested everything that was foreign to it, but his strongest aversion was to the French, whose light and frivolous character forced a perfect contrast with his own.

"That contradiction only augmented my amour, for it irritated my vanity, and I conceived almost as much pleasure in triumphing over an unjust prejudice as in possessing the hand of my beloved. It was not the same for the young woman. Women's hearts are, on that matter, generally diametrically opposed to ours. There is no honest maiden who, in my position, would not have regarded the resistance as a shameful defeat, and flight as a striking victory.

"The regrets of my young inamorata, in quitting a man whose desires she had welcomed, were doubtless as keen as they were sincere, but they were stifled by the pride of her mother, and they both departed without my being able to obtain any other information than that they were returning to Paris, their birthplace.

"You know, my friends, what a first love is, and the dolor of a first separation. Every man, in such circumstances, seeks subjects of consolation analogous to his tastes, a hunter

81

in pursuing wild beasts in the forest, a warrior in launching himself into the midst of battles. For me, nourished on the charms of study, I only found relief in reading the poets who had best given voice to the language of love: Catullus, Tibullus and, above all, Virgil in the fourth song of the *Aeneid*. I made their harmonious lines resound, not from the hills and the valleys, but from the walls and ceilings of my classroom.

"I taught my young pupils to respond to my tones, and had it only depended on me they too would have becomes Timaretes and Tircis. The shadow would perhaps have replaced the reality, and my heart, by virtue of being softened to fictions, would have ceased at length to be sensible, but a cruel mockery escaping the mouth of my father suddenly dissipated the illusion that was consoling me. From that moment on, the enchanting dreams vanished, never to return; the awakening was frightful, and it was henceforth impossible for me to sense my loss without an unbearable laceration of the heart.

"After futile combats, my feeble reason was finally forced to give in, and I quit the paternal roof in order to try to find the person from whom I could not live apart. I arrived in Paris and tried to pick up her trail. Having no idea of that great city, I imagined that simply by pronouncing the name of Madame Delaplace, which was that of the mother of my beloved, anyone would be able to indicate her residence to me. I therefore descended from the coach after having passed through the walls in order to seek information regarding her dwelling at the city gate, but no one knew her.

"Still led by hope, I went from door to door asking for Madame Delaplace. My foreign accent, very remarkable then, often excited nothing but laughter and astonishment. Twice, however, I thought I had finally found the person for whom I was searching so ardently, but, either in good faith or out of malice, it was the dwelling of prostitutes that had been indicated to me. That scorn, which could not have any unfortunate consequence for a heart filled with veritable love, ended up making my renounce me vain research. My only hope for success then was chance. But when I had exhausted the money I had brought with me I found myself no further advanced than the first day, and it was necessary for me to make a serious decision.

"After Mademoiselle Delaplace, the Muses were the unique object of my amour, and I flattered myself that I was one of their favorites. It was, therefore, from them that I sought some consolation, but the extreme penury of my finances did not permit me to pay gratuitous court to them. Convinced that my literary knowledge merited being distinguished in Paris, as they had been in Worms, I went to offer myself to the Royal College as a professor of philosophy. I was asked whether I was in favor of Descartes or Aristotle. On my response, which clearly demonstrated that the philosophy of the Stagirite was mistaken, and that I was for truth and against error, the door was slammed in my face.

"The same question having been asked of me in the other colleges at which I presented myself, I received a similar welcome for the same reply that I gave. I finally understood, after so many disgraces, that it was necessary for me to renounce the state of professor of philosophy. As long exercise had nevertheless rendered me philosophical, before deciding on another course of action, I reflected on those that were on offer.

"Among all estates, two in particular were distinguished to my eyes; the object of one was to spread enlightenment, the object of the other to extinguish it. By embracing the first, that of a man of letters, I would be exercising the most beautiful of all magistracies. Elevated above all the professions, and all the classes of society, everything would be submitted to my examination and censure, from the scepter to the crosier. I would identify evil, I would indicate good, I would spread enlightenment and the love of humanity everywhere.

Thus passionate for higher learning, I attributed an exaggerated influence to it in my youth. At the age when the senses have the greatest empire, I devoted them entirely to thought. I imagined that genius emanating from and participating in the divine essence, must dispose of events, and bring about those that we desire most ardently. Age and experience have certainly disillusioned me; it has been incontestably proven to me that a host of occult causes determines the affairs of this world, and that in that upheaval, it is not the man of intelligence but the fool most often triumphs. Poor petty beings that we are! We read the heavens, we know the courses of the stars, we can trace their daily march several centuries on advance, but we are incapable of being assured of our own from the present moment to the one that will follow it!

"How could I foresee in my noble enthusiasm that the rival of Demosthenes and Virgil was about to fall to the rank of a simple soldier?"

"What are you calling a fall?" asked Dom Antonin. "After the rank of legislator, I know of none finer than that of defender of the fatherland."

"Undoubtedly," replied the old soldier, "a brave soldier is a precious citizen. But you will agree that it is very cruel for a man who loves justice and humanity to serve as an instrument of injustice and tyranny. It is to that, however, that the military man is most frequently exposed, because, for every reasonable war commanded for the salvation of the state there are ten criminal ones that are only ignited by ambition and the foolish ardor for conquests. I served under the two greatest captains of the century, Turenne and Condé; both were distinguished by their probity, and yet both have not only torn the bosom of their fatherland but have undertaken and sustained foreign wars that, if they had been submitted to the judgment of an impartial tribunal, would only ever have made a noise in the council by which they would have been rejected.

"Condemned by my birth to serve in the humblest ranks, it was only after fifteen years of service that I was made an officer, and you shall see by the action that obtained me the recompense in question and the one that nearly lost it for me, how different civil virtues are from military virtues.[24]

---

[24] Author's note: "This distinction is false. The courage that defends the state is no less honorable than the wisdom that governs or administers it. The error arises from the fact that

"You will recall that during invasion of Holland, the enemy lowered arms when we had passed the Rhine after the atrocious words of the Duc de Longueville: *No quarter for that rabble*,[25] for which he justly paid with his death. The following day, I was sent to reconnoiter the country at the head of a detachment. On arriving in a village, without having encountered a single armed man, we perceived a crowd of women and children, who ran away from us and took refuge in a church, The detachment wanted to set fire to it, but I opposed it with all my might, and it was not without danger to my life that I saved those unfortunates. Would you believe that I was denounced as a traitor for that act of humanity, and the command of the detachment was taken away from me in the following expedition?

"In despair at such bloodthirsty ingratitude, I sought death, and in an engagement that happened not long afterwards I launched myself at a battery of six cannons that was protecting a defile. By an extraordinary good luck, the blast did not hit me, and, hurling myself on the battery I took possession of it before a second discharge. The finest deeds of a soldier, if they are not witnessed by a leader worthy to appreciate them, are lost in the obscurity of his rank. Fortunately, that one was noticed by Monsieur de Turenne, and I was immediately promoted to lieutenant.

"In the next campaign I captured an enemy flag and was elevated to the rank of captain. In the absence of a talent or extraordinary hazard, that grade was the *nec plus ultra* of of-

---

the matter at stake is insufficiently explained. The soldier was doubtless culpable if the order had been given to spare no ne, but it is, on the contrary, very probably that his commiseration had been calumniated, because there is reason to believe that, in conformity with the rules of war, the order to kill only applies to those who had taken up arms. [Editor's Note]"

[25] The reference is to Henri II d'Orléans, Duc de Longueville (1595-1663), who was reported by Turenne to have uttered the words in question immediately before being shot dead.

ficers of fortune, but, far from being ambitious for a superior position, I only hoped to retire from the service. I had only embraced that estate by necessity; it was becoming more odious to me from day to day. That unjust and cruel war in Holland filled me with horror, but I only wanted to leave with honor, and for that it was necessary for me to wait for peace. It was still a long way off, and shortly after the flooding of Holland I was obliged to march, still under the orders of Monsieur de Turenne, to the burning of the Palatinate.

"Imagine my state of mind when, having returned to the gates of my native city, which I had not seen for twenty years, I was commanded, along with the regiment of which I was a part, to burn it. I ran to throw myself at Monsieur de Turenne's feet, imploring him to spare my homeland, or, at the very least, the roof under which I was born, where my family dwelt. 'This is impossible,' he said to me, coldly, 'but I hold you in esteem and I will compensate you for your loss. I only recommend you not to say anything about it, for I am not in a position to do as much for everyone.'

"Less touched by the Maréchal's generosity than his refusal, I replied to him curtly that I did not want anything, and ran inside the city wall. I launched myself through the tumult, the blood, the fire and the most frightful and frantic disorder; I reached the paternal house. What a spectacle was presented to my eyes! My two sisters were fleeing through the flames, their children in their arms, and my brother was striving, with my old father, to save his daughter from the brutality of the soldiers.

"One of those wretches was about to thrust his bayonet into my father's breast when I laid him at my feet with my saber, and tried, by having myself recognized, to arrest the fury of the others. A vain effort! Intoxication and rage was at their peak, and no longer knew any brake. Reduced to defending my life, I succumbed to the weight of numbers and fell, pierced by several bayonet-thrusts.

"I was carried unconscious to the general headquarters. The men of the art judged my wounds to be very grave; they orders me to the waters at Barèges, and on their report that I would never be in a fit state to resume service, I obtained my retirement with the pension of my rank.

"My father, already infirm and languishing, died of the effects of that horrible scene. The rest of my family, having had the good luck to escape and to rejoin me, had not left me. I recommended them to the Maréchal, who came to visit me several times. He promised to realize in their favor the offer he had made to me, and as soon as I was in a condition to support the fatigue of the journey, I left for the Pyrenees.

"Since that time on I have lived there, in summer at the waters and in winter in the village nearby, which I preferred to any other refuge. The good air and the mild tranquility, for which I sighed for such a long time, the assurance of the return of my family to its hearth, the reestablishment of its property and its former fortune, thanks to the cares of the good Monsieur de Turenne, all completed my cure and contributed to rendering my retirement delightful. I had resolved to finish my life there, if cruel politics had not chased me away with the worthy villagers who formed my new family.

"A few good books, a beautiful countryside and peace— that was the happiest thought that was present in my reveries after the tumultuous years of military service. All that my felicity lacked, which I have found since I have been with you, was the society of amiable and educated individuals."

VII

Several inhabitants returning from cutting wood on the mountain came to tell us that they had seen bear tracks in the snow. We thought at first that they were mistaken, because the governors had assured us that after the rupture of the cornice, none of those animals, nor any wolves, remained in the Valley, and it was certain that none could have been introduced after the rupture. However, we investigated the tracks in question, and verified that they were, indeed, the footprints of a bear. In consequence, the governors charge five men, among the most expert and bravest hunters, to complete the destruction of what still remained of those harmful animals. I was appointed head of the expedition.

We left at first light, each of us armed with a good rifle and four cartridges. After an hour's march following the animal's racks, we perceived it in the distance, retreating at a slow pace. Judging that it was near to its lair, where we would trap it more easily, one of us climbed a tree in order to observe its direction. He saw it go into a cavern. I then ordered three of our men to go around the cavern by way of a long detour, and to approach it when we did, so as to catch the bear at the same distance between two fires when it emerged from its shelter.

The order was executed perfectly. We all stopped some twenty paces away to either side of the cavern. In response to the shouts we uttered the animal appeared, roaring. It was immediately felled by three rifle shots. The noise of the discharge drew another bear out of the cave, at which three further shots were aimed. The latter, less grievously wounded, got up from its fall and hurled itself in our direction, but we had had time to reload, and it was finished by a second fusillade.

Two little cubs, barely able to walk, then appeared at the entrance to the cavern. We approached them cautiously, and having assured ourselves that the two animals we had killed were a male and a female, and that none remained but the two cubs, still being nursed by their mother, we took them away.

The education of those animals has confirmed the opinion that I have held for a long time, than in general, the instinct of carnivorous animals is far superior to that of herbivores. Our bears are perfectly domesticated, as faithful and as vigilant as the best guard dogs. They protect our sheep from attack by eagles, the only enemy that we now have to fear. They acquit that function all the better because an eagle has no adversary more redoubtable than a bear; they flee at top sped as soon as they perceive or hear one.

That superiority of instinct in the animals that live on flesh is necessary in order that they can find and surprise their prey. If the wolf were not more cunning than the ewe, the species would not have been able to survive. I am thus disposed to believe that the most intelligent of animals is not, as is claimed, the strongest of the class of herbivores—to wit, the elephant—but the most redoubtable of carnivores, to wit, the lion.

Several facts come to the support of this opinion. It is known that in Asia, lions are trained for hunting, and that no other animal can compare with it for skill. Who does not know the story of the hungry lion, launched into the arena against a slave, whose feet it came to lick, recognizing in that wretch, who was expecting to be devoured, the benefactor who had once cured it of a dolorous wound? The ancients possessed the art of taming that terrible animal. Those enjoying triumphs harnessed them to their chariots; they have been seen following their masters like dogs, and perhaps one might succeed, with time, patience and a few precautions, in making that class of animals domestic, attached to the service of humans like that of dogs, which were originally savage and ferocious, and still are in some countries.

That occasion was the last on which use was made of firearms for hunting. The governors, judging that some need more important for their employment might arise, had all the powder and al the rifles that remained in the valley collected and locked away. The bow has been substituted for the rifle. The use of that weapon, so widespread before the discovery of gunpowder, was initially very awkward, but in a short time, exercise and competition produced archers who would have been able to match themselves against the most celebrated in Crete.

Game is quite abundant in hares, partridges, capercaillies, pigeons, grouse and, in certain seasons, various migratory birds. Prudent measures have nevertheless been taken in respect of the permanent residents to conserve the species. The eagle is the only enemy against which there is no truce.

Everyone, after the completion of the agricultural excavations, having been occupied in the construction of cabins, our new town was completed in the course of the winter. We followed for its form the plan of the town of Versailles. The governors' house is on a small eminence from which a row of twelve cabins extended to either side. Those cabins are designed solely for human accommodation. Behind them are the common stables for the animals. That separation, contrary to the custom of the region, which mingles the human species with animals in the same habitation, was preferred because of its salubrity.

Every cabin is divided into two parts. The beds of the girls are in one, the beds of the boys in the other; it was thought that purity of mores, the most efficacious of all laws, depends principally on modesty and innocence in early age.

Meals are taken in common in each family, but every Sunday, the governors invite ten inhabitants to their table. These invitations are ordinarily made in the natural and successive order, without distinction of age or sex, unless some circumstance demands a deviation from that habitual order. As the object of those banquets, somewhat similar to that of the seven sages, is to maintain peace, union and virtue by exhortation, praise or reprimands, according to circumstance, the order is sometimes disturbed, but it is unheard of for an individual punished by non-admission to the chiefs' table in his turn to merit the same mortification for a second time.

After having provided for the conservation of the society, we occupied ourselves with the temporal end of its members. Death can inspire great thought to the profit of the living. It is in the bosom of a cemetery that the most eloquent lessons in morality sometimes arise. Our sage governors have established, for all individuals without distinction, the law that only applied in Egypt to kings. In consequence, the memory of a person whose career has just ended is subjected to an examination before their body enters its last refuge. An inscription raised over the grave contains the judgment that has been pronounced. Their descendants participate in this world in the recompense or punishment that the judges assign in the other. Virtue is the only stock of nobility, but woe betide the off-shoots of that fine stem that bear degenerate fruit; it is degraded pitilessly and relegated, if it is merited, to the lowest class.

The field of rest is some distance from the village, in a field surrounded by a ditch and a living hedge. Above the entrance gate the words can be read: *It is here that human beings quit their terrestrial remains in order to dwell in the celestial domain from which they descended.*

At the birth of every child, a tree is planted in the field of death which bears their name. That marks the spot that they will occupy at the end of their life. They often visit the plant with which they will one day be united forever. They delight, in childhood, in surrounding it with the most beautiful spring flowers; the two of them grow and develop at the same time, and both, perhaps, will conclude their careers together. Thus the terrors of the final moment are appeased, and people become accustomed to seeing the growth, decay and dissolution of the material part of their own being with the same eyes that they observe the successive changes in the tree that bears their name.

If I were writing a book that was to pass into the world that we have quit, the inhabitants of that world, who have no notion of ours, might ask me with the most ardent curiosity for details of education, marriage, our work, our pleasures, or laws, our costumes, etc. All these different subjects would be the subject-matter of other chapters susceptible of greater interest, but I am writing for the posterity of our Valley, which will be eternally isolated, and an uninterrupted tradition will transmit precise instructions to them on all these subjects. There is, however, one subject that does seem to me to require written information, in order that routine, always a trifle vague, does not take the place of regulation, and that the plan traced will always be followed, and that subject is education.

The education of our children commences at the age of seven. Until that epoch, where the first glimmers of intellect commonly appear, announced by curiosity, questions and the desire for knowledge, they remain in the sole dependency of their mothers or their relatives. That precious curiosity is then directed toward useful objects. Five of the people most distinguished for their wisdom and knowledge are charge with that responsibility; the first ones named for that purpose were the two governors, the former minister, the old soldier and me.

From the age of seven until that of eighteen, the male children live under the same roof, eat at the same table and are continually under the gaze of one or more of the five masters. They learn to read and write, and as their intelligence develops, they receive a few elementary notions of physics, geometry, astronomy, geography and history. They are even given an idea of the fine arts, painting and music.

"What purpose does such instruction serve in a desert?" one might ask in the world, if this writing were known there. Not to make the persons who possesses it shine, I would reply, but to make them happy. The pleasures of the senses are not only extinguished with the senses themselves, but even in the time of their greatest energy they are almost always mingled with bitterness and regret. What a difference there is between that sad enjoyment and that produced by thought! It is there, truly, that the pure and continuous voluptuousness exists that is said to be the lot of angels.

It is by the energy and elevation of the mind that humans escape the blows of fortune, and even the dolors of the body. It is by that means that they acquire the celestial philosophy of the Stoics, the most perfect class of humans ever to appear on the earth.

As all the sciences are connected, I have now reached the one that is the principal subject of study of your youth: morality.

Religion is morality reduced to precepts. As there is only one morality, so there ought to be only one religion. Christianity was made to serve as its model. That institution was so simple and sublime that the entire world would have ended up adopting it if it had not been denatured. We have tried to reestablish the primitive order. The two bases of our doctrine are, as in the earliest times, the love of God above all, and the love of our fellows equal to that we have for ourselves.

All the consequences of these two principles are developed in our catechism. As it is in the hands of all our inhabitants, there is no need to talk about it. I only think it appropriate to recall the motives for each of those principles. The first, the love of the creator, is a natural sentiment of gratitude for the greatest of all benefits, life. The love of our fellows derives from the very plausible opinion that all humans, being composed of the same substance, and all having the same organs, ought to be considered as being part of the same mass of elements, and that division into various separate molds that form as many distinct individuals dies not destroy that primitive identity; that the sentiment that affects every human being of the wellbeing or distress of another is a confirmation of that identity; and that, in consequence, the love of our neighbor is, strictly speaking, nothing but the love of ourselves.

The catechism that I have just mentioned informs the rule of all duties, and traces the route of all virtues, but as the first poet of antiquity remarked, for the graces as for reason, actions make more impact on the mind than words. The masters' concern is, therefore, to make an application of precepts to the various events of life; if ordinary conduct does not furnish enough proofs, they give rise to them; they try to cover, in the short space of youth, the entire career of a human being, and to accumulate in a few moments the vicissitudes of fortune and adversity disseminated in a long sequence of years. Thus, our young people have an apprenticeship in the human estate, and they arrive at that estate already instructed by the best of masters, experience.

VIII

One of our recently arrived brothers has just terminated his career. He was an old man of ninety-five named Jacques Saintgès, distinguished throughout his life by his temperance, his assiduity in his work, his domestic virtues and his probity.

The entire population of the Valley accompanied his mortal remains to their last refuge, but the prescribed examination and judgment could not take place in regard to a man whose life, although so long, only lasted very briefly in our midst. During the funeral march, the consolatory hymn was sung, which softened the tears by giving a hope to the regrets, and an inscription recalled the esteem that he enjoyed constantly in his homeland.

In this month of February two male children were born three days apart. As we all form a single family, the subjects of joy of one of our brethren are common to all the others, and births are placed in the first rank of public celebrations. Two trees have been planted in the field of souls, and the names of the new-borns engraved on a plank paced beside each tree until they are strong enough to bear the inscription. The days have been celebrated by dances, various games and the exercise of the bow; communal meals crowned the festivities.

Several of our young men, who have made a choice among the young women of the Valley, desired to consecrate it immediately by marriage, but one of our laws specifies that no one can marry before the first of November or after the first of April. Two motives inspired and protect that disposition. The first is to leave the couple more time to get to know one another well before the engagement; the second is not to interrupt the agricultural labor, and to postpone all individual festivities until the time that nature has marked for repose. A third advantage follows from that delay in the most important act of life, of which the lovers usually only now the value a long time afterwards, and that is the prolongation of desires and hope.

Dread and hope are two sentiments that seem to be reserved to humans. There is no future for an animal; born to present sensation, it seems deprived of the imagination that rejoices or suffers in an idea, often with more energy than in reality. If the anticipation of pain is a cruel privilege of the human species, that of happiness is a very precious compensation. It would be extravagant to think that it might be possible to extinguish entirely the sentiment of dread while leaving access to our souls for that of hope. Both of them necessarily have the same degree of intensity, and anyone who might die of the fear of harm might also expire of the hope of pleasure. The only thing that is sometimes with the power of human being is to abridge the duration of one and prolong the duration of the other.

The more than a hoped-for happiness increases in the imagination, however, the more it excites the ardor for enjoyment, and the more difficult it is to postpone the moment. That is why the constraint is salutary, and the tyranny benevolent. Our young people are chagrined and curse the cruelty of the law every day, but in the meantime, their heart is full of the most delightful sentiments; one day, they might experience sharper ones, but never ones as pure and as continuous.

There were, however, two young people among the number of lovers for whom the delay was an unbearable torment. They were two rivals, both ardent and presumptuous, flattering themselves aloud with the anticipation of a complete victory, and trembling in the silence of solitude with the fear of a shameful defeat. The young woman with whom they were smitten was firmly decided in her choice, but whatever insistence were made, she refused to declare it. The impetuosity of their character made her shiver, and she preferred to impose a silence that tormented them than cause, by explaining herself, the eternal unhappiness of one of the two.

The governors decided that this case merited an exception; that one was required by the same motive that had dictated the law, the happiness of the interested parties; that the young woman could not declare her choice too soon and that the declaration ought to be made with the greatest solemnity

In consequence, they invited the young woman, in an assembly of all the inhabitants, to let her heart speak freely. Perceiving that the presence of the two rivals intimidated her and closed her mouth, however, they asked them both to step outside momentarily. When she was able to express herself without fear, she admitted her penchant. The two rivals were then called back in, before whom she was emboldened and confirmed that admission.

As the future spouses had known one another for a long time, their union was concluded the same day. After having signed the certificate, one of the governors made the rejected lover an exhortation full of sentiment and reason. Our brethren are habituated to hear the voice of heaven in all the circumstances when success has not crowned their desires. But unless one is absolutely insensate, how can it be misunderstood when all the voices of the earth manifest it, and there no longer remains any object of hope? Thus, the same day saw the happiness of two people commence and completed the unhappiness of a third.

Until now we have made use of hand mills for grinding the wheat, but that process is slow and the flour that it produces is neither clean not fine. Fortunately there were workers among the newcomers instructed in the construction of watermills; they have succeeded perfectly, and we now have a mill that is easily sufficient for the consumption of the Valley.

Nothing is more striking in the mountains than a beautiful spring day after the snow, the forests and the ice of winter. We saluted the first one that appeared to us with the liveliest effusion of joy. The governors yielded to the general desire and instituted a solemn feast to celebrate that cheerful epoch of the year. It was allocated to the month of May, without any other fixation than that of the day of the month when the cloudless sky and the radiant sun seem to announce the reconciliation of nature with humankind. At the first rays of the sun that shines on that great day, we all assembled—men, women, children, and the elderly—with the two governors bringing up the rear. With a verdant branch in hand, we made a tour of the Valley, celebrating with hymns and canticles the return of the beneficent star, the father of warmth and life. After a banquet, at which the most intimate and sincere unity reigned, the festival concluded with dances and games.

Refrain carefully, my friends, from taking our expression regarding the power of the sun too literally. We are firmly convinced that that celestial body is submissive, like the entire universe, to the law of God alone; the sun is merely one of the organs of his benefits. It is to the Supreme Being, the unique creator of all things, that the formation and maintenance of all that exists in nature is due; he alone merits the adoration and homage of the human species.

After the day of celebration our work of cultivation recommenced. Those labors are pleasures, because they are moderate, and it is to us alone that their fruits belong. The repose that follows them is also a pleasure, and is equally one of the fruits of the labors: an admirable alliance of occupation and wellbeing, of health, the contentment of the soul, and the expansion of all the affectionate sentiments. Sloth and idleness never know such delicious joys!

That reflection would doubtless be out of place outside the Valley, in those desolate rural areas where chagrin, cares and anxieties are combined with the rudest labors. There, the unfortunate cultivator, half dressed in rags, comes back from the fields covered in sweat, succumbing to fatigue. Coarse black bread, and water that is often muddy, are his only nourishment, while his hungry children utter heart-rending cries and his mind is tormented by taxes, obligations, bailiffs and the barbaric despotism of his landlord. What a state! And those unfortunates are the brothers of the great landowners gorged with riches and honors, all of whose says are spun in gold and silk!

That disastrous inequality does not exist here. We are all dressed in the same garments, nourished on the same food, and if some of us sometimes devote ourselves to different occupations, it is for the common interest—and as soon as they are finished, they return with pleasure to the amicable cultivation of the fields.

Thus, in the peace of God, in his powerful blessing, implored every morning by pious canticles as we go to our agreeable labor, in the perpetual presence of his fortifying gaze, having confided to the earth the sustenance of our life, the harvest that we have collected surpassed our expectations. We have obtained enough to nourish us for two years; that surplus is necessary in the state of isolation we are in, deprived of the means to substitute for a famine is one occurs.

The extent of the cultivation that produces the quantity of subsistence in question is proportionate to our population. If the population is augmented, we shall augment the cultivation in the same measure. There would have to be a prodigious increase for all the land in the Valley to need plowing.

Three people have died; to wit, one man and two women. Henceforth, I shall not mention deaths or births, because we keep a separate register for each object, in which everything concerning the person who is coming into the world or leaving it is inscribed with exactitude. We also have an individual register for marriages. After the opening of the interval devoted to that union, however, three have been celebrated that require further detail than those of dates, names and genealogy.

The first of these unions was between the children of the two governors. No political union between two crowned heads has excited a keener and more widespread joy. It is not that the slightest division existed between the two families, it was desired that power, thus far shared, should be united in a single individual, such seems to be the desire of nature in all things. Different opinions, and hence several counselors, are required, but what would become of government if decisions were opposed? Reason and public interest are united in favor of simple monarchy, the supreme authority of a single individual. Particular circumstances had caused us to set aside that law, but ulterior events have brought us back to it and we are fixing it permanently in place. The son of Dom Simeon, in marrying the daughter of Dom Antonin, has been named as the sole successor to the government of the Valley.

The second marriage that I think I ought to mention here is that of the old soldier with the daughter one of our new cultivators. Finally, I too have taken a wife. In any well-governed country, marriage has no need of encouragement. Woe betide

one that is obliged to accord recompenses to that sweet inclination of nature; it supposes that nature is thwarted by large
obstacles! But everything in our fortunate Valley favors that
desire so powerfully that our attention is limited to directing
choice, matching spouses and, often, moderating their urgency.

We therefore had reason to be astonished in seeing that
the minister of the Protestant village who had come to join us
was the only one who refused to take a wife—but we were
even more surprised when, to our insistence that he explain
himself, he declared that he was a Catholic priest and that
nothing in the world would be capable of making him perjure
the oath he had made to remain celibate. This is the summary
of his life that he recounted to us.

IX

"I was born in the class that is qualified as superior,
known as the high nobility. As I was the last of three children
who were destined to sustain the status of the family at Court
and in the army, my place was fixed at birth in the ecclesiastical estate. However, I was born with tastes entirely opposed to
the duties of that estate.

"I was told that the opposition in question was not an obstacle, and that scandal was no longer a crime, except for the
people. They examples I had before my eyes proved that verity only too well. A host of abbés of quality, celebrated for
their libertinage, succeed to the highest dignities, but in the
city of Athens I had the soul of a Spartan. Passionate for
study, I had attached myself to the philosophy of the Stoics,
and the love of virtue held sway over the love of pleasure.

"At the seminary those sentiments attracted the disdain
of my masters and the mockery of my comrades. They treated
the austerity of my principles as pettiness of spirit, and the
purity of my conduct as ignorance of the world. One professor
of theology perceived my surprise at the contrast between the
morality of Jesus and the doctrine of some of his ministers,

and gave me the explanation for it. He was a man very different from his colleagues; as distinguished by his virtues as by his enlightenment, he lived in that mild neglect of society so dear to people who sincerely love study. He had a few obligations to my family, and it was by opening his heart to me that he gave evidence of his gratitude.

"'All the religions of the world, my friend, are covered in a mysterious veil. I shall not examine the question so much discussed of whether the mystery is useful, and whether it would not be more appropriate if no veil were imposed between the eyes of the people and the truth. That question is one of those that ought only to be decided by experience. Now, I could prove by reasoning that nothing ought to be hidden from the people, but if that principle were adopted it would follow that I, a mere individual, had toppled the edifice of twenty centuries; but if I had done that so easily, another innovator could do the same just as easily by preaching a doctrine different from mine. Thus, the people would be floating eternally in uncertainty, never sure that the religion of today would not be dethroned by the religion of tomorrow.

"'You might say to me: how can one give one's assent to mysteries that the human mind is unable to comprehend? I would reply to you: do you understand the system of the world, the causes of the winds, of light, of fire and a host of other things, any better? Over all these things, we do not blush at our ignorance. The one that occupies us, religion, is far more important. Is not the genius of its divine founder of the greatest weight? The suffrage of nearly twenty centuries has sanctioned that sublime institution. It is for us to submit to it with no further examination. If, by virtue of one of those events that sometimes led to political revolution, the base of the religious institution were to be shaken, it is then that examination might be permissible. Until then, that which is remains the sacred ark; let us give the example of obedience and submission.

"'The double precept contained within Christianity is abused. People pretend to believe in everything about it that is mysterious, and color that belief with the most criminal actions. That is hypocrisy, and is doubtless a great evil. But what have the wicked not abused? It is beyond the strength of the human mind to produce anything perfect; and among the different religions of the world, I do not see one that combines, like ours, as many advantages balanced by so few inconveniences.

"'Conserve your principles, then,' the good priest went on, 'continue to love the truth, but don't refuse to submit to the religion any more than to the government of your country. Did not Jesus himself submit to the religion instituted by Moses, although he recognized its falsity internally? Did he not fulfill all of its rites, some of which were evidently residues of paganism? How would he have been able to preach his divine morality if he had commenced by castigating all the established usages? Following the example of that sublime model, respect the work of the centuries, but like him, build on the foundations of eternity.'

"The advice of the estimable Doctor affirmed me in the career from which I was ready to exit. I completed my course of study at the seminary, and after having stayed for two years with one of my uncles, who was the Archbishop of   , I was summoned to the court in order to occupy a place of confidence with the only son of Louis XIV. I arrived in the famous epoch when the conquest of Holland was intoxicating the monarch with incense. Fine minds, scholars and artists of every order and every class, seemed to be disputing the prize for the vilest flattery. They raised above Marcus Aurelius, Trajan and Henri IV the author of the most unjust, disastrous and futile of all wars.

"Men of genius are rare, and when nature produces one, it not ordinarily on a throne that she places them. The flattery succeeded in persuading Louis XIV that he had superior views and a talent for execution in all things. War, politics and finance: he was capable of guiding everything by himself; on the most mediocre subject, he was capable of playing the most skillful minister. He served as the model in everything, including dancing. His stature was that of Apollo, his gaze that of the sovereign of the gods; men lowered their eyes in terror in his presence, women in modesty and desire. How, with a precise mind, but devoid of genius or education, could he not have been perverted by a poison that kills the strongest minds?

"He had a taste for great things; it developed into a fondness for the gigantic, and forced nature at Versailles and Marly. He liked war; he was persuaded that he ought to be the arbiter of Europe, and all the powers irritated by his ambition drained their treasuries and the blood of their people. He believed in God; he was told that as there was only one sovereign in his empire, there ought similarly to be a single religion, which as his own—and he became a fanatic and a persecutor.

"How long will kings sacrifice the wellbeing of their people to the avidity of their courtiers, the solid and immortal glory of vivifying agriculture, commerce and industry to the frivolous and bloody laurels of conquests, and the title of father to that of oppressor of the fatherland...?"

At this point the old soldier interrupted the former abbé. "I ask your permission," he said, "to make a great authority on that matter heard. I was once a guard in the antechamber of the Prince de Condé, on a day when he was alone with the celebrated Racine. It was very hot, and the door was kept open to let in a little fresh air. This is the dialogue that I heard between the two great men. I copied it word for word as soon as I was relieved of the sentry duty.

"The Great Condé said: 'Your very human opinion, my dear Racine, is not very political. It is necessary in France for a king to be an oppressor in order not to be oppressed. I have made war as a matter of duty, and now I make it by inclination, because I have learned to make it, and one ordinarily obtains pleasure from things in which one succeeds; but I confess to you truthfully that I would have preferred peace—and it seems to me that in that condition I would have even more means of obtaining the esteem of my fellow citizens,'

"'You astonish me, Monsieur,' said Racine. 'Your Highness seriously thinks that war is necessary to France? Is it not sufficient for her to be in a state to defend oneself if she were attacked?'

"'No,' said Condé. 'History demonstrates to us that the reigns of those sage and peaceful monarchs who only aspired to be able to repel the enemy if they were attacked, correspond precisely to the times when France was invaded and torn apart by ambitious neighbors. It is frightful to say that a man must be a tyrant or a victim, but without civil laws, force—that great law of nature, would exercise all its empire between simple citizens; savages experience it in all its harshness. Sovereigns, in regard to one another, are in the condition of savages; without laws that repress them, force alone is above them, and in the contest of armed ambitions, the one who is the last to take up arms almost always becomes the prey of his rival.'

"'And the victor subsequently devours his subjects!' said Racine.

"'It seems to me, my dear Racine,' said Condé, 'that you are arranging all that as scenes of a tragedy, which ought to finish with the punishment of the crime and the triumph of virtue, but your imagination is misleading you; it is not the most peaceful of monarchs who create the greatest wellbeing for their subjects. Being surrounded by the force of opinion, far superior to real force, they do not even grant them that which they possess; for such is the nature of the people: they exaggerate what escapes their gaze as that which it embraces diminishes. From that widespread and accredited opinion, conspiracies and civil wars are born. Ardent spirits rise up on all sides attempting to overturn the colossus that one insults as soon as one ceases to respect him. It is then that the sovereign sheds blood, or allows the throne to be bloodied by factions. That terrible alternative does not arise with a conquering monarch; his glory is the Medusa's head that paralyzes with fear and respect. God and peaceful kings are besieged by conspiracies. Louis XIV has never seen one during his reign.'"

"Yes," the former abbé continued, "that is indeed the character of the great Condé. I have seen the same man weep-

103

ing at the lines: 'Let us be friends, Cinna, I say to you./As my enemy I have given you life;/I give it to you again as my murderer,'[26] who said so lightly the day after the Seneffe affair, on seeing twenty-five thousand men lying dead on the battlefield: 'One night in Paris will repair those losses.'[27] But don't you think, my friends, that kings only make their subjects fear them because they don't know how to make the love them? The Prince de Condé seems to me to be confusing the weakness that one scorns with the moderation that one respects.

"The meaning of expressions is construed differently according to the character of the people who employ them. Thus, an extravagance appears reasonable in the eyes of a madman, and tenderness is regarded as weakness by a despot. The Vicomte de Turenne thought very differently from the Prince on that subject. Of the two great captains, one was as economical with the blood of his soldiers as the other was prodigal. But let's get back to Louis XIV.

"The pride for which that prince is so often reproached is accompanied by so much nobility of soul and accuracy of mind that one is inclined to regard his faults as the result of his poor education, and his good qualities as those of his natural character. If his good qualities had been better cultivated, he would not have imagined that the nobility is the only portion that belongs to the human race, and that the remainder, comprised under the name of *the people*, is inferior by nature. He would not have sacrificed the wellbeing of his people to his personal glory so lightly, and would be not only the greatest of kings but the best. At any rate, posterity will never forget thus he obtained, in spite of his enemies, the title of the Great, and it will be confirmed; but it is doubtful that similar confirmation will be given to the title of Restorer of Letters, which has been given to him by the scholars he has pensioned and the courtiers who did not know its value, because it will judge with more impartiality that the letters he protected as a means

---

[26] The lines are from Corneille's tragedy *Cinna* (1641).
[27] The Battle of Seneffe was fought on 11 August 1674.

of grandeur, without either knowing them or liking them, would have achieved by themselves the gleam with which they shone under his reign.

"When the time devoted to the education of a prince has passed, when his ideas have acquired consistency and he has reached the age at which one considers that one has the right to see with one's own eyes and judge for oneself, the slightest censure is a calumny; only praise in the truth. The vices of Louis' education at least had the good result that they contributed to ameliorate that of his son. The most honest man in the court, the Duc de Montausier, presided over the formation of his heart; that of his mind was directed by one of the greatest geniuses in France, Bossuet.[28]

"The dauphin's tutor enjoyed a consideration in the Church equal to the confidence that the government testified to him. I judged by the research he made of my conversation and the questions that he addressed to me on a few religious opinions that eyes were upon me and wanted to know my principles. I revealed my entire soul to Monsieur Bossuet; he saw a perfectly pure morality, but a somewhat equivocal faith. In vain he strove to destroy what he called my prejudices; he ended up by desiring the grace of which he thought me worthy.

"While awaiting the favor of heaven, however, I lost that of the king; instead of the bishopric that I had the right to expect, a mission in the Calvinist provinces was offered to me; it was evidently a test or a trap. I only saw it as an opportunity to be useful to the unfortunate targets of persecution, and I accepted.

---

[28] Charles de Saint-Maure, Duc de Montausier (1610-1690) was given responsibility for Louis XVI's eldest son, Louis "le Grand Dauphin" (1661-1711) in 1668. The latter died before his father, so the throne passed to his own son, who did not have the same educational advantages.

The department of conversions was confided to Monsieur Pellisson.[29] Although newly converted himself, Monsieur Pellisson had obtained public esteem by his courageous attachment to Superintendent Fouquet. He was charged with employing gentle means to bring strayed souls back into the fold; he counted greatly on the most persuasive of all: interest, and I wish to God that he had been as efficacious as was hoped, or that the futility of all those means of conversion had put off the government forever.

"Monsieur Pellisson offered me all the money I wanted and let me choose the region to convert. I chose the Languedoc, because it was one of the most distant from the center, and where, in consequence, the abuses of authority were most to be feared; but I refused the money, convinced that consciences ought not to be made into an object of traffic. I was, however, as animated my self with the desire to make proselytes for the Roman Church, not, it is true, because I thought that one could not be a good man in the Protestant church, but because, spiritual power in France being distinct and separate from temporal power, it appeared to me to be impolitic that subjects of the same empire were not submissive to the same authorities. It is religious schism that has rendered civil wars for religious causes so long and so bloody; that is what still maintains the fire that is not hidden. The government thus had good reason to try to extinguish it, by recalling all citizens to the same unity of belief and submission, but the means it was employing did not seem to me to have been properly considered.

"My friends, in the moral and in the physical realm, bad seed only produces poor fruit. As long as it was sought to deceive the Protestants, far from converting them, they would be driven further away. All the appearances of union, amity and fraternity would be rightly suspected by them; beneath the apparatus of fêtes, under the garlands of flowers, they would always see a hidden St. Bartholomew's Eve. Instead of cun-

---

[29] Paul Pellisson (1624-1693)

ning and lies, I was determined only to proceed in my mission with frankness and verity.

"I began by admitting the first misdeeds of the Roman Church, the principles of the schism of the Protestant Church, such a luxury and libertinage of its ministers and the sale of indulgences, but I explained that those misdeeds had not relationship to the spirit of the religion, that the Roman Church was the first to condemn them, and that they ought to be considered as only of the maladies of the body politic from which no corps on earth is exempt. I insisted on the indulgence that all Christian communions ought to have for their sisters: an indulgence that the legislator of Christianity had recommended so strongly to his disciples.

"Now, you say, given that we are divided in opinion on the principal articles of the religion, which of the two should retract, Rome or us? You see, I reply, like brothers going to law over a trifle, we end up squandering half the patrimony thereon. Your common morality still being the same, you only have to reconcile yourselves to the rest.

"That was the ordinary text of my discourse. I added commentary, I tried to find striking applications of it, for the language of the people consists of proverbs and exemplars, as that of philosophers consists of principles.

"Those means prospered beyond my hopes, and I saw the proselytes of a henceforth purified religion increasing in numbers by the day, which no longer seemed to be animated by anything other than its divine institutor's spirit of mildness and reason. However, either because other means had been employed elsewhere that moved the Protestants to rebellion instead of wining them over, or because too ardent a zeal cannot tolerate the slightest delay, the government suddenly changed its measures. It ordered the imprisonment of the ministers of the proscribed sect and removed children who had reached the age of seven in order to raise them in the dominant belief.

"The Archbishop of the province was a prelate of enlightened clarity, a worthy friend of Fénelon and an enemy, like me, of rigorous means.[30] He had supported me with all his power, striving to moderate that of the intendant, whose character and principles were entirely opposed. On learning of the new orders from the court, he urged me to remove myself to the heart of these mountains, which were about to be delivered to subalterns of the authority, always more insolent than their masters. I went.

"Already, the local minister had disappeared, and preparations were being made to tear the children from their mothers' arms. My name, the credit of my family and the power with which they believed me to be invested, imposed themselves on the satellites of tyranny, and I contrived a suspension of the execution until I had received a reply from the minister to whom I was about to write. What I requested was granted, but on condition of directing the children myself and affirming them in the path that their culpable forefathers had abandoned. I therefore remained the sole spiritual leader in the village. Experience fully assured me too fully of the bounty of my methods for me to think of employing any others. Thus, in order to gain the confidence of my flock and bring them back to the old route on my heels, I followed theirs, at least as far as that which was common to their religion and mine.

"I preached the morality of Jesus. I read them the Gospel. I showed them in their misery the God of the whole earth, who recompenses resignation and virtue. They looked upon me as their own pastor, and would inevitably have ended up as a flock of the Roman Church, but the fear of the dragoons destroyed all those hopes. It was necessary for me to flee with my good Calvinists, for whose minister you mistook me. I cannot make myself any reproach; I have forgiven the crimes

---

[30] François Fénelon (1651-1715), some time before writing the *Aventures de Télémaque*, was appointed to a mission to convert protestants in Saintonge in 1686-87, and used a mild approach that contrasted strongly with the violent and oppressive methods applied elsewhere

of France, and I would have submitted to her spiritual authority the most zealous support of her glory and prosperity."[31]

X

We heard cannon fire down below this morning and numerous rifle shots. We immediately went up on to the rampart, and from there we saw war, with its horrible cortege. France and Spain are shedding blood at the limits of their empire. Two troops of combatants are already at grips; the path is heaped with the dead, the wounded and the dying. They can only continue murdering one another by climbing over that funereal barrier. Snipers of bodes parties have scaled the slopes of the mountains; they are burning cottages, killing the elderly and raping weeping daughters on the bosom of their dying mothers.

Whence came the spark that has produced such a conflagration? What is the motive for a war that will engulf a million men, and might perhaps set fire to all Europe, extending to all parts of the New World? In appearance, public good; in reality, doubtless, the ambition of a minister, the intrigue of a courtier, or some other equally important subject. Cruel individuals, is that how you play with human lives? You sacrifice an

---

[31] Author's note: "I am omitting here various events of an interest concentrated within the Valley; this story comprises the history of several years, but it is evident that there are few objects of general interest in the story of a people devoid of ambition, devoid of distinction of wealth, power and honors, and, in consequence, devoid of battles and heroes. Tranquil in the midst of the bloodiest wars, it only had knowledge of the one between France and Spain occasioned by Charles II's will, in which all Europe was embroiled at the beginning of the eighteenth century. What follows is what is said about that war in the *Annals*. [M. de Montagnac's note]" The war in question was part of the Nine Years' War, usually designated as the Catalan campaign; the fighting reached a peak in 1693.

entire generation to the conservation of your power or your pleasures!

How many seeds of discord and hatred sown all over the world will render even more precious the sweet peace that we enjoy in our Valley? It is the only place on earth that human wickedness cannot penetrate. In vain, long chains of mountains rise up to the heavens; in vain, profound seas separate the continents; nothing stops frenetic ambition. We alone, in the midst of the servitude and the destruction, withstand the fury of the genius of conflict. Ours is the true empire of the ground over which we soar; we could be avengers, and in the excess of our indignation we were violently tempted to roll the boulders that we had to hand down the slope and crush the French and Spanish troops, victors and vanquished, alike.

"We could have carried out that act of justice with impunity, which would indeed have been thought to be an act of celestial justice. Already, rocks weighing more than three quintals were on the edge of the abyss; already they were lifted up, ready to fall upon the heads of the tigers which were disputing the prize of ferocity at the foot of our mountain.[32]

---

[32] Author's note: "One might be indignant at the expressions of the Aerial people, every time they have occasion to talk about war. It is necessary to pardon those extraordinary people, absolutely foreign to our mores, for not having more accurate ideas regarding the duty imposed on sovereigns to maintain their empire in such a state of strength and courage that it would be impossible for their neighbors to attack them successfully. When one is assured of perpetual peace, one can mistake the value of warriors. Everywhere else that language would be reprehensible. The placid Quakers, faithful to their religion, do not take up arms, but they are nevertheless penetrated with a profound esteem for the defenders of their homeland. Those who have studied history know that the most unfortunate of all peoples are the enervated peoples who have ended up being subject to the law of a conqueror. Such, in remote ages, were the Persians, the Carthaginians and the

We were only waiting for a signal from the governor—but instead of giving it, he made us party to a reflection that disarmed us immediately.

"You know," he said, "that the peoples of Europe are the slaves of their sovereigns; those soldiers have been removed from their plows and their métiers. They have come here to fight for a quarrel that is unknown to them. Are we going to bring down on the innocent the punishment of the guilty? No; heaven alone has the power to distinguish the crime; heaven alone has the right to punish it. For ourselves, let us be content to separate the combatants and suspend the carnage; if only for the rest of the day we can obtain a great advantage, and the only one that is at the disposal of humans, for it is beyond our power to do good, and fortunate is he who can only prevent evil.

"A stratagem that seems infallible to me for that purpose is to convince both parties that they are cut off and surrounded by a superior force. Now nothing is easier; it is only necessary to advance all together on to the rampart, uttering loud cries and firing a few rifle shots; we shall not have to repeat that intimidating game twice for our triumph to be complete."

The governor's hopes were fully confirmed. At the noise we made, all eyes turned toward us immediately, with the greatest surprise; a few signals of recognition were made on both sides, but on seeing that we did not respond, each party imagined that the reinforcements that had arrived we for its adversary, and when we had ceased to show ourselves, each of them took flight, doubtless convinced that we were coming

---

Egyptians, and in modern times, the Italians and the Portuguese. While wistful philosophy sees in the distant future peace and amity reigning over the entire earth, the experience of centuries will always retain the terrible phrase in the ears of subjugated peoples: *Woe betide the vanquished!* Honor, esteem and gratitude, then, to the brave men who protect their fellow citizens, at the expense of their own blood, from that extreme of opprobrium and misery!"

down the mountain to envelop them. We thus succeeded, with the aid of innocent artifice, in stopping the effusion of human blood for a brief interval.

We foresaw that the interval would not be of long duration, and that as soon as the two parties had realized that their anxieties were unfounded, they would return to the assault with more fury than ever, but the noise of firearms that recommenced the following day did not draw us on to the rampart again. Although we were placed out of danger, those bloody combats did not provide for us, as those in the Circus did for the Romans, an object of curiosity and amusement; we were not tempted to witness them a second time.

On hearing those voices of terror and death, we bemoaned the sad result of the progress of the human mind, which, for want of direction, has produced over time a host of evils and so little good.

Meanwhile, the solemn day was approaching for us that presides over the rebirth of spring. Garlands of flowers were suspended from the cabin doors first thing in the morning. Soon, groups of young men and women, clad in their best clothes, began dancing to the sounds of flutes and oboes. The council of elders gathered with other elderly people. Finally, the governor appeared, and was welcomed by all the testimony of respect and love. Then we set forth to make a circuit of the Valley, acceding to custom, while singing the praises of the Eternal, who renews the flowers and fruits of the earth every year, and provides for our needs as well as our pleasures.

The strong and sonorous voices of the men, and the silvery tones of their companions, supported by the harmony of the instruments, formed a celestial concert. When we had arrived on the rampart that overlooks Spain, we perceived a troop of Spanish soldiers at the foot of a little fort recently built on the mountain that overlooks the path of transport or passage in that part of the Pyrenees.

Those unfortunates, fanaticized by the false ministers of the simplest of religions, imagined on seeing us that we were divine messengers sent by the Supreme Being. They dropped to their knees and begged us to accord them our mediation.

"Celestial angels," the cried, "pure and sublime spirits, deign to speak for us to the sovereign arbiter of combats; we are defending His cause; may He enable it to triumph over his superb enemies."

Scarcely had they finished when French troops, having scaled their mountains, fell upon them like eagles on feeble doves. Immediately, the language changed as fortune shifted, and the vanquished heaped imprecations upon us.

"Perfidious creatures," they cried. "You came to seduce us, to dazzle our eyes with a deceptive glare, in order that we might fall under our enemies' swords. Angels of darkness, quit your false light; return to the abyss into which you were precipitated. And be forever cursed by us as you are by God."

Thus led astray by superstition, which judges everything by the appearances that are contrary to reality, they adored us as angels and cursed us as demons on the same day.

For more than a year, the noise of war and combats made themselves heard incessantly, almost every day. The same mountain passed alternately from one adversary to the other and back, but the conquest was accompanied by so much pillage that it ended up being devoid of value. The victors no longer dared graze their flocks there; the pasturage, the objective of the quarrel, covered the ground in utter futility, and was not harvested by either competitor.

The heart of our old soldiers was reanimated by the noise; they talked about their old wars, and sometimes still yearned to figure in the new one, but it was only a simple bodily habit; the slightest return to the present effaced the memory of it. If they had had their country to defend, they would have returned to their former estate with pride.

There are no idlers in our society, no drones to devour the honey of the bees. Everyone works, but although the products of labor are common, not all labor is similar. The foremost is, beyond a doubt, agriculture, but along with agricultural workers one needs millers to grind their wheat, blacksmiths to fashion their implements, and weaves for their clothes. An accident has just given birth to a new class of workers.

One of thatched cottages in the village caught fire, and one of our brothers who had gone up to the roof to extinguish it fell with the covering and broke a leg. From the bosom of the crowd that surrounded him and lavished him with sterile expressions of sympathy, a man suddenly emerged who, after examining the fracture, guaranteed its cure. The man was known for his useful and adroit treatment of the sick. A treatise on anatomy that he had found in the library had fortunately revealed his inclination and aptitude for that science and everything related to it. He had often applied it successfully to animals; several had been cured by his care of ulcers, dislocations and fractures.

In general, surgery is the most certain of all the branches of the science relative to the cure of human maladies, and perhaps the only one that is reliable. It only operates on visible ills and by similarly evident methods: no conjectures or palpations, no diversity of opinions and theories, as in medicine. If a man has a broken arm there is only one way of repairing the fractured bone; in consequence, there is no contestation, unless between the zeal and skill of the surgeons summoned.

But it is not the same for a man attacked by an internal malady. What is the malady? What causes it? What is the invalid's temperature? And so on: so many questions to resolve. Then come as many different curative systems. Each physician has his opinion, founded on experience; all the opinions differ, but all are nevertheless right, because temperaments are not the same and the remedy that cures one patient might kill another. How can one discern, among such a great variety of temperaments, the remedies appropriate to seemingly similar maladies that are really as viable as the subject?

It is that uncertainty which, in all times, has spread clouds over the utility of medicine. Good minds have regarded it as a conjectural science, as often deadly as salutary. Thus, all things considered, it is at least dubious that our ignorance in that matter was a misfortune—but we had all the more reason to cultivate surgery, which, independently of the cures of external evils that are particular to it, is often more familiar with, and cures more reliably than medicine, those born of internal disorders. It has therefore appeared to us to be necessary to form a school for that useful art. Young Laurent, whom hazard has presented to us in such a favorable manner, has been appointed its professor.

A few pupils, chosen from among the young people who show most disposition for it, will be attached to that establishment. The nourishment and sustenance of those disciples of Aesculapius is a further burden on our agricultural workers, of which they are far from complaining, since it will only be an indemnity of essential services which might be necessary to them at any moment. Thus, in our society, all individuals are useful to one another, and all work contributes to the common prosperity.

Until now we had only known the advantages of our isolation from the rest of the world; this year, we have experienced its inconveniences, Our wheat-fields, partly frozen by heavy frosts that occurred at the beginning of spring and partly drowned by deluges of rain that fell as it was about to be harvested, have only yielded a quarter of their accustomed produce. In all the parts of the civilized world, such a difficulty could be easily repaired through the channels of commerce. Constrained here to obtain all our resources internally, instead of seeking to augment our provisions in conformity with our needs, we have been forced to regulate our needs in accordance with the quantity of our provisions.

It is in that terrible necessity that the philanthropy has developed that renders to every individual the misfortune of his brothers. Weakness and malady have rights that are nowhere more sacred than among us; pregnant women, nursing mothers, children and convalescents have not experienced any dearth. All those to whom nature has given strength and courage have competed for the honor of supporting a part of their lot in the general distress.

Struck by that sad event, our Englishman, Monsieur Odgermont, keenly regretted the potato, long naturalized in his homeland, which was absent from our valley. He has often told us about the great advantages of that root. The rain that caused our wheat to perish would have been very favorable to its growth, and the same cause would have produced the ill and its remedy. The root was unknown in our mountains when our fathers left them in order to settle here. Perhaps it is there now, but how and my what route could we procure it? It would be a hazard bordering on prodigy.[33]

XI

For some time now, a violent desire to have news of our fathers' fatherland has been widespread in the colony. It is nearly fifty years[34] since they left it to come and settle in the valley; death has harvested almost all of them since that time, and there bones are resting honorably in the abode of eternal pace. Only four individuals of that generation are still alive.

Those four elders had opposed the stir of curiosity for a number of reasons. "You can only satisfy it," they say, "by sending one of our brothers to our former homeland. Even admitting that an exit from the valley and a return might be practicable, who would be our traveler's guide in an unknown world? Might the evil men that chased us away not have been reproduced in their race? What would become of our worthy

---

[33] Author's note: "The omission of a few events devoid of any kind of interest outside the enclosure of the Valley obliges me to leave another gap in the manuscript here. I shall resume the story with one of the great events consigned to the Annals of the Aerial people. [M. de Montagnac's note]"

[34] Again, this figure is slightly odd; given that the valley was certainly first settled in the late 1680s and the indication given shortly is that it is now 1729.

brother in the midst of those devouring wolves? If he escapes their ferocity, would he not have to dread the poison of their equally murderous voices? Do you want to expose yourselves to the pestilential contagion that the innocent victim might bring back among you?"

These various objections were easily demolished. We would only make use of the rope manufactured to let our brother down to the ground after having tested it with a considerable weight. Our brother would have for a guide the least aged of the four survivors from the old world, who has already asked to accompany him. If the two voyagers perceive the slightest appearance of trouble they will immediately retrace their steps. With regard to the vices of the society that they will be obliged to frequent, it is impossible that they would ever seduce the people of the Aerial Valley.

One motive more powerful than curiosity encourages the voyage. The population of the Valley has increased considerably since its establishment, and we anticipate, albeit in the distant future, a moment when the number of inhabitants will exceed the extent of the terrain. It will be as well, before emerging from our Ark, to send forth an exploratory dove; it will come back swiftly, sad and fugitive, without having seen anywhere to rest its feet, or it will bring us in its beak a green branch, and we shall learn in that manner whether the earth is habitable, or if water still covers its entire surface.

While we were occupied with that important objective, a weary falcon came to land near one of our cabins. It was easily caught. It was wearing a collar around its neck on which these words were engraved:

I belong to the king of France, year of grace 1729, epoch of general peace throughout Europe.[35]

---

[35] Author's note: "It will be remembered that in that era, Europe had enjoyed peace for nine years, and that the general peace in question was untroubled for a further five years."

That news seemed to have been sent to us from Heaven. The words "general peace" clearly announced not merely an end to political quarrels but also that of the war of religion that had obliged our ancestors to abandon their fatherland. Thus, France, tranquil internally as well as externally, was now enjoying all the favors of her rich soil and her beautiful sky, and the motherland, repenting its persecution of our fathers, would open her bosom and extend her arms to her fugitive children.

Our elders were not the last to adopt that opinion; all views were in accord; it was merely a question of determining who among us would be confided with that great mission.

The suffrage fell almost unanimously upon our governor. He was a man of middle age who had received from nature a decided taste for the study of government and the religion and mores of different peoples. The books of history, as many ancient as modern, that our fathers had brought with them had guided him in that research. He theory was profound; he ardently desired to verify it with facts. In any case, being the son of Monsieur de Montalègre,[36] a counselor of the parliament of Toulouse, one of the founders of our colony, it would be easier for him than for anyone else to instruct himself as to the present politics of France.

He was replaced during his absence by the deputy governor. He was accompanied by one of the four old men born on that earth. The latter was still capable of supporting the fatigues of the journey, and had not forgotten the patois in usage in the mountains of the Pyrenees.

---

[36] This must be Simeon's son Rubens—and subsequent events confirm that hypothesis—although it is odd that only his older companion is said to have been born outside the valley, given that he and his wife Dina were both among the original settlers. Rubens was in his teens in the late 1680s and would now be in his fifties, provided that the text's twice-repeated interval of "fifty years" is ignored.

While the Council was occupied in drafting instructions for the voyagers, another party of our brothers worked on their Aerial vehicle. This is what it comprised:

Among several trees that shadowed the circular rampart of the valley, growing on the side facing France, was a gnarled and robust beech. That tree had grown at a slant, projecting outwards, but was attached to the rock by vast and profound roots. It was capable of supporting the heaviest burdens all the way to the top. Several of our brothers had tested it be advancing far enough along the trunk to plunged their gazes all the way to the foot of the rampart. That tree was cut half way along its length; the bushy crown detached by the ax fell with an enormous noise. The extremity of the trunk was then opened by two saw-cuts to form a mortise; a wheel and pulley were introduced into it, fixed there by an iron axle.

The hempen rope that had been woven was passed through the pulley, and one of the ends of the rope was attached to a stone weighing between three and four hundred pounds, which was lowered to the foot of the mountain and hauled back up again without the slightest accident.

The proof of the apparatus having been made in that manner, we were perfectly tranquil regarding the success of our voyagers' descent. Their departure was fixed for two days thereafter.

However, on seeing the moment of their separation so imminent, the voyagers were besieged by troubles and anxieties. They were about to quit a country where all physical needs, and all those of the heart and mind were completely met, and the pain and pleasure of an individual were felt by the entire society. In brief, the same soul seemed common to all the brothers of that great society.

What would they find in exchange of an abode heaped with so many favors? A country entirely unknown for fifty years, which, in that epoch, exhausted by long external wars with all the powers, was completing its destruction by a persecution as unjust as it was bloody against the most industrious and most useful portion of its own inhabitants. Was it not reasonable to suppose that that country, expiating its pride, might have fallen prey to the vengeance of rival powers or the despair of its unfortunate citizens?

Those reflections were less dolorous for the older of the two voyagers; he no longer had a wife, his married children saw before them a numerous posterity, and their gazes turned less frequently toward their father. But our brother Montalègre was the unique object of the love of his tender spouse; tears flowed abundantly in the secrecy of the nuptial bed.

Among the objects necessary for the great voyage, money was not forgotten. All the cash that had been brought, as much by the founders of the colony as by the citizens who came to populate it, had been gathered together and deposited in the governor's house. The sum was quite considerable, but, money being of no utility for the needs of the Valley, the box in which it was contained had not been opened for more than forty years. Three thousand livres was taken out, which seemed sufficient for the expenses of the mission; a further three thousand livres were to be employed for the purchase of objects that might present themselves.

It was agreed that our voyagers would sound their horn three times to announced their return to the foot of the mountain; at that signal, the rope would be sent down that would haul them back up into the Valley.

At dawn on the day appointed for the departure, the voyagers went to the rampart, surrounded by their families and fooled by all the inhabitants. Curiosity, surprise and fear were panted alternately in their expressions.

Meanwhile, a seat was attached to one of the ends of the rope on which the voyagers could sit. The other end was coiled around a windlass in order that the descent might be more gradual and less perilous.

The elder, Andossy, took his place on the seat first. While he descended, the people sang a hymn, asking Heaven for a favorable welcome on the ground, and a happy and prompt return. The old man, suspended over the abyss, joined his voice with the concert of his brethren.

When he had reached the ground at the bottom of the mountain, the seat was brought back up and the younger man placed himself upon it, after having hugged his desolate wife for the last time. The songs never ceased to resound in the air until he too reached the ground. Then we saluted again, and followed them with our eyes, until they disappeared entirely in the distance.

XII

This is the relation of the voyagers, written by our friend Montalègre:

We descended to the earth on the third of July 1729, an hour after sunrise. After having followed a shaded path to the left and then the stream of a cascade, we arrived on a vast plain covered with gravel and the debris of rocks. Our plan was not to stop on that first day, until we reached Garringue, Andossy's natal village. Although it was more than forty years since he had left it, he had not forgotten that it was situated on a high hill above the torrent. Thus, we were sure of finding it by not losing sight of the waters. We had encountered on our way a few shepherds, who had reminded our brother of his native tongue.

Finally, after three hours of marching, we discovered Garringue, elevated on a plateau. We climbed up by a sinuous path carved into the rock. But what was our brother's surprise when we found his village abandoned and deserted, all the houses denuded of their thatch and most of the walls fallen into ruin. He searched for his paternal roof; the interior was full of brambles and piles of stones that served as retreats for snakes and scorpions. The land around, once ornamented with beautiful wheat-fields, was covered in gorse and heather. There was hardly any trace of the ancient furrows.

It was only half a league further on that we found a commencement of agriculture. Until then, the mountains, closely approaching on either side, only left a passage for the torrent. The sun only appeared for a few hours in that narrow defile, where cold vapors reigned almost constantly. Afterwards, the slope became less steep and presented some surface for exploitation, but cultivation is exceedingly difficult on soil inclined by seventy-five degrees. It was accomplished by means of oxen, which, in spite of their small stature and extreme lightness, would not have been able to maintain themselves upright on the precipice without the support of the laborer.

We stopped at the first hamlet. My brother Andossy was immediately recognized by a few old neighbors who wept with tenderness and joy on seeing him again. We sat down at their frugal table, and slept beneath their hospitable roof. They told us the story of what had happened after the flight of our brothers from the village of Garringue in these terms:

"Shortly after that event, the government put the fugitives' property up for sale. Although the possessions would have suited us principally, we were too attached to our unfortunate neighbors to take possession of their spoils. The same sentiment of fraternity united all the mountain folk. So, throughout the Pyrenees, people thought like us, and none of the inhabitants presented themselves as buyers. A few foreigners were the only ones who came to look at these domains with a view to acquiring them, but we struck them so vividly with the dread of our friends' return that they all renounced their plans. Then we resumed the cultivation of your lands, but after several years of waiting in vain, the hope of seeing you again vanished, and we ceased our work. Your uncultivated fields testify to our regrets as well as the absence of the rights of their masters."

Such was the discourse of the good mountain folk. We could not doubt their sincerity; they all had their hearts on their lips. All along the mountain road, we found the same cordiality, mores and almost the same habitudes as our Valley. We were given excellent dairy produce everywhere, with a very tasty bread made with maize flour, which they call *mistra*. They were the gifts of the purest hospitality. The first time, following the instruction we had been given, we tried to pay, but they were astonished as we would have been in our Valley. In brief, it still seemed to us that we were among our brethren, and the only difference we perceived between that country and ours was the thickness of the air that we were breathing. That air seemed heavier to us the further we descended toward the plain. We were no longer animated by the delightful sensation of existence that perhaps suffices in the ethereal region for the existence of pure spirits. Thus the fish that swims full of joy in descending from the height of a river has difficulty in penetrating into the heavy and viscous waters of the sea.

When we arrived in the plain, we were offered two places in a public vehicle that was departing for Toulouse, but we preferred to continue our route on foot. We perceived that we were no longer among brothers, but among strangers who made a traffic of the needs of passers-by. The meals and shelter or which we paid were not as good as those we had been given.

The country to either side was flourishing with a rich culture, but we were surprised to see almost as many women as men devoted to laboring in the fields. That disturbance of the order of nature, which has so clearly marked by the strength, character and inclination that she has given to each sex the kind of occupation that befits them, is evidently one of the most deplorable effects of the preceding wars. Several consecutive years deprived of their spring had attacked generation at its source, and the women had been obliged to quit their spindles in order to take up the spade and guide the abandoned plow.

What will result from such disorder? If the women are hardened; if they lose the exquisite sensitivity of which the great part of their intelligence consists; if they become men, who will replace them in the gentle functions of wives and mothers? The Amazons made themselves warriors, but they renounced marriage. These peasant women, hang become men, will not remain celibate, but they will be wives devoid of

123

modesty, mothers devoid of tenderness, and will have lost the advantages of their sex without acquiring those of ours.

XIII

We entered Toulouse through the Muret gate, and we traversed the Garonne over a beautiful bridge constructed in the reign of Louis XIV. Scarcely were we within the city walls, however, that our senses were struck by the most frightful confusion; the noxious air of the streets, the tumult of carriages, the shouts, the friction of an insensate crowd, two ranks of tall houses that scarcely permitted us to see the sky—everything redoubled our astonishment, embarrassment and alarm at every step.

We walked in silence, clasping hands from time to time with tears in our eyes, and every time, we experienced the same desire to retrace our steps; but the gaze of God, ever present in our thoughts, affirmed our courage, and we advanced as far as the Grand Monarque inn, which our friends in the mountains had indicated to us. It required some time for us to recover our normal composure. How many time an involuntary memory returned us to our peaceful retreat! Oh, my worthy friends, if we had had any doubt about the incomparable felicity of our abode, that voyage would have dissipated it irrevocably. No, God has not created anything more perfect than the Aerial Valley!

The principal object of our mission was to inform ourselves of the present condition of France and its political and religious principles. In seeking that instruction, it was necessary to be wary of making ourselves known. To that effect, we introduced ourselves into several societies of the quarters of estates, conditions and relationships entirely opposed, and as soon as we became the object of curiosity in a house we did not return there.

One day, passing along the Rue Nazareth, I was struck by an inscription on the fronton of a coaching entrance: *Hôtel de Montalègre*. As I stopped to consider the house that bore my name, and reflect on the fluke of chance that had led me, for the first time, after fifty years, to my forefathers' residence, I saw an old man running toward me, his arms extended, shouting: "It's him, it's him! It's my good master's son. Yes, there on his wrist is the mark of the burn. Oh, forgive me, Monsieur, but I saw you when you were very small, I carried you in my arms. How you resemble Monsieur your father! Oh, what a father! What a man he was! Alas, I was the only member of his household who did not accompany him in his flight. He forbade me to do so; he had his reasons..."

At the old man's exclamations, and the name of Montalègre, which he repeated several times, the neighbors and passers-by had assembled; the courtyard was filing up with every passing moment. At a window on the house, however, a fat man suddenly appeared, who shouted furiously: "François, François, what's all that rabble doing? Get rid of them and close the doors."

The good François obeyed, and said to me with tears in his eyes: "Oh, Monsieur, I once had a father in yours, but now..." He held on to me, and begged to be allowed to come and see me at my lodgings. I consented with pleasure.

News of that adventure, however, spread through the town, and the next day I received visits from several people, among others an old friend of my father who had been his colleague in the parliament, of which he was still a member. That acquaintance allowed me to make others in the highest class of society, for the parliaments, since the death of Louis XIV, had usurped a portion of the sovereign authority.

It is doubtless indifferent to you to know how the parliament of Toulouse is made up, and if you desired to know, would it be possible for me to give you an idea of it? How can you, my friends, my brothers, who live in a perfect equality understand that there are societies where wealth and power are on one side, misery and servitude on the other? The class of despots is perhaps even more unhappy than that of slaves. You would surely never consent to a part of our population one day increasing the number of tyrants or that of victims.

At any rate, liberty of conscience is no more assured in that city than justice, and this is what the venerable old man I met, who was a friend of my father, told me:

"My friend, religion is subject in France to all the instability of the ministry. When your father was obliged to flee, bigotry was on the throne; the depositaries of authority declared war on the intelligence that they did not have, and which they feared. Reason hid, philosophy dared not appear and hypocrisy was a virtue. That sad epoch was succeeded by impiety and the most immoral and most abject license. Persecution had already been revealed in the general dissolution that followed that disorder, and the executioners took up their instruments of torture again. Now, a sage ministry holds the reins of the empire, but the monarch is devoid of strength, and his authority might pass into other hands at any moment and change its principles."

I had informed that worthy old man of the death of his old friend, my father, but I had hidden from him, as from everyone else, the place to which he had retired with the fugitive inhabitants of the village of Garringue. It is necessary that our dwelling, like the celestial abode, not only remains accessible but that no one knows its location, its form and its nature. In any case, after a few fruitless attempts, I was left perfectly tranquil in that regard.

XIV

We often heard mention in the societies of a stranger who had taken refuge in Toulouse some time ago, as astonishing by virtue of his benefits as by the care he took to conceal their author. His wealth seemed as inexhaustible as his generosity and modesty. He anticipated the needs of all the indigents of the city, every year putting a large sum at the disposal of the parish priests, and it was by chance that the source of the alms had been discovered. A frightful famine would have desolated the locality the previous year, if provisions had not been brought in from afar by a businessman who was honest but devoid of fortune and in whom, by the considerable sacrifices that the largesse in question cost, was able to divine the hand that was secretly distributing them. However, he had obstinately refused public recognition, and when he was pressed on the subject he said that he was not giving anything to anyone, but only returning a deposit confided to him.

That friend of humanity avoided people. When he went for a stroll, it was far from public places, in the deserted countryside or along the solitary bank of the Garonne.

One day, as we were passing a garden that he had outside the city, we stopped to look through the gate at a large number of hives for which he cared with marvelous success, for no one understood the education of bees better than he did. As soon as he saw us he came toward us and invited us to enter.

We were charmed to encounter an opportunity to inform ourselves concerning the exploitation of those precious insects. Since we had discovered the honey that they produced, we had thought about introducing the practice in our Valley; a honeycomb that we have brought will allow you to judge for yourselves whether that new production might be as useful as agreeable.

The conformity of tastes naturally links men together. That one saw us as savages of a sort which lived in some remote desert in the Pyrenees, and it was in some such retreat that he desired to bury himself. He offered to transport his hives there if we would consent to receive him with them.

As he made us that proposal, the most tender affection shone in his eyes. Everything that we had learned thus far about that man was to his advantage. His mores were pure, his character mild, his knowledge extensive on numerous objects, and profound on the administration of bees, which interested us particularly. However, before making any reply, we desired to know who he was, and the motives for the mystery in which he enveloped himself.

At first he seemed troubled by that request, but a moment's reflection convinced him of the innocence of our curiosity, and he accorded us his confidence in the following terms.

XV

"You see in me a man who, with the purest heart, carries the weight of all the misfortunes of his century. I am devoured by remorse without having committed any crime; I try in vain to efface the past by means of the present. Ardent coals beneath my feet would not torment me any more than my memories. Permit me, then, Messieurs, only to tell you as much of my life as is sufficient to make myself known.

"I only learned the secret of my birth on my mother's death, a few years ago. Thus, I had reached maturity when everything relating to that event was revealed to me. I shall thus be anticipating in time in that part of my story.

"My father was a simple artisan, my mother an honest peasant. Both of them lived in obscurity for a year, at the end of which my father, tormented by an ambitious presentiment, quit his wife in order to go and seek his fortune in Paris. They agreed before separating that the wife would change her place of residence and her name.

"Cleverness, a spirit of intrigue and a talent to please and flatter the passions soon opened to the husband a familiar access to the prince, too facile and too fond of pleasures, who governed France. Ecclesiastical dignities were in the hands of the regent, and to make one the recompense of the minister of his lusts appeared to him to be a piquant novelty that made him smile in advance.

"Then, he sent one of his accomplices to detach the page from the register kept by the curé containing the certificate of the celebration of his marriage. The same man then stole the minute of the contract from the office of the notary. As soon as those two documents were in his possession, he destroyed them. Thus entirely relieved of his first bonds, he established my mother in a rich domain in the vicinity of Tours. She continued to pass herself off as the widow of an officer named de Ville-Franche.

"I was fifteen years old at the moment of that augmentation of fortune. The virtuous education I had received had fortified the innocence and purity of my inclinations, and I as only sensible to the wealth because it furnished me with more means to instruct myself and to help the unfortunate.

"Some time after our establishment in Touraine, my mother had a desire to see Paris. It is rare that a woman, enjoying such great opulence, does not yield at least once in her life to the curiosity to visit the capital of Europe, enriched by the glory of so many great men and ornamented by the graces of so many beautiful women; but she did not think that she ought to undertake the voyage without having obtained the agreement of her husband. The latter, having become the prime minister,[37] consented to my mother's request, but under the most rigorous condition of the profoundest discretion regarding everything concerning him.

"On arrival in Paris, my mother, in conformity with the Cardinal's order, took the title of Comtesse, and I was known as Monsieur le Comte. We had a town house, two carriage and numerous domestics.

"Among the people attracted by our fortune was a very discreet and guileful abbé, who exposed with a great deal of artistry the traps that were extended for me in society, and ended up proposing that he serve as my guide therein. Fortunately, that proposal was not at all to my mother's liking, for, although I was too young to judge men accurately, the man displeased me precisely by virtue of the efforts he made to

---

[37] This datum leaves no doubt—and later information confirms it—that the reference is to Guillaume Dubois (1656-1723), who rose to power during the regency of Philippe II d'Orléans and retained his position after Louis XV became king, but the information given about his supposed background bears no resemblance to the biography of Dubois recorded by history.

please me. She replied that her son, never quitting her, was not running any risk of taking a false route.

"The abbé insisted that at least I should go to visit the Cardinal; it was, he said, an indispensable duty for any distinguished man arriving in Paris, and offered to introduce me to His Eminence, with whom he had the honor of being acquainted. That priest, so great in terms of his position was so discredited by his conduct, and was so notorious throughout France for combining the most abject baseness with the most impudent pride and the most crapulous libertinage, that the second proposal displeased my young and simple innocence as much as the other, but the abbé caused dangers to be glimpsed in my refusal, and my mother, alarmed, demanded the sacrifice of my repugnance.

"To begin with, we were introduced into a drawing room where several individuals of the highest rank were assembled. The abbé whispered in the ear of an usher, and Monsieur le Comte de Ville-Franche was soon called. The abbé went with me into the cardinal's study.

"I expected to see the face of a monster who bore all his vices written in his features, but I perceived, on the contrary, a mild face, a fine and intelligent gaze, and the most affable welcome. After having considered me with a great deal of attention, he asked whether I did not want to acquire a position, either in the army or the magistracy.

"I stammered a few words in a timid tone. He came closer and patted me on the cheeks with the flat of his hand. 'Come, come, my young friend,' he said. 'You have need of a support; regard me as your father, I am absolutely of a mind to serve you.'

"I said: 'Monsieur...' and stopped short. I was torn between two conflicting sentiments. When I looked at him I was tempted to take him for the most honest man in the world, but when, reentering into myself, I recalled what I had been told about him, he filled me with horror, and I was impatient to get away. The abbé strove to make me listen by signs that he was my best friend, and I might perhaps have allowed myself to be gained by his concern, when the Maréchal de Villeroi was announced.[38]

"At that name, the Cardinal's face suddenly changed. So mild and cheerful before, it was alternately animated by anger and baseness, vengeance and perfidy. The mask had fallen and I saw, in all his ugliness, the scoundrel that had been described to me.

"We left without being noticed, so preoccupied was he by receiving the visit of a man that he detested, and whom he would have liked to strangle while embracing him.

"I shall not tell you, Messieurs, what happened during the fifteen years[39] that I spent in Paris. A stranger in the midst of the events and tumult of the capital, my ardent mind was at first entirely absorbed by a single chimera: the quest for the perfectibility of the human species. The attentive study I had made of the writings of philosophers, ancient and modern, had convinced me that a means existed of raising humankind above the limits within which it had thus far been confined. I thought that it was uniquely for want of searching for it where it was that the means in question had not been found. The glory, intoxicating at my age, of such a sublime discovery, filled all my faculties.

"It seemed to me that the three constitutive parts of our being—the body, the mind and the heart—ought to collaborate equally in the acquisition that that perfectibility. From that derived the necessity of perfect health, a broad education and the purest morality. All my research tended toward those three

---

[38] François de Neufville, Duc de Villeroi [or Villeroy] (1644-1730) had been exiled from Paris after plotting against Philippe d'Orléans, but was recalled when Louis XV came of age.

[39] Yet again, this figure is odd; the regency began after the death of Louis XIV in 1715, and it was not until then that Dubois became chief minister, so the speaker cannot have been in Paris for fifteen years, given that he has already spent several in Toulouse.

objectives, and you can imagine how much work was involved; but the results were very different from what I had hoped. Obstinate in improving my physical existence to an ever greater degree, I fell ill; I became almost stupid by dint of trying to elevate my mind; and the profound study of morality perhaps ended up even taking away the sentiment of the just and the unjust.

"There is no point in telling you about the various follies that occupied me thereafter; I am in haste to arrive at the event that determined the rest of my life.

"The Cardinal was afflicted by a malady, the fruit of his debauchery, which took him to the grave. Before then he underwent an operation, which, far from returning him to health, accelerated his terminal decline. In those dire moments, he summoned me, but when I arrived in his presence he was already no longer able to speak. He recognized me, however, and he put in my hands a sealed paper, which he indicated by signs that I ought to take away with me. It was addressed to my mother.

"I took it to her, but instead of telling me what it contained, as she habitually did with everything she received, she maintained the most profound mystery with regard to that writing. Her health, which was already depleted, deteriorated day by day after that event.

"When she sensed her last moment approaching, she summoned me to her bedside, and revealed to me the sad secret of my existence. She told me that my father—and you have doubtless suspected it, Messieurs, since the beginning of the story—was that same prime minister, Cardinal Dubois, too unfortunately celebrated thought France. She unveiled to me at the same time her husband's intrigues to remove and destroy the evidence of his marriage and oblige her to silence regarding that circumstance. Finally, she confided to me that the letter that I had given to her was a testament by the Cardinal, which assured her of the possession of immense wealth.

"My mother's sole inheritor after her death, which followed shortly after that revelation, I found myself the possessor of a fortune that would have sufficed for the subsistence of a province. I detested its origin, and seemed to hear myself incessantly reproaching myself for enjoying the fruits of the sale of my fatherland to its enemies, of that of the functions of government, of financial positions, of the dignities of the church, of the infamous traffic of modesty and innocence. Even if it had not been impossible for me to return all those stolen goods to their various original sources, I would not have been able to repair the harm he had done, and it not have lessened or reduced the term of the chagrins attached to their possession.

"What made matters worse was that the secret of the marriage, which had been so well hidden during the Cardinal's life, became public, and the subject of conversations, as soon as he was dead. How can one confront such a tempest? How can one bear the all-too-just reproaches of a host of victims, and the even more bitter censure of so-called patriots? How, in sum, can only be impudent when one is not culpable? I preferred to disappear from the midst of humankind and to make restitution, by means of an invisible hand, of the wealth whose enjoyment seemed to me to be a crime.

"When that project was settled in my mind, I founded, without making myself known, a hospice for indigent orphans and another for the elderly. After having dismissed all my domestics, while assuring them of bread for the rest of their lives, I took a public carriage in the name of Renou, carrying in my modest luggage, in diamonds and other precious stones, the remains of an odious fortune that I have consecrated entirely to the relief of misfortune.

XVI

"My design, in leaving Paris, was to bury myself in some corner of the Pyrenees, in order to associate myself with the wretched and peaceful mountain folk, and share the favors of Providence with them, of which they are so often deprived. On arriving here, however, I learned that the snow was already obstructing several of the roads leading to those frontiers. Thus, I was forced to spend the winter in Toulouse.

"I devoted all of my leisure time to the study of natural history. What a vast field of meditation! I went all the way back to the birth of the world in order to contemplate the picture of nature.

"In that primal epoch, when evil did not yet exist, the tiger was devoid of rage, the serpent had no venom and the earth was a paradise covered in fruits and flowers; thus, hand of God continued to direct his work, and in that Golden Age, the memory of which is celebrated, under different names, by all peoples, the excellence of the human race would never have had occasion to be observed in their own works. But if, in this age of iron, humans were suddenly to disappear from the earth, the brambles, the vipers and all the destructive animals would immediately take possession of their empire, and life would be nothing but an animate death.

"In the midst of that frightful chaos, let humankind be manifest for a second time; they speak, and all order is restored; the monsters of the forest flee, the earth is embellished by the flowers of spring and the treasures of autumn; they are the envoys of Providence; the miracles without number they produce are evident proof of their mission. It is in vain that the legislator of Parnassus has conspired against that sovereign of the Universe.

"The beautiful verses of Boileau charm the ear without obtaining the suffrage of the mind. As long as reason holds sway over instinct, the preeminence over all the creatures of the earth will belong to humankind. All beings are submissive to them. There is none, however wild it might be, that does not faithfully obey human will, when it is able to make itself heard. There is sufficient proof of that in my experience alone. I have domesticated the most apparently indocile quadrupeds and insects; for instance, these bees, which humans sometimes treat in such a barbaric manner, for which they sometimes avenge themselves so furiously, I have made my most zealous servants; they come to me and go away at my command, caressing me, kissing me and taking their nourishment from my lips."

At those words, Monsieur Renou perceived on our faces a few marks of surprise and curiosity, and was immediately disposed to convince us of the reality of what he had just said. From a hothouse in his garden he took an unctuous white paste, and rubbed it on his face, neck and hands.

Immediately, the bees emerged from their hive in a host. He drew away; they followed him, heaping themselves up on his face and all over his body. He could have transported them like that to the ends of the earth. When he wanted to send his guests away he uncorked a little bottle that he was holding in his hand and poured out a few drops of the liquid that it contained. Immediately, the penetrating odor that it exhaled served as a signal for retreat; without exception, all the bees returned to the hive.

After that experiment, Monsieur Renou continued in these terms:

"For some time I have been absorbed in the study and the concerns of that single insect species; I have saved it from cruel proscriptions. Before me it was common practice to destroy the entire population in order to collect the produce of its labor; I have found the means of obtaining the same result without committing murder, and I believe that I have benefited humans and bees equally.

"These solitary occupations have prolonged my sojourn in Toulouse, and I had almost decided to end my days here, if I were still able to remain unknown—but for some time, people have been observing me with more attention; someone has doubtless discovered who I am. Thus, instead of an object of esteem, I shall become one of scorn.

"Save me, for pity's sake, from that infamy. Take me into the most obscure depths of the Pyrenees. I only ask one thing from people, for the good that I can still do them, and that is that they do me no harm."

We consented to his desires, which procured our hermitage the double acquisition, equally precious, of a useful insect and a brother, in accordance with our heart, endowed with a perfect vocation.

We were constrained to suspend our return journey until the first frosts of winter, in order to be able to transport the hives without fear of losing the inhabitants. We employed the time that elapsed before that season in visiting the useful or simply objects that were to be found in Toulouse. We have brought with us all those that appeared to us to be susceptible of some utility in our solitude.

Among those objects is a plant of the greatest value, the potato. The root in question, which was unknown in France when our fathers left, has been introduced there since, with great success. It furnishes a very healthy aliment and resists almost all the bad weather that causes other productions to perish. Thus, it is an inappreciable aid in years of dearth. With that generous supplement, we would not have suffered the horrors of famine ten years ago.

With regard to items of pure pleasure, they are only suitable to a people composed of two distinct classes, one very numerous that labors, and the other very small, which enjoys and only occupies itself with pleasures. Those things have been brought to a point of perfection that can perhaps only be appreciated and savored by that small class of rich people. Can you, inhabitants of a world that has nothing in common with the earth, conceive of the importance of dancing, the luxury of garments, of carriages, of furniture and a host of similar superfluities?

I confess, however, that there are in the fine arts cultivated down below parts that would be susceptible of pleasing you. I have brought engravings and a few statues that will give you some idea of the art of painting and that of sculpture; but what will interest you most of all is a few pieces of religious music that will suit our celebrations.

I would also like to talk to you about the theatrical performances of the beautiful tragedies of Corneille and Racine; another writer, Monsieur Voltaire, marches close on the heels of those great men. I have seen the masterpieces of those poets played. The pleasure of hearing the beautiful lines of Iphigénie, Cinna, Oedipus and Brutus from actors who know how to make their magic felt is beyond any idea that I can give you.

When the flowers nourishing the bees had withered and the lack of nourishment in the surroundings, with the return of the frosts, confined them to their houses, to live on the provisions that they had amassed during the summer, Monsieur Renou occupied himself with their transportation, and we set forth.

The day of our departure from the earth for our heaven was the most beautiful of our lives. Adieu, superb and unfortunate earth, abode of pride and poverty, accumulation of gold and mud, atmosphere of perfumes and smoke; be proud of your arts and your genius; all the masterpieces of your great men are not worth the innocence and peace of our Valley.

It results from our voyage that if our population is augmented to the point of being obliged to end a colony outside, the only place that is suitable for its establishment is the one where our fathers once lived. It is the only one where their descendants will still find friends and brothers.

Here ends the journal of the travelers returned to our midst. After having transcribed it, I am taking up the pen in order to deplore the terrible consequences of that unfortunate voyage.

XVII

Until that day, we only knew by the tradition of our fathers the malady that attacks all nascent generations on earth, and harvests such a great number of them every year. Smallpox was as foreign to us as the plague or war. One of our voyagers, our governor, brought us the germ of that cruel scourge; it developed almost immediately after his return. We succeeded in saving his life, but that new poison has spread through our population; it has already cut back a large part of the excess by reason of which we had sought another abode in advance. What completes our chagrin is that it will be a source of destruction for our posterity that it will be impossible ever to exclude.

To that physical evil, a moral evil was joined, perhaps more deadly still. That Monsieur Renou, who had desired with so much ardor to join our society, and who, in accordance with the report of our voyagers, we considered at first as one of our most cherished brothers, suddenly changed his language and his conduct. He became somber and misanthropic, living alone in the woods outside of the time necessary for the care of his bees. He even ceased to take his meals in common with us, and, taking with him the nourishment necessary for the day, often only reappeared in the evening to sleep in his cabin.

When bad weather or some accident forced him to remain among us, he occupied himself solely in castigating our conduct and customs; inveighing against the doctrine of our catechism, he preached another, which he claimed to be wiser. His zeal was bitter, and his egotistical and concentrated philosophy tended to isolate human beings instead of identifying them with their peers.

We discovered, however, that that grim man had a great penchant for women, and from that moment, we thought that we were assured of being able to cure him, for it is impossible for the most obstinate man, if he has a sensible heart, to resist the ascendancy of the truth when it is presented to him by a sex that ornaments it with its own charms. If it is from the thought of man that reason emanates, but it is the grace of woman that ensures its triumph. Wisdom might have been astonishing, emerging fully armed from the brain of Jupiter, but she only obtained the homage of the earth be appearing in the features of a goddess.

The person distinguished by Monsieur Renou had a beautiful face imprinted with a hint of melancholy analogous to her lover's character, but, raised in the habitude of our labors and our pleasures, the superior intelligence with which Providence had endowed her only rendered more appropriate to serve as a model. The two lovers became close, declared themselves, and were satisfied by their mutual confidence.

Their union seemed to be consecrated under favorable auspices, for, in the early days, the husband, inseparable from his wife, appeared to have renounced his solitary tastes, and reentered the bosom of the society from which he had banished himself. When the charm of the senses had partly dissipated, however, character resumed its empire; his wife, who adored him, followed him into his solitude, and, either by amity or the attraction of novelty, always very powerful in women, a few others joined her.

Monsieur Renou's natural penchant for a retired life had been fortified since his earliest childhood by a passion for study and rural life. When circumstances had introduced him into society he had immediately lost his taste for it, on seeing that the science of his books bore no fruit there, and often only attracted new lessons instead of eulogies. The misfortune of his birth completed the souring of his sprit. No longer wishing to live with humans, he thought that he might at least obtain their homage by pouring his fortune into the bosom of society. He found a large number of ingrates and an even greater number of discontents; hence his profound misanthropy. The world, according to him, was only made up of madmen, imbeciles and the wicked.

In quitting the earth, he had imagined that he was about to enter the celestial abode, but if he saw in us humans better than those from whom he had separated himself, he perceived nevertheless that we were not angels. From then on his head was completely lost, but, as he had a beautiful soul and a good deal of intelligence, he attempted to justify his system and his conduct, and, unfortunately, he had some success in that among women and young men.

The governor and the Council, alarmed by the number of his proselytes, put to work all means of persuasion to bring Monsieur Renou back to reason. Above all, they represented to him the conditions to which he had agreed in order to live in their society, which he was essentially betraying in seeking to trouble its union and its peace, but he replied that he had never been able to alienate his liberty, that he consented to allow everyone the faculty of living as they wished, but that, in what only concerned his own person, he desired similarly to be able to act as seemed good to him.

People obtained from him the bad example of antisocial conduct, and the offer was made, in order to give more scope to the independence of which he was so jealous, to lower him to the earth that he had quit, and even to leave him his wife for a companion, provided that she consented freely to go with him. He replied that he had not yet decided, and that when he did, he would find a means of leaving the Valley without anyone's aid. After those final words he withdrew abruptly.

It had already become commonplace that in his fits of melancholy he would disappear for an entire day, but in the evening he would return to his cabin. This time he did not come back. His wife, desolate, wandered around all night, calling to him in vain. The next day, the governor, taking pity on her pain, set forth with several of our brothers to search for him. Finally, after long investigations, one of them perceived a piece of paper suspended from a branch of a tree on the rampart overlooking Spain. This is what the paper contained:

The dissolution of my body to organize its substance in a new form is a law of nature, the conserver of movement and life. I am advancing that metamorphosis by a few moments, because my existence is a burden to me. But I ought not to leave my remains in this celestial abode; that would be too poor a recognition of the bounty of the angels who have received me here. Let them return to the accursed earth from which I came, to give birth to another being. If there is any justice, I will have sufficiently acquitted its portion of misfortunes; and there will only be, after my stormy life, serene days to savor.

After that fatal writing, we had no doubt that the poor fellow had thrown himself from the height of the rock. That

conjecture turned to certainty when, on looking down, we perceived a cadaver at the bottom of the precipice. A few shepherds surrounded it; we called to them and threw them some
money, indicating to them by signs that they should take the
sad remains away and give them a sepulcher.

Monsieur Renou's letter revealed a frightful secret; it evidently proved that its author was of the sect of materialists,
who think that the senses of humans contain all their existence, and that nothing remains of them after the dissolution of
their physical envelope.

How can a man who does not believe in the existence of
the soul, nor, in consequence, in that of God, nevertheless be
good, compassionate, charitable and loving? How with the
most decided system of egotism, was he nevertheless not only
the best friend of humans, but also the most zealous protector
of animals? That contradiction can only be explained by supposing both an exquisite sentiment and a false reasoning, a
great sensibility and a bad logic, an excellent heart and a mind
gone astray. Monsieur Renou had one by nature; the other was
the result of his misfortunes.

It would have been the end of our institution of such a
doctrine had propagated among us. We seek to elevate human
beings, to spiritualize even those actions that seem to be the
most dependent on matter; and the other system tends, on the
contrary, to reduce them to the rank of brutes, to annihilate
even the idea, so incomprehensible and spiritual, of God himself.

However, it is so easy to degrade the firmest human being when one flatters his passions and his natural idleness, that
it is not without reason that we feared the progress of that
murderous doctrine. In fact, we perceived that a few young
people were already reasoning instead of acting, smiling at our
religious practices and amusing themselves instead of working.

At first, the Council tried exhortations and the path of
persuasion; they had no success. When it was certain that
speech was futile, we had recourse to action. "You want to

separate yourselves from our society," we said; "you do not think or act as we do; you apparently believe yourselves to be wiser than your fathers; that is what the future will determine. In the meantime, as soon as you do not support our burdens, you ought not to share our benefits. In consequence, we declare from this moment that you are excluded from our community. Here is your portion of land and livestock; extract from them the product you judge to be appropriate, and live henceforth in your own fashion and as you intend."

Sociability is a prerogative of the human mind. Animals, concentrated solely in their own interest, cannot know the virtue that consists in the sacrifice of one's own personal advantage to that of another, because their existence is entirely material, and there is nothing in them capable of transporting itself outside themselves and identifying with another being, of seeing and sensing with other organs than their own.

Our innovators, therefore, in conformity with their doctrine, isolated themselves completely in their narrow sphere. Without laws, without religion, without any common principle, they were soon divided. They had separated themselves from us cheerfully; they came back sad and confused; in tears, they asked us to forget their errors and receive them once again into our society, the most difficult burdens of which they would oblige themselves to support in expiation of their sins. We extended our arms to them, as brothers who had momentarily gone astray.

XVIII

Those dangerous innovations were not the only ones produced by Monsieur Renou's residence in our midst. We had not had any suspicion of that stranger, because our souls were pure and the long felicity that we had enjoyed had appeared to us to be unalterable. He had been penetrated with admiration for our mores, but although he had been keenly animated by the desire to do good, his mere conversation was capable of producing evil. People listened with avid curiosity to his accounts of the novelties of his homeland; the attention that was paid to those stories inflamed his imagination. The simplest things seemed to us to be admirable marvels; he became passionate in recounting them, and, doubtless without intending to do so, inspired the design nevertheless of adopting them. It is thus that a single drop of colored liquid poured into a large jug of water immediately communicates its color to it.

One of the establishments of his homeland that obtained the particular suffrage of Monsieur Renou's listeners was the division of wealth. The community established among us, the sharing that aligned all the inhabitants of the Valley irritated, from that moment on, those who felt endowed with some superiority of strength, talent or industry. If they had had their distinct property, they would have been able to enjoy their natural advantages. The community of wealth put the strong under the empire of the weak, the industrious under that of the idle, the man of talent in the dependency of the inept. Was that not a revolt against the law of nature? Was it not better to follow her inclination and allow a man distinguished by some superiority the disposition and employment of the particular favors that had been accorded to him? The society would find its profit therein, as the individual would find his satisfaction.

A few sages replied that the society of the Valley, having no neighbors, and, in consequence, no rivals or enemies, had no need of talents to give it glamour, strength or glory; that those talents, born in the bosom of physical inequality, and favored and developed by political inequality, lacking subjects of exercise outside, would sow trouble and discord within; that they would destroy the equilibrium produced by the perfect equality of individuals, wealth and power; that they would give birth on the one hand to opulence, pride and despotism, and on the other to poverty, humiliation and servitude.

Those representations were full of reason, but reason being no longer heeded, passion awoke all interests; the very people who, by virtue of their physical or mental weakness,

143

would have been the first victims of change, solicited it with the ardor of blind ignorance.

That conflict of opinions became further inflamed with every passing day, threatening the gravest consequences. The sole means of putting an end to it was to leave to the society itself the judgment of the quarrels that rose up in its bosom, to that effect to count all the votes, and to allow the greater number to triumph.

That opinion was in favor of division. There was then a question of how the division ought to be made, and after some discussion it was decided that the division, of land as well as animals and other effects, would be made per head. It was agreed at the same time that the return to the former order of things would take place as soon as it was requested, and that it would similarly be by virtue of a majority vote.

It is thus that, in all times and all lands, political revolutions, changes of government and administration, or even simply of ministry, have always presented in prospect a great attraction in the eyes of the people. Ancient history is inexhaustible on proofs of that verity. The imagination loves to stray into the vague obscurity that covers the future. If one has experienced some displeasure in the present situation, it is because the order of nature has been disturbed; it can be reestablished, one hopes, and one is convinced. However, the change so strongly desired has scarcely arrived than one begins to regret, bitterly, the estate from which one has emerged.

The satisfaction of the inhabitants of the Valley was, at first, similarly unanimous. It seemed to them that they were entering for the first time into liberty. The robust, vigilant or industrious individuals were finally able to profit from the development of their particular faculties, and the idle, the feeble and the inept to enjoy the comforts of repose. Of those two species of people, two distinct classes were formed, one of which multiplied its means of existence beyond its needs, the other, more numerous, unable to produce enough to provide for the simple necessities of life.

Both of them demanded the creation of a symbol of exchange; it was indispensable, especially for the latter class, that of paupers, who could only procure the subsistence that they needed by alienating their property. Gradually, therefore, the bulk of property passed into the hands of the laborious and the industrious. Then there was a very pronounced physical inequality, which soon gave birth to a mental inequality. The rich people, having an assured existence with an abundance of free time, employed that time in cultivating the minds of their children. Those who were reduced to the necessity of working in order to survive, could not enjoy that advantage. Thus, the superiority of fortune was supplemented by that of intelligence. That double power gave birth, on the one hand, to pride and despotism, and on the other to baseness, abjection and servitude.

That would have been the end of the colony had it been more extensive and richer, or if it had been located on the earth neighboring other states with which it had been able to open communications and establish commerce, but in that virgin land, virtue was still energetic and personal interest had not been able to stifle it. The enriched owners had not been hardened; they often blushed at the augmentation of their fortunes. Natural justice rose up against circumstantial ambition. In brief, their enjoyment was troubled, as if they had had the sword of Damocles suspended above their heads.

Artfully, the governor seized the moment. Thanks to his insinuations, the numerous class of the poor requested and obtained the convocation of a general assembly. Several of them appeared there in the most wretched state, and they all demanded loudly the revocation of the division of wealth and the reestablishment of the old community of property. There were a host of excellent reasons in favor of that opinion, but they were presented in a repulsive manner. Misery is less well able to express its needs the more sharply they are felt. Nevertheless, the most persuasive eloquence would not have obtained more success, if it had only had purely human motives to support it. So the governor, who had foreseen the evil and

145

was frightened by its progress, hastened to put a stop to it by the only means capable of triumphing.

"My friends," he cried, "remember that you promised, before God, to consent to the reestablishment of the community of wealth as soon as it was requested by the majority. I take that same God as the witness of your promise, and of the general demand that has been made, and I order you in his name to keep it."

Those few words, produced in a solemn tone, produced the desired effect, so imposing is the majesty of the Supreme Being, present in our lives at every instant!

However, although property reentered into community, the people remained in the particular order that their distinguished means had assigned to them. They had given too evident proofs of their superiority for them to have the false modesty of not believing themselves to be a veritably superior class. That sentiment was not pride but an accurate consciousness of their value.

In all the great states of the earth, that difference between the mental faculties would have created, as among the Romans, an order of Patricians who, imagining themselves to be privileged by nature would have arrogated all powers and honors to themselves; but the inhabitants of the Valley, who had more rights to that distinction, endowed with a spirit of rectitude and order unknown elsewhere, considered the advantages that nature had accorded them as a musician appreciates the high notes that contribute to the harmony of a concert. Thus the different kinds of mind contribute equally here to form social harmony, without it seeming reasonable to attach more nobility to some than to others.

However, whatever care has been taken to efface the line of demarcation between the two classes, the classes themselves will probably exist for a long time. The first will always be superior, since it can subsist without the help of the other, while the latter, essentially dependent, cannot do without the first. Thus, it is from that first class that the members of the governor's Council are taken.[40]

XIX

Meanwhile, the widow of the unfortunate Renou was inconsolable. Her profound dolor had rendered even dearer the savage tastes and melancholy character of her husband. She had accompanied him in his solitary wanderings, and when he was dead, she resolved to take up residence near the tree where he had deposited his final thought, which we had named the tree of despair. She requested that favor from the governor as if her life depended on it.

When she had obtained it, she went to establish herself at that extremity of the Valley, accompanied by her sister, who had never quit her. Her two brothers, who loved her tenderly, and who were not yet married, brought her the things necessary to her existence every day.

Madame Renou had only been living in the vicinity of the tree of despair for a short time when she brought into the world a testament to her husband's love. As was customary, a tree was immediately planted in the refuge of eternal peace, which was named the tree of hope.

---

[40] Author's note: "If these Annals are accurate, it is necessary to agree that the people of the Aerial Valley are superior to all the other peoples, ancient as well as modern, that we know. Everywhere else, such a revolution would have caused torrents of blood to flow. If perfidious suggestions had led our mountain folk astray, they came back immediately as soon as they surrendered to their own reasoning. That reason granted to humankind is a powerful guide. It would have the same empire everywhere if it were not stifled by social institutions. The great merit of the regulation of the Aerial Valley is that of conserving all the rectitude and all the force that the infallible guide in question obtains from nature. [Editor's Note]"

When the child reached the age of seven, the Council demanded him, in order to give him the education common to all the inhabitants of the Valley and to form him for the kind of life most appropriate to his own happiness and that of his brethren, but the mother was struck by such chagrin on learning that they wanted to separate her from her son that they dreaded taking her to the final excess of despair, and they consented to leave the child with her, if she promised to raise him in conformity with the rules of the community.

Is there any rule, though, that can prevail over the love of a mother for her son? After him, the object that was dearest to her was the memory of her husband. The profound solitude in which she lived concentrated all her sentiments in those two affections. They were the only principles of her conduct, and her promise, although made with a sincere intention of keeping it, vanished as soon as she found it in opposition to the tastes of the son or the theories of the father.

One can judge from the character and habits of the latter what kind of mind he had. As bizarre in his literary opinions as in his conduct, he was on that subject the most confirmed anglomaniac. Young, Milton, Addison and Pope were his favorite authors; he had brought along with their works those of a few English contemporaries. A few interesting passages improvised in his conversations with his wife had similarly inflamed the woman's mind in favor of that foreign literature. Her son was born with intelligence and a great deal of the English sensibility that we call melancholy. Those dispositions, which were only fortified as he grew older, caused him to acquire an aversion for the rustic labor of the Valley.

His mother and the women of her society, marveling at the sight of an intelligent and sensitive young man who composed ballads and songs, decided his vocation. He wanted to be a poet and a philosopher; the titles of that double merit were easily accorded to him by his judges. They never wearied of listening to him; but he often escaped them by plunging alone into the middle of forests or wandering on the ramparts of the Valley. He was sometimes seen sitting on the projecting ledge of one of the rocks on that wall, transfixing by his tones a crowd of shepherds assembled down below.

From the talent of speech he soon tried to pass on to that of style. Glory was nothing to him; he had no idea of it, but the beautiful verse of Racine and the beautiful prose of Fénelon resounded in his ears, and the pleasure procured for him by the reading of those celebrated men caused him to conceive a very great desire to imitate them. The inheritor of his father's tastes, he had also studied the English language, and to form his style he translated various highly esteemed morsels from that language.

I shall only transcribe one of them, but I ought to say beforehand that the talents of young Renou had no merit for us. Several times, the governor advised him to abandon all his writings in order to occupy himself with one of the labors useful to society, but the advice was rejected with disdain. It was then necessary to come to the ultimate expedient.

"There is not one métier in the Valley," it was said to him, "that does not have its value; agriculture is the foremost of them, but the others work for it, and the weaver, the blacksmith and the carpenter produce things that are necessary to it, and for which is pays in exchange. But of what utility for any of our workshops can the art of aligning punctuation or rhyming words be? Your pretended talent, far from being useful, might be harmful, since it might furnish a text to contestations and to disputes. Leave your verbiage alone, believe me, and work like us, or I warn you that you will end up only having sounds and the wind in exchange for our words."

Young Renou was deaf to the voice of wisdom. It required, in order to correct him, that a lesson should come to him from experience, which is always the best master in such things. His audience, which had initially assembled in large numbers, abandoned him as soon as he had lost the charm of novelty. The distribution of wheat that they had shared with him ceased with the pleasure they had in listening to him. Thus, the orator was soon reduced to preaching in the desert— but he could not, like Saint John, accustom himself to living on grasshoppers or roots; he was then forced to take up some useful work.

That purely manual labor was repulsive to him at first, but gradually, he adapted to it, and after a few months he was one of the good agriculturalists of the Valley. In the meantime, literature did not lose its rights over him, but he only devoted the moments of his leisure to it, and became by virtue of that a model that no one any longer blushed to admire.

XX

Here, now, is young Renou's translation.

The Hermit, by Mr. Parnell.[41]

In the depths of a desert unknown to the world, a venerable hermit had been living since his youth. His abode was a cave, his bed a little moss, his nourishment fruits, and his beverage a mountain spring. Far from men, he was ever in the presence of God; his sole occupation was prayer, and his sole pleasure adoration.

That calm, so pure, and that life, the very image of Heaven, came to be troubled by an idea. If vice were triumphant on the earth, and if virtue was subjugated by it, what would become of the wisdom of Providence?

---

[41] "The Hermit," by Thomas Parnell (1679-1718)—the archdeacon of Clogher and a friend of Jonathan Swift and Alexander Pope—was not published during his lifetime, his works being collected and published posthumously by Pope. It is a long narrative poem in heroic couplets, but "Renou's" version is in prose, and is a paraphrase and a digest, not a translation in any strict sense of the term. It therefore seemed appropriate for the present text to back-translate that version rather than reproduce the English original—which is, of course, easily available for consultation on line.

From that moment on, the future darkened in the pious sight of the solitary, and his soul lost its repose. Thus, while the waters of a lake present a placid surface, nature reflects therein a tranquil image; the shore is distinct at its edge, the trees shade it with their suspended crowns, and the firmament sends down the paint of its various colors; but if a stone falls into the bosom of that humble element, the troubled crystal is immediately split by circles that extend in all direction; the sunlight is broken into fragments; the bank, the trees and the firmament flee is frightful disorder.

Impatient so clarify his doubts, to know the world himself, to know which of his books or the shepherds of the desert he ought to add faith—for he had not yet seen any of the human species but a few pastors gone astray in their nocturnal march—he quit his cell, took his pilgrim's staff in his hand, lowered his hood over his forehead, and departed at sunrise, resolved to examine everything with a profound attention.

The morning was well advanced when he emerged from the vast desert in which no past had been perceptible, and the sun was in the middle of its course when he saw, paused on the high road, a young man properly dressed, whose charming face was ornamented by blond hair falling in loose curls.

"Greetings, Father," said the young man, drawing nearer.

"Good day, my Son," replied the respectable old man

A conversation is engaged; questions and replies succeed one another rapidly, and the pleasure of a thousand various remarks charms the tedium of the route. Enchanted by one another, if they differed in years, they were united by sentiments. Thus, an old elm supports a tender ivy; thus the young ivy embraces the old elm.

Meanwhile, the sun was near to setting; the final hour of the day advanced, enveloped with its modest colors, and nature was silently inviting the earth to repose when the travelers saw a superb palace not far from the road. They directed their steps toward it, in the moonlight, along an avenue of tall trees that formed crowns of verdure to either side.

The noble master of that palace had long given hospitality to strangers. His generosity, however, adulterated by praise, was no longer anything but the vain display of a spendthrift luxury. The companions arrived; liveried servants were waiting for them and the lord of the manor came to welcome them at the door. The supper table was groaning under the magnificent profusion of dishes, and everything was shining with a gleam that good and simple hospitality does not have. Taken thereafter to their apartment, they forgot the fatigues of the day and plunged into a profound sleep on silk and down.

The next day, at first light, as soon as the light breeze came to play on the surface of the long canal, caress the flowers in the cheerful beds and agitate the bushy crowns of the nearby trees, the guests got up, docile to nature's signal. They found an excellent breakfast served in a magnificent room. The affable master did the honors, and invited the travelers to drink an excellent sparkling wine from a golden cup. Finally, they emerged from the portico, satisfied and grateful. The lord of the manor was the only one who had cause to complain; his precious cup had vanished; the younger guest had stolen it covertly.

Sometimes a traveler encounters in his path a snake with brilliant skin, lying in the sun; full of anxiety he stops, and precipitately moves away from the danger; then he resumes his march at a timid pace, darting anxious glances to either side. Such was the old man when, already far from the palace, he perceived the stolen object glittering in his sly companion's pocket.

Nonplussed, he stops; he is burning, but he dreads proposing that they separate, and continues the route with a tremulous heart, his eyes raised to the heavens, mournful that generosity should be so poorly recompensed.

While they were walking dark clouds covered the firmament and veiled the glory of the sun; noises in the air announced the approach of rain, and the livestock traversing the plain ran for the stable. Warned by those presages, the traveling couple hastened their pace to seek shelter in a nearby edifice. It was a tower flanked by turrets, raised on an eminence surrounded by a wide ditch. The inhospitable, grim and repellent spirit of its owner had made a desert of the surrounding area.

As they approached that sad dwelling, the fury of the wind augmented; rapid lightning flashes flickered among the torrents of rain, and the loud thunder burst above their heads. They knocked at the door for a long time; for a long time their shouts combined with the noise of the hammer, while they were prey to the precipitate assault of the deluge and the wind.

Finally, a slight hint of pity slips into the barbarian's heart. For the first time, he goes to exercise hospitality. With a chagrined hand he causes the door to rotate on its rusty hinges and regretfully receives the travelers, shivering with cold, under his roof. A miserly faggot illuminates the cold heart. A little brown bread and acidic wine is served as their dinner, and the tempest has scarcely begun to appease when a prompt adieu instructs them to go in peace.

The observant hermit cannot understand why an individual as rich condemns himself to such a miserable life. What motive, he wonders, can lead one to lock away, to go completely to waste, the subsistence of a thousand unfortunates? But what new astonishment bursts forth in his expression when he sees his young companion take from his pocket the precious cup that he stole from their previous host, so generous, and pay with it for the miserable welcome of the second, so sordid and so harsh.

But the storm clouds have already dispersed; the sun is rising in an azure firmament, the green meadows exhale sweet perfumes, and the leaves shiny with dew mark their joy at the return of day with their tremors. At that signal the travelers quit their sad refuge, as the master contents himself with closing the door carefully.

While they drew away, the pilgrim's mind was profoundly agitated by various thoughts. The action of his companion, deprived of their motives, appear to him now as a crime and then as an extravagance. Penetrated with horror for the one

153

and compassion for the other, he lost himself in the explanation of so much eccentricity.

Meanwhile, the shadows of night returned to veil the firmament, and the travelers, already occupied in seeking a retreat, perceived nearby a very proper house in the midst of a perfectly cultivated field. Beneath its simple exterior, which presented neither the spectacle of sorry indigence nor that of vain grandeur, the dwelling responded to the character of its master, a happy man who loved virtue and fled praise.

Our pedestrians turned their wary feet in that direction, and, blessing the modest manor with their good wishes, bowed before its worthy possessor, who replied to their salutation: "Without pride as without envy, I render to the one who has lavished a part of his benefits upon us; he it is who sent you; receive, therefore, on his behalf, a frugal meal given with a good heart."

He spoke the hospitable table was served. Then he entertained them with wisdom and virtue until the sound of the bell, reassembling the honest domestics, came to close the day with prayer.

Eventually, dawn broke, nuanced with a thousand colors, and the world, renewed by tranquil slumber, recommenced the cycle of its works. But before the departure of the travelers, the younger of the two approaches the cradle where a child is asleep, seizes him and strangles him. O ultimate horror! O monstrous ingratitude! The only son of such a generous host, the nascent pride of the house; his face turns black, he shivers; utters a sigh and dies.

What becomes of our hermit at the sight of that horrible murder? No, Hell, Hell itself, opening its profound abysms before him and enveloping him with its devouring flames, could not have struck him with more terror. Bewildered and confused, he wants to flee, but his trembling knees betray his desires. The young man pursues him and catches up with him.

The road intersecting with several others, a domestic had come to serve as a guide. They arrived on the edge of a torrent that traversed the road; the passage was difficult.

The domestic goes ahead, over the long oak branches that take the place of a bridge. The young man, who seemed to be on the lookout for an opportunity for a crime, approaches the unsuspecting guide and precipitates him into the abyss. The unfortunate man disappears immediately, rises to the surface again momentarily, and then falls back forever into the gulf of death.

The old man can no longer contain his fury. With sparkling eyes, he cries: "O execrable monster...!" But scarcely has he opened his mouth than his strange companion has quit the human form. His young face is imprinted with a mild majesty; his robe, having become a dazzling white, floats down to the ground; a brilliant aureole crowns his head; the air around him is perfumed by a celestial odor, and dazzling wings cover his shoulders with their tinted plumes. In brief, he has taken on a divine form, and his gait in that of an angel of light.

At the sight of this prodigy, the fury in the hermit's heart gives way to admiration; his tongue is immobile, his mind struck by a profound astonishment. The amiable angel, with a voice similar to delightful music, is the first to break the silence.

"Your prayers, your homages and your innocent life, have risen on the wing of a sweet memory to the supreme throne. Of such perfections are the joy of the celestial empire made; an inhabitant of that brilliant abode, I have descended at the behest of the Omnipotent to calm your anxieties. Cease to prostrate yourself before me; I am merely your equal.

"Learn the secret of the government of the great Being, and your conscience will cease to be alarmed.

"The just creator, in forming the world, desired that it should be submissive to laws of nature, and that it would be in passing via secondary causes that everything here should progress to its goal. It is thus that, retired far from the terrestrial sphere, the sovereign master exercises his power. He makes the actions of humans concur without contradicting his will; he demands above all that they trust firmly in his wisdom.

"Doubtless nothing is more surprising than the events that have just struck your eyes. However, when you are instructed as to their motives, you will recognize the justice of the Omnipotent and you will learn to submit your reason to things that we cannot explain.

"That superb man surrounded by a pompous luxury, whose life was too sumptuous to be innocent, who receives his guests at a table encrusted with ivory and regales them in the morning with an exquisite sparkling wine in golden cups, in losing one of those precious cups, has been corrected for his impudent ostentation; he will continue to be hospitable, but with more simplicity.

"It was to the wretch tormented by eternal suspicions, whose worm-eaten door never opens to a poor traveler, that I gave the cup, in order to make him know that heaven is able to recompense kindly mortals. At the sight of that vessel he recognized the price of the virtue that he had abjured, and his grateful soul has opened itself to pity. Thus a mineral, penetrated by the active heat of the burning coal packed around it, soon melts, and disengaged from its matrix, the silver that it conceals flows into the crucible.

"After long years of virtuous conduct, the heat of our pious friend had been partly detached from his God, drawn away by the love of a child in a cradle. For him he lived in anxiety, and already he was recommencing with his eyes the course of his troubles on the earth. Into what extravagances might such a delirium have precipitated him?

"God, to save the father, has taken possession of the child. Thanks to my skill, everyone, except you, thought that he had died of a convulsion. Now the father, in tears, humiliated in the dust, recognizes the justice of his chastisement.

"However, all would have been over for the fortune of that man had his perfidious servant set foot in his house again; he would have stolen his master's treasure this very night, and what a loss that would have been for the poor!

"Such are the enlightenments that Heaven has charged me with giving you. Return in peace, be resigned, and no longer accuse Providence."

With those words, the young Seraph deployed his sonorous wings and took fight before the wonderstruck eyes of the sage. Such was Elisha when his celestial master rose above the clouds in a celestial chariot. Thus, at the sight of the chariot of fire rising into the heavens, was the dazzled prophet inflamed by the desire to rise after it.

"O Lord," cried the prostrate hermit, "let thy will be done on earth as in Heaven!" Then, turning back with his mind satisfied, he returned to his ancient dwelling and finished his life in piety and in peace.[42]

---

[42] Author's note: "This small production by Parnell, which appeared at the beginning of the last century, is, in the original, a masterpiece of precision and grace. The subject is taken from the old tale of the Hermit, which every people dresses in its own fashion. Voltaire framed it in his charming romance of *Zadig*; he seasoned the philosophy of the English poet with cheerful and humorous jokes. But it is necessary to agree that that justification of human miseries is no better than all the other theories that have been imagined to explain the ways of Providence. One does not see Prodigals becoming more sage because their gifts have been abused, or misers rendered generous because an impulse of pity has turned to their advantage. The death of a tenderly cherished infant has more often inspired despairing fathers to murmurs against Providence than sentiments of gratitude and love. In general, passions, like characters, depend in part on the nature of temperament, and are not susceptible to simple modifications, but if one cannot change the elements, at least one can direct them and employ them usefully. Thus the skillful groom who subjugates an unbroken charger to the bit, takes a portion of its insensate impetuosity and converts its caprice and recklessness into noble courage. [Editor's Note]"

I am only consigning that writing here as a monument to the power that the Aerial Valley possesses to rise to the glory that immortalized the finest centuries off Athens and Rome, and simultaneously as a proof of its wisdom, not only in not having aspired to that glory, but in having extinguished the desire for it permanently. In fact, what would have been the fruit for us of that intelligence so vaunted on the earth, which consists in vain phrases? We have no idlers to amuse; all the members of our society, without exception, are devoted to useful labor. They would listen gratefully to the man who taught them some means of improving agriculture or the métiers that occupy them. They need common sense in action and not intellect in words. The States that have a superfluity of population can squander it at their whim, but for the sake of our interest as well as our prosperity, we need to inspect in each individual the employment of his time and his faculties. It is necessary that everything works to the common advantage of society.

Meanwhile, the Council assembled in order to weigh up the advantages and inconveniences of the journey outside the Valley, and to decide whether there ought to be any further communication with the earth. The expedition had procured the introduction of the potato and bees. The former was an infallible guarantee against the dearth of wheat, and in that regard and of incalculable value. The honey of the bees not only furnished us with an agreeable foodstuff, but a salutary remedy against several maladies.

The evils of which the expedition had brought the seeds, however, were at least equal, if not superior, to the benefits that it had introduced. What advantage could compensate for the smallpox, which had destroyed a part of the population, and whose poison, now incurably, threatened all posterity, and for the moral vice, more disastrous still, that had attacked the government and mores in their principal root?

Physics and chemistry, it is said, are now the most flourishing sciences in Europe; the progress they are making every day promises humankind useful discoveries and precious se-crets. But the corruption of morals that always increases in a proportion superior to the improvements of the arts, doubtless also produces some new seed of evil, which would be import-ed here along with that of good, and we do not want the reme-dy, since it would necessarily be inseparable from the malady.

In accordance with these considerations, the Council has decided that the Aerial Valley will have no more communica-tion with the earth by any channel whatsoever.[43]

---

[43] Author's note: "There is a contradiction here that is bound to strike all attentive readers. It is said that the Council decid-ed not to have any communication with the earth, and yet, fifty years after that decision was made, Monsieur de Montagnac received the most amicable welcome from the inhabitants of the Valley, as we have read in his account of his voyage; and it was only after being treated for more than a day with all the marks of benevolence that a single individual came to give him the order to leave.

Struck myself by that contradiction, I asked Monsieur de Montagnac to explain it to me. He replied firstly that the Council's decision had never been made public, because they were waiting for another expedition to be proposed, which had never happened and perhaps never would. Then he told me that it was necessary not to judge the people of the Valley too rigorously. That people has few memories because it has few troubles, for it is chagrins, primarily, that fix the epochs of the past; in that regard they are like the savage who sells his bed today without foreseeing that he will have need of it tomor-row.

Monsieur de Montagnac had conformed until now with the principle that he had very judiciously established of only giv-ing the public the part of the Annals of the Aerial Valley sus-ceptible of general interest. I have seen with sorrow that he had removed in transcribing it, at this point, in addition to the list of governors, the writers of the Annals and the members of the Council for several years, two adventures whose subject

Military music has made the echoes of our mountains resound. Having climbed on to the rampart, we have heard songs united with that music, and those songs seem to be a hymn to liberty, for that word has often been repeated, always with the greatest respect. Sometimes, we have even seen the entire army fall to its knees on pronouncing the word "liberty." How have people enslaved for so many centuries suddenly been able to break their chains? What spring has been powerful enough to impel them with such a movement? Is that great revolution the result of the philosophy that was beginning to agitate in the milieu of the eighteenth century? Or is it religion that has concluded its work?

---

and style respired the antique simplicity so admirable when one encounters it in Homer or some other author of the earliest times, but which is no longer anything but ridiculous when it is applied to recent events. It then resembles a modern palace build in the Gothic genre.

I have to make Monsieur de Montagnac another reproach in the opposite direction. There he has published something that ought to be suppressed, and the passage immediately following it, which it would have been interesting to make known, he has retrenched. The passage in question relates to the war of our Revolution between France and Spain. That is the last public event of which the Valley had cognizance. I thought I ought to apply to the suppression an unnecessary or disparate filling, and render publicity to the singular manner in which the Aerial people envisaged that revolutionary war. That war was doubtless the object of the keenest curiosity of the inhabitants of the Valley, about which they must have asked the most pressing questions of Monsieur de Montagnac. However, the aeronaut does not say a word about it in his narrative. I cannot imagine what his reasons were for passing over in silence everything relating to that great event, but at any rate, I have appended what is said about it in he Annals of the people. [Editor's Note]"

We were seeking to determine which of those two explanations was the more plausible when we heard a eulogy to fraternity resounding with that to liberty. From then on our uncertainty was at an end; we no longer had any doubt that that beautiful union was the work of religion recalled to its primitive purity. That alone, of a people of slaves, could make a population of brothers.

Several battalions passed successively before our eyes, all singing the double triumph of liberty and fraternity. They were carrying at the tip of a pike the bonnet, the symbol of liberty, and their flag was dived into the three principal colors: a union that evidently announced that of the three great orders of the State, once so divided: the clergy, the nobility and the third estate. We were talking about those pleasant ideas, and we could already see the temples of Janus closed all over the world, and all the peoples embracing one another, at the invitation and the example of the French.

But what a horrible awakening has just dissipated that enchanting dream! The very next day, those brothers, so tender, transformed into ferocious tigers, were at grips with the Spaniards. After a battle of short duration, the French were victorious; the vanquished, on their knees, begged for their lives in imploring voices.

"Fraternity or death!" was the reply their received, furiously. The sign of acceptance was to display on the hat a cockade in the three colors. At the slightest delay, or the slightest hesitation, the cherished brother was slaughtered pitilessly.

What, then, is this new association, the amity of which can inspire the greatest tenderness and the most ferocious range? Instead of being ameliorated, has the human mind in France fallen back into barbarity? Is not this the delirium that took possession of the entire Roman Empire, on the eve of its fall, when its citizens murdered one another over theological quarrels while the Barbarians were at the gates, ready to consummate its ruination...?[44]

---

[44] Author's note: "Then concludes what the Aerial Annals present of interest. It appears that the people of that corner of the Pyrenees believed that the revolutionaries of the end of the eighteenth century had been afflicted by madness. That opinion was doubtless very honourable for them; it is, however, the most plausible, for the wickedness that turns to the profit of its author is self-explanatory, but depravity taken to the excess that was then manifest. The depravity that tends to destroy everything, without a plan, without a goal and without projects for the future, is evidence of a derangement of the intellectual organs—in a word, true madness.

"It requires a very powerful reason to re-establish an entire great people in the possession of what it has lost. It has found one, and the reparation as prompt as it was unexpected of the evil caused by the dementia will be the most striking and most admirable prodigy in general history.

"In any case, one ought not to be surprised by the limited extent of the Annals of the Aerial Valley. A fortunate people that has no external political relations furnishes very little material to history. In that regard, it is the same for peoples as for individuals; the happier they are the less noise they make. The example of the Aerial people cannot serve as a model for any other people in Europe; its mores, its government and its social constitution are too different from everything that we know; but it is an agreeable spectacle to see the price that virtue can still obtain when it is united with courage and the love of liberty. [Editor's Note]"

Turrault de Rochecorbon: *The Year 2800, or, The Dream of Recluse*
(1829)

> *The exercise of social virtues carries the love of humanity to the depths of the heart.*
> Jean-Jacques Rousseau, *Émile*, Book 4.

I have slept for nine hundred and sixty years, and I awake on the first day of May. What an awakening! How astonished I am! All the cities are deserted; all their inhabitants are in the country; everywhere, the first of May is a public holiday.

Even the king has quit his throne and his court; he is in the country, accompanied by his ministers, surrounded by his guard. His hand is on the handle of a plow; he is laboring the earth. The people assembled around their king are applauding the encouragement that his is giving to agriculture. The four oldest laborers in his kingdom, each clad in a white simar and girdled with a red belt, surround the king, who is clad in his royal vestments; he traces four furrows.

That operation concluded, a banquet assembled under a tent receives the king and the four oldest laborers; two are placed to his right and two to his left. The ministers are facing him; the guard surrounds the tent. When the meal is over, everyone retires; the king returns, with his ministers and his guard, heaped with the applause and the blessings of the people.

The same ceremony takes place in all the towns of the prefecture and the sub-prefecture; the prefects and the sub-prefects furrow the earth with the plow, in the presence of the four oldest laborers in their district, the judges of the tribunal and the maire of the commune.

But what do I see? The ministers are dressed in a very particular manner. Like the four laborers, they each wear a white simar circled by a red belt; on the back and the front of the simar these words are written in golden letters:

Friend of the People and the King

I ask someone why the ministers are wearing such inscriptions.

"It is," he replies, "in order that they never forget that they are depositaries of the confidence of the people and the king, who have chosen them."

I ask them how they are chosen by the people and the king.

"For several years," he replies, "the electors of our départements, before naming députés, are obliged to choose five candidates per département, to compose a list of candidates for the ministry; they have the orders of the sovereign to take the most honest and capable men from all the classes of the French, without distinction of birth, rank or fortune. All virtuous and capable men are eligible for that important position. The king does no longer wishes to name his ministers by himself, for fear of being mistaken; he prefers to choose them from the list of candidates that is printed and presented to him by the députés of the kingdom at the opening of their session.

"Those ministers can be reelected for three years in succession. The ministers who unite for three consecutive years the wishes of the king and his people have honored the fatherland; they are awarded a cross of merit and a retirement pension. It is the same for all financial positions, the levying of taxes, administrative and judiciary positions; as all these positions are salaried, the king wants them to be filled by honest and capable men. The fear of being mistaken has determined His Majesty to charge the electors of the départements of his kingdom to form lists of candidates in each category, in sufficient quality and quantity for the service to be done well and not interrupted. These lists are also printed and presented to the sovereign, who appoints those who fill the vacant places. All the lists last until they are exhausted; then they are renewed in the same fashion.

"The lists of candidates for the administrative posts can only be selected, for prefects and sub-prefects, from among the number of maires of each département, and for maires from among the members of the council of each mairie."

"That is change!" I exclaimed.

"You have seen nothing yet," my man told me. "Come with me to the temple; you shall see something new. There is only one religion in Europe now. The kings, weary of making war over differences in religion and the limits of their kingdoms, have finally adopted the project of the Abbé de Saint-Pierre;[45] they had created a European Diet composed of a delegate from each kingdom; that Diet holds its sessions alternately in each capital of a kingdom or empire. All the differences between nations are brought before it; the nation condemned by the Diet is obliged to execute the judgment it has rendered, or all the other powers would unite against it and execute by means of arms what it refuses to do of its own free will—but that never happens; all the verdicts of the Diet are respected and immediately executed by the powers.

"Those same powers have charged the delegates to the European Diet of agreeing between themselves a single religion, to be adopted generally, in order to avoid disastrous was

---

[45] Charles Castel de Saint-Pierre (1658-1743) was a social theorist most famous for proposing an international organization responsible for maintaining peace between nations. Although he was briefly at Louis XIV's court when he was chaplain to the king's sister-in-law, the Princess Palatine (whose husband, Philip II d'Orléans subsequently served as regent during Louis XV's minority) his reformist ideas got him expelled and kicked out of the Académie. Much of this futuristic vision is a popularization of his ideas.

165

that offend the divinity by destroying the human species, which is his work. They were also charged with proposing the abolition of all customs and rights of entry and exit between kingdoms; all the proposals have been adopted, and commerce is now free throughout Europe.

"Before going into the temple it is as well that I inform you about the religion that has been adopted by all the powers. In Europe, only one God is recognized, the protector of human beings and everything that exists. Every church or mosque is a temple consecrated to the divinity; that temple is only open on the first of the month; it is served by an old man over fifty years of age, chosen by the electors of the department, from among the most capable and renowned men in the département.

"That minister gives a moral reading in the temple; afterwards, he thanks the Supreme Being for the conservation of everything that exists. Two young men and two young women carry offerings of flowers and fruits to the steps of the altar every month; the baskets are taken by the minister and distributed on the altar. The minister, surrounded by the bearer of the offerings, intones in the vernacular language a hymn to the Most High, to offer him the presents of the earth; the hymn is repeated enthusiastically by the people."

My guide had not finished speaking when I saw a group surrounding two young men and two young women in the temple; I followed them and was delighted by the god order that reigned in the assembly. The minister edified me with a discourse as simple as it was sublime, which dealt uniquely with the love of God and one's neighbor. Here are the words, which I have remembered:

"Messieurs, brothers and friends.

"The task that I have to fulfill in your regard is very important, since it is intended to help you understand your duties toward God, toward your sovereign and your neighbor. If I only had to remind you of your duty toward God, I would content myself with saying to you: open your eyes; contemplate everything that surrounds you; elevate your actions of grace toward the great Being who conserves everything; who makes all the globes move to which he imparts a regular rotation that has never been deranged for an infinity of centuries; who makes spring succeeds winter, summer succeed spring, and autumn succeed summer, and assigns to each seasons its functions; who conserves the seed of vegetation in all the seeds during the winter; who develops it and brings it into flower in spring, fructifies it in summer and ripens it in autumn to nourish everything that exists.

"Do we not have enough in that talking picture to elevate our adorations and actions of grace to the great Being? We owe them to him every morning when we open our eyes, since every day we see again the dazzling spectacle of nature, which does not vary and is always the beautiful *par excellence*. Oh, my friends, let us therefore dedicate all our actions and offer all our endeavors to that Supreme Being, as the principle that conserves everything and from whom all the good flows that is spread over this globe.

"Let us love our sovereign and our neighbor as ourselves, and let us do to our neighbor all the good that we would wish him to do to us. The sovereign is a chief devoted to his people, he is born to conserve them, to protect them, to defend them, to provide for their needs, to have wise laws execute that can render them happy; one cannot, therefore, be too attached to one who devotes himself to the happiness of others; one cannot respect him too much, since he sacrifices all the moments of his life to conserve the people confided to him; after God, let us render our sovereign al the homage that is due to him; let us respect him as the nation's chief. The happier and wealthier the nation is, the more respectable is its chief, the more the glory of his government reflects on him.

"Our neighbor comprises our fellows, men like us; we ought to return to others the good that they do to us. We would not want anyone to speak ill of us; let us not speak ill of others. We would not want anyone to do us harm; let us do no harm to others. We would not want anyone to steal what is ours; let us not steal from others. Finally, if we are in need, we would be very glad of aid and assistance; let us aid and assist others. Those, my friends, are all the duties of society; those are all the obligations of human beings toward their peers; fulfill them with exactitude; obey the laws, love your sovereign and your neighbor as yourselves; you will find in the accomplishment of these precepts your interior contentment, and you will be happy."

"Every month it's the same sermon," the man accompanying me told me. "By dint of repeating the same thing, the people understand easily; they become better."

"But what has become of the sovereign of Rome?" I said.

"He still exists," was the reply. "He is no longer called the pope, but bears the title of great patriarch; he is married, as are all the ministers of the temples; in order to be a minister of altars or the king, it is necessary to be or to have been married. Bachelors are excluded from all functions; it is thought that they are more borne to egotism than other men, and in consequence less apt to fulfill public functions."

As he finished speaking, the maire of the commune arrived in the temple; he joined the four young people who had carried the baskets; there, in the presence of all the people, he married them and gave each of them a dowry of three thousand francs.

I asked the reason for that ceremony, and from where the money came.

"You are about to learn," he told me. "The human race, in growing old, has recognized by experience that humans are naturally borne to ambition, cupidity, avarice and egotism; that they seek to enrich themselves at the expense of their peers *per fas et nefas*. Sensible people have imagined ways to make use of human vices to give birth to social virtues; thus, a maximum has been established for fortunes. Each father of a family, on dying, can only leave to his children a hundred and fifty thousand francs each; the surplus belongs to the state, which is obliged to distribute that surplus to young men and young women in the commune to which the deceased father belonged, and who have distinguished themselves by some evidence of virtue, either toward the fatherland, the sovereign, their parents or their fellows.

"Every year, lots of three thousand francs are composed, in goods or in cash, from that excess of fortunes; those lots are destined to endow young men and young women who have distinguished themselves by some evidence of virtue or benevolence; they are married with great pomp in the temple, before the altar of the divinity. On the first of every month, other marriages also take place in the temple, in the same manner, but the state does not endow them.

"Since the promulgation of the law of the maximum of fortunes and the sage employment of the excess of those same fortunes, bankruptcies are no longer seen; the fathers of families augment their fortune by labor, by economy and by commercial industry, and compete with one another to leave the largest amount to recompense social virtues.

"Only the royal family is exempt from the maximum, because it is considered that the throne and the persons attached by blood ties to the chief of the nation can never be too rich, in order to exercise benevolence and represent the nation worthily.

"The sovereign also nominates those French people of both sexes who have a right to public benevolence, and who ought to be endowed by the state, from a list of candidates drawn up by the council of each commune where there are sufficient successions and legitimate levies to provide for that legal disposition. That list is also presented to the sovereign by the députés of each département. Since that order has been established, France has flourished, and the French adore their king, whom they regard as their father; for his part, the king loves his people as his children.

"When, in a commune, the father of a family leaves a greater fortune, after the removal of the children's legitimate entitlement, than is necessary to endow marriages, the state applies that excess to the hospitals of the principal towns of the prefecture and sub-prefecture that are most in need, in order to liberate people from the excessive duties they were paid at the customs-posts of towns for comestibles, which once had to be established for the hospitals whose property had been inappropriately sold. People only pay half now of what they used to pay, and soon, if the same order subsists, they will no longer pay anything; there will be no more customs-posts, no more shackles on the internal commerce of the kingdom; the people will be happy, and the excess of the fortunes of the rich will then be turned entirely to the profit of social virtues by the augmentation of the marriages of those who have been their authors."

"But how are the successions of those who die as bachelors divided?" I asked my informant.

"If they are nephews and nieces who inherit," he told me, "the legitimate entitlements in those cases are reduced to sixty thousand francs; if the bachelor's heirs are cousins, the entitlements are reduced by a further fifth, and a further fifth for every degree of distance from the direct line. Just as fathers of a family can divide their inheritance between their children, however, bachelors, while alive, can divide their fortune between collateral heirs, while leaving the state the portion affected by the law to the recompense of virtues. The government usually approves these dispositions, although they will not always be equal in value; it is only in cases of excessive differences of rewards that the government permits itself to level the shares of children, collateral heirs and those destined to the recompense of social virtues—but that rarely happens, so jealous are fathers and bachelors of endowing their children and heirs equally, and satisfying the law remunerative of virtues."

"Tell me, you who are instructing me, what have you conserved of the ancient institutions?"

"Finance," he replied. "I mean land tax and property tax, stamp duty, auditing, mortgages, and waters and forests. These taxes were deemed necessary for the conservation of the realm, in order that the king can make indispensable expenditures every year, for the maintenance of his troops, the payment of functionaries, the encouragement of the arts, the maintenance of granaries of abundance and highways. Every year, the government buys wheat to garnish the granaries of abundance; that wheat, if it is not consumed in the year by famine, is resold at the end of the year and replaced by new wheat, because it has been recognized by experience that there are years of sterility caused by bad weather, and that it is wise government to ensure the lives of the people by means of provisions.

"The highways are no longer maintained by labor gangs; it is the government that has them maintained by convicts sentenced to a certain period of hard labor. Convicts are no longer relegated to seaports where no one sees them and where they cannot serve as an example in the interior of the realm; it was deemed more appropriate to mores for the example of those sentenced to a period of hard labor to be renewed every day, in public view, in order that the public might be warned on a daily basis that crimes against society are punished with the full rigor of the law.

"Since that sage institution, crimes against society are hardly committed any more, because no one wants to be exposed to the gaze of the people. Those condemned to death under the old criminal code are presently condemned to perpetual hard labor; they alone are sent to seaports to serve in the galleys. Before going there they are marked on both hands with the letters GP, in order that in case of escape they can be immediately recognized by the police. It was deemed disadvantageous to kill men from whom useful services could still be obtained. In that we have imitated the people of the north; the Russians gave that example of humanity to France.

"There is only one case in which the death penalty is invoked, and that is the crime of lèse-majesté; those who attempt to assassinate the sovereign are punished by death, because France loves her kings, and wanted to extirpate at the root the crime of lèse-majesté. The same penalty is applied to those who attempt the lives of princes and other members of the royal family, which is regarded by the nation as a sacred family in which, in default of the lineage of the reigning king, the nation finds chiefs to govern it in accordance with the Salic law."

"Those are great changes," I said to my guide. "I admire them. But what do I see on that road? What is the significance of that group of men and women?"

"It is," he replied, "the chain of laborers going to work on the roads; men, women and children are following them. The children are asking their parents: "Why those chains? Why those iron balls? Why those public corrections by the overseers?"

"It is," the reply is made to them, "because they are thieves, fraudulent bankrupts, crooked tax-collectors—in sum, bad lots of every sort who did not want to submit to the laws."

"Ah," say the little children, "we shall be careful not to do likewise; we shall respect the laws, and will not do what they forbid. That example, repeated almost every day, produces the best effect, changing mores and preventing crimes."

After that, we went into the establishment of a school-teacher. I asked him what his plan of education was.

"The reading of the laws," he told me. "That of the moral code that contains what one owes to God and one's neighbor, and mathematics. No one can occupy a position in the state unless he has a certificate of completion of three years in our schools."

When we left the house of the teacher, the man who was accompanying me took me to the law court. I went in, and saw a curtain hanging at the back of the hall like that of a theater, on which was painted a Themis holding a sword in one hand and scales in the other. Weary of always seeing the curtain extended, I asked my guide when it would be raised.

"Never," he replied. "The judges in this court as are invisible as the divinity; they render their judgments; the clerk you see outside writes them down; there is a ten minute interval between the pronouncement of one judgment and the next, during which the interested parties have the right to go and see the record of the judgment pronounced. The king's prosecutor, who is also outside the curtain, facing the clerk, has the right to order the policing of the hearing, and has a copy of the judgments made in the session made by the clerk; at the end of the session the copy is signed, as well as the register, by both the clerk and the president..."

My guide was still speaking when I heard a loud voice shout: "Silence!" and all the members of the public fell silent. A moment later, another voice, not as loud but very clear, pronounced the words: "Number nine, codenamed Rose, has won his suit against number twenty, codenamed Carnation."

Ten minutes later, the same voice pronounced: "Number thirty, codenamed Tulip, has won his suit against number fifteen, codenamed Jasmine." Ten minutes later, again, the same voice pronounced: "Number fifty, codenamed Wallflower, has won his suit against number sixty, codenamed Tuberose"—and so on.

When the session had finished, I asked the man with me to explain that enigma; I had not heard any speeches, as in my own time, and did not know how to interpret what I had seen and heard.

"Justice is no longer rendered as it once was," he told me. "Advocates no longer conduct the civil cases of their clients by means of pleas and procedures; the judges are no longer known. Suits are classified; in the first class are those whose value does not exceed two or three hundred francs; in the second class are those between five hounded and a thousand francs, in the third, those between one thousand and ten thousand; in the fourth between ten thousand and a hundred thousand. Any case that surpasses in interest the range of the fourth class is treated in the same manner as those in that class.

"In the first class, the two parties can each only present one document containing two written sheets on stamped paper taxed at three francs a sheet; in the second, a document of four sheets taxed at six francs a sheet; in the third, a document of eight sheets taxed at eight francs a sheet; and finally, in the fourth, a document of ten sheets taxed at twelve francs a sheet. The parties have a week after the assignation to submit their documents; those documents contain a number in the margin, under the name of a flower, which is the badge of the contending party. A duplicate of the number and the badge are added to the document on a piece of blank paper; the two documents and their badges are brought together; the whole is sealed by the interested parties, who send the packet to the president of the tribunal, who is required to send it to the minister of justice within twenty-four hours.

"In his turn, the minister of justice sends the documents for and against, within a week of receipt, to a distant tribunal at least thirty leagues away from the one in which the suit originates, known to him alone, and relative to which he maintains secrecy. The tribunal to which the case has been sent has a month in which to judge it. When the judgment has been pronounced, the documents are given to the clerk and sealed with the tribunal's seal, and a copy of the judgment sent to the minister conceived in these terms: Number nine, codenamed Rose, has won his case against number twenty, codenamed Carnation. The minister then takes the badges of the two contending parties, has the judgment transcribed under the two badges, sends a copy of that transcription within a week to the tribunal where the case originated, and has the transcribed judgment sealed again under the two badges, which are immediately deposited in the ministry's archives. The tribunal to which the decision is sent is obliged to pronounce it within a week.

"When it is a matter of properties resulting from titles for greater or lesser areas of land, each party joins his title-deed to his document on a sheet or half-sheet of stamped paper; the contents of that sheet or half-sheet are certified by the notary, the proprietor of the minute, who adds his signature and his seal. It is the same for all notes signed by debtors to their creditors or money-lenders; the notes are transcribed in their entirety on stamped paper and the signatures of the lenders must be placed beneath those of the borrowers or debtors; the signatures of creditors or money-lenders must be certified as veritable by the notary public of the district—every district has one—with whom the signatures of all money-lenders and individual creditors must be deposited, on penalty of the annulment of the loan or debt; witness-statements and expert reports are subject to the same formality.

"There are, as before, two stages of jurisdiction in civil matters. When one of the parties is not content with the judgment rendered in the first instance, they can lodge an appeal before the tribunal where the suit originated, to which they present their case, and which is required to notify the adverse party, who must respond within a week. At the end of the week the tribunal sends the documents back to the ministry of justice; the documents in question can only be augmented by one sheet; they are subject to the same tax and bear the same badge as in the first instance. The ministry, with the same interval, obtains the relevant documents from the tribunal that judged the case, and sends them, along with the grounds for appeal and their rebuttal, to a tribunal at least thirty leagues distant from the one that judged the case, and still with the same distance from the one where the suit originated, which, in its turn, sends its decision, in the same form, back to the ministry of justice, which returns them in the same manner to the tribunal where the suit originated, which, in its turn, with the same forms and delays, pronounces the judgment of the appeal court.

"In that fashion, as you see, justice is good and promptly rendered; the plaintiff does not know his judges; the advocate accelerates the affairs of his clients; that is another benefit of our government, which is eager to prevent abuses. Like the ministers of the altars, the judges are chosen from among the most enlightened and upright men in the nation, without distinction of birth, rank or fortune, because it is considered that one cannot be too knowledgeable or too just to instruct or judge people. Even the priests, who are subject to the new law, can be appointed, if they have the qualities required. Justices of the peace and criminal tribunals have been conserved without any change.

175

"To accelerate the course of justice, His Majesty has thought it necessary to veil the process and reduce the mechanism, so the royal court and court of cassation have been abolished; all tribunals have been rendered equal and able to judge one another; the ministry of justice alone chooses the appeal courts, in civil and in criminal matters, in the fashion indicated above, which cannot be changed. Criminal courts replace the court of cassation.

"His Majesty names for life one candidate per département to replace the great patriarch in case of decease, choosing the candidate from among the most renowned ministers of the altars. Each European power also names a candidate for each province of its kingdom. The list of these candidates is printed and presented to the European Diet, which chooses and names the great patriarch's successor. That list lasts until it is exhausted, and then it is renewed in the same fashion.

"The great patriarch is a power in Europe; he is a delegate to the European Diet. He is the only elective, because it is considered that one cannot be too pure, too religious toward the divinity and too much a friend of humans to be chief of all the ministers of altars in Europe. The great patriarch is the sole depositors of the decrees of the European Diet. The original of the code of the religion of Europe, that of perpetual peace and that of the liberty of commerce, signed by all the delegates of the powers, composes a single book, which is deposited in the great patriarch's temple. On the first page of that book one sees the religion, which is represented holding in one hand a ribbon bearing the words *Perpetual Peace in Europe*, and in the other, a ribbon bearing the words *Liberty of Commerce in Europe*. Faithful copies of this book are also deposited in all the temples and mosques of the ministers of altars of every power.

"The maires or their deputies are obliged to witness gratuitously the funerals of all the individuals who die in their communes; they register deaths, births and marriages as before. Cemeteries are no longer adjacent to temples; they are places at least two thousand paces from the habitations of communes. Cadavers are no longer taken into temples; it has been recognized that it is insufficiently respectful to the divinity to carry dead bodies into his temples; only the living can enter therein, because only they can sing hymns of gratitude to the Supreme Being who conserved everything.

"Women married to merchants, traders or businessmen no longer have the liberty to separate their property from their husbands' in order to protect their dowries from the risks of commerce; that ancient custom is regarded as abusive, opening the door to fraud and rapine. Today, the endowed property of the wife, and any that she acquires by succession, donation or otherwise, become the collateral of creditors. The children of a bankrupt father cannot, for fifty years, exercise any branch of commerce; the intention is to punish the crime of bankruptcy even to the second generation. Since that fortunate law, fraudulent bankruptcies are no longer seen, and one no longer sees bankrupts becoming richer than they were before their bankruptcy, as was often seen before.

"The law that restricted the number of notaries in each commune and advocates at tribunals has been repealed as destructive of competition and talent, and contrary to the public good, to the interests of which it is injurious, depriving many young people of a status to which they have the right after receiving a certificate of qualification after spending three years in the office of an advocate, solicitor or notary. The list of candidates in that party is drawn up by the council of the commune, presented to the electors during their assembly, but the electors to the députés, and by them to the sovereign, who chooses from the lists, makes the appoints and has provisions delivered."

My guide then took me to the capital of the kingdom. I saw written on the door of St. Denis, in large letters: *Tomb of Kings*. "They alone," my companion told me, "are buried in that place; the chief of each nation are respected throughout Europe; they all have similar tombs. Since the plan of the Abbé de Saint-Pierre has been carried out, and they have agreed a single religion and the liberty of commerce, they are adored in all nations; all the peoples of Europe regard them-selves as brothers, the Salic law has been adopted throughout Europe, the kings are consolidated on their thrones, no longer fearing invasion or dethronement; general peace is a political bond that unites all the nations and attaches them to their chiefs. Everyone gains from that fortunate change; agriculture, industry and commerce of every sort have redoubled their activity; the people enrich themselves in laboring; they are happy, and the chiefs find their people more willing to pay taxes.

"The day when that fortunate convention was adopted and signed by the delegates of the powers is celebrated every year throughout Europe; that celebration lasts for three con-secutive days. The needs of the state have diminished in each power, and taxes with them; our king no longer has more than ten thousand regular troops, eight thousand of whom are in-fantry and two thousand cavalry. A hundred cavalrymen and two hundred infantrymen compose his guard. Each power has reduced its military force; having much less expense therein, all the kings have come to the aid of their peoples, diminishing taxes proportionately every year."

"Those are very wise reforms!" I exclaimed. "There are, then, no longer any wars, no longer any lost crops trampled under the hooves of horses, cut while green to serve as their pasture; no more towns subjected to contribution to slake the avarice of warriors; no more massacres of men, women and children by ferocious soldiers, no more pillage, no more rape, no more burning, no more crimes of every sort, no more fam-ine, no more plague, no more kings dethroned by rogues and ambitious men who want to take their place; in sum, no more brigands of any sort recompensed for their crimes by impuni-ty."

"The human species is better directed," he told me. "It is occupied in agriculture, in commerce and industry of every sort. A man who has made a discovery useful to society, of whatever kind, receives from the government a patent if in-vention with an *ad hoc* medal and a small annual pension. He no longer has, as before, the exclusive privilege of practicing the objects of his invention for several years; his discovery falls into the public domain, which profits from it; that advances the perfection of the arts by as much, and does not harm artists.

"In sum, the same order exists today between the powers that compose Europe as in the constellations that illuminate that beautiful art of the world; the order is immutable in the globes that illuminate the world and in the governments of Europe; they all have the same operation, the same laws, the same religion, and they work toward the same goal, the happiness of the human race. Providence had doubtless desired that reform, since it has inspired certain humans with analogous ideas—for it is necessary not to dissimulate; the ideas are not ours, they are inspired in us by an invisible power that we cannot resist, and we are only satisfied when we have manifested those ideas; the good that must result therefrom is the sole recompense that pays those who have the courage to render them public."

"The sweetest music is not more agreeable to me than your words have been. I have only one regret, that of being too old; I shall not be able to enjoy for a long time the harmonic system of Europe But what do I see? A superb column in a little garden, in front of a house of modest appearance—what does that column signify?"

"You shall find out," said my companion. "I know the owner of that house; he will explain everything to you."

We entered the house; the master took us to the column. The column was made of hard stone, twelve feet high, with four faces in its base; it was borne by twelve steps representing the twelve months of the year; four pots of flowers placed and the four corners of the fifth step, descending from the foot of the column, represented the month of May, by the flowers born in that month, with which the pots were filled.

"It was a man without children," the inhabitant of the house told me, "who wanted that column to be erected after his death, for the sustenance of the poor. He made provision in

179

his will to give to the poor of his commune on the first of every month twelve hundred livres of white bread, which made twelve livres each; he affected all the revenue of his land to the service of the rent; the fund cannot be sold except to the charge of the service of that rent, which is inalienable by nature, nor transportable to any hospice or house of charity. On the first of every month the testamentary executor is obliged to place four pots of flowers at the four corners of the step that represents the month, filled with flowers of the month, to open the garden and make the distribution in question, at midday precisely, to the hundred poor people, half of the chosen by the minister of the altars of the commune, half by the testamentary executor. The meaning of the testament is inscribed in the four faces of the base of the column. On the first, on the eastern side, is written: *Column elevated by N* ; on the second, the northern: *For the support of a hundred poor people of the commune*; on the third, the western: *To which will be distributed, in equal portions, twelve hundred livers of white bread*; and final, on the fourth, the southern: O*n the first of every month of the year, in perpetuity.*

"All travelers and curiosity-seekers come to visit this column, and several have erected similar one in their own lands. Sages claim that the bases of the religion of Europe are calculated on this mysterious column; the kings of the earth have admired this simple and sublime idea. They wanted to surpass it by making use of the column as the basis for the religion of Europe; they have all adopted the religion of which he had spoken, the project of peace of the Abbé de Saint-Pierre, and agreed the liberty of commerce between nations. Since those three points have been established in Europe, the kings of the peoples have been happy; the former are filled with glory, the latter with respect and attachment for their princes.

May 1829.

Jacques Fabien: *Paris in Dream*
(1863)

I. Fantastic Voyage

It was ten years since I had left Paris and France. Disembarked at Marseilles on 30 December, a single bound took me from the extinct ship to the carriage that lit up in order to take me to Lyon. It was there that I had arranged a rendezvous with a friend, a Parisian like me, who would come to meet me.

On the platform at Lyon the first face I saw, blue with cold, was that of my man, waiting for me. We embraced two or three times, and shook hands—a momentary affair. On contact with my cheek that blue cheek reddened with pleasure.

We dined together, as two good friends glad to see one another do; then, impatient to return home, we left that same evening by the express train that would reach Paris at five o'clock in the morning. A night in a carriage—what's that? So many things to say to one another. We would hardly have enough time.

The whistle blows. We pull away.

Here we are, installed in our first class compartment, face to face, fatigued, wrapped up to the ears, legs crossed, a hot water bottle under our feet, a corner for each head.

"You'll be very surprised when you see Paris again."

"Why?"

"Because I defy you to recognize it, my dear. It requires a no more and no less than a compass to find one's way around."

"Well, if Paris is no longer the same, at least you haven't changed. Still the eye behind a magnifying glass!"

"I dine with a friend—very good. A week later, I set out politely to visit him—but the house, the street, everything has

181

vanished. And many other stories too. What can I tell you? There's a splendid change of scene by Ciceri."[46]

"Enough exaggerations. Paris is my homeland; a son has no difficulty recognizing his mother."

"You'll see, you'll see. In the meantime, I'll take responsibility, when we arrive, for serving as your cicerone, Monsieur Stranger."

"Well, so be it..."

Suddenly, a transfiguration has occurred around us.

Our compartment is enlarged. How? I don't know. Previously gloomy, it has become radiant. Instead of two sleeping companions, a wide awake company, select and well-dressed. One could believe oneself in an elegant boudoir in some rolling Faubourg Saint-Honoré. Over there, a notary, if I can believe his white cravat, is reading a newspaper, as he would read it in his study beside his Carcel lamp. To the side, a young couple; in front of the young couple, a mobile table, and on the table, two fuming carafes, and Bavarian cream desserts. How the devil have they been able find such a hot delicacy, not of a nature to travel, in their overnight bag?

But there's something else: for five minutes, the eyes of my female neighbor, a little too wide, seem to have been sighing. For whom? For me, undoubtedly. Conceited as that I am!

The eyes are extinguished, my unconscious neighbor slumps gently into to my arms.

"Press the button, Monsieur!" people shout at me from all directions.

"What button?"

"There, beside you, in the corner of the compartment."

Meekly, I put out my hand. Surprise! A uniformed attendant appears, disappears and reappears with a glass of water in his hand.

---

[46] Pierre Ciceri (1782-1868) was a leading set-designer who worked at many of the Parisian theatres.

People cluster around the lady. The faint resists. I'll wager that she finds my arms softer than those of her armchair. A gentleman arrives, as neatly dressed as the lawyer, doubtless a physician. He has her carried out of the compartment. Everyone follows.

Meanwhile, the train speeds on and on, with no concern for what is happening inside. No *hold on!* Not even a hesitation. The air whistles past, as before.

I follow everyone else. My neighbor is deposited in the physician's office. There, she decides to open her eyes. With that, reassured, I slip away, curious to know how this placid coming-and-going of passengers can be affected at top speed without risk of broken necks.

This is what I observe:

Our train is flanked, throughout its length, by two lateral galleries, uncovered, and lighted like the interior. They finish at the two ends. To the fore, there is a buffet, the physician's office and the conductor's; to the rear, seats useful on many occasions, particularly on the railways; the ladies go to on one side, the gentlemen to the other. On each gallery a kind of valet-attendant is on sentry duty, ready to respond to the appeal of a bell.

During my admiration, the victim of the faint went back the compartment with our traveling companions. As she went past me she darted a glance at me that was not at all grateful. Why? My conscience was clear, as pure as the early morning air chilling my face, and the sky, in which the stars were vanishing one by one. I thought it as well not to follow her, so I was strolling, my cigar lit, along the cold gallery, when the conductor came to ask for my ticket.

The train was going into a station; we were in Paris.

II. Arrival in Paris

In Paris, no, I'm mistaken; we're only at the gates of Paris, within sight of the ramparts, in the place where the Château de Bercy once stood.

The station, expelled from the Boulevard Mazas, has retreated all the way here. It is spacious and comfortable. As we are chatting, sitting casually in a well-heated and well-lit room, a uniformed employee approaches us, cap in hand. He asks us for our baggage-tickets, our instructions and our keys, arranges to have the trunks delivered, submits them to customs inspection, pays the duty, loads everything into a hired carriage, and then receives payment for himself and his assistant in accordance with a tariff displayed on the wall. He explains to us that it is forbidden for porters to enter into personal contact with travelers, and that it is forbidden for them, as for him, to accept any tip, under penalty of dismissal.

Our nocturnal entry into Paris was affected via the new Boulevard de Lyon, a broad thoroughfare, with fresh air, as full of light as in the middle of the day, bordered to the left and the right by buildings in a uniform style. I did not even suspect the existence of that boulevard. It was nothing other than the course of a former railway track, connecting to the old Rue de Lyon.

The public clocks chimed six. The belated and chilly dawn had not yet broken, but let us not forget that it was the thirty-first of December.

III. Popular Progress

"Stop here, Coachman!" cried my friend, in the middle of the Place de la Bastille. Then he turned to me.

"I promised to be your cicerone, to show you the prettiest Parisian magic lantern slides. Let's get down—we'll start here."

"What a spectacle!"

"Oh, don't get excited so soon. It's not time yet. We'll come back here. For the moment, let's occupy ourselves with what concerns the working classes, and only that.

"You see those two rows of open-fronted shops that extend along the Boulevard Beaumarchais. They have for guests, from the twenty-fifth of December to the fifteenth of January, workers of both sexes, raised to the ranks of traders for the Christmas season.

"Let's go closer. You'll notice that they're all the same, picturesque in their elegance, well-covered and well-closed, illuminated by gas. The petty merchants are at their posts already. Dawn hasn't yet broken, and the displays are ready. Look, what jolly presents, bright and tempting for the passer-by."

"One might think that they were rows of Swiss chalets made of fir-wood. It's like a child's colored toy fresh out of its box. I can scarcely explain that elegant ensemble.

"Nothing simpler. The city of Paris put the entire block—whose design was furnished by comic opera villages—up for auction, and the right to hire them for a certain number of years. It assumes responsibility for their storage, and furnishes the gas.

"The entrepreneur rents each shop, fully furnished, keys in hand, for a franc a day—which is, therefore, for the duration of business, twenty francs, payable by the week. All professional tradesmen are excluded; preference is given to old men, women and households with children. As for merchandise, those who are too poor to procure any can apply to a benevolent society established in each quarter, which buys in bulk and sells them on to the unfortunates on easy terms. It is, say the poor people, *our winter harvest*."

"The city doubtless allows an annual subsidy to the entrepreneur."

"I don't believe so, but all right, let's admit, if you wish, a subsidy; it would still be economical. You can judge for yourself. At the end of January the hospital was once the rendezvous of those poor folk, exposed during the day to the wind, the rain and forced by night to go to sleep as sentinels on their meager treasury. And the hospital is expensive! Today, it's no longer the same, as witness the faces that respire health and satisfaction."

185

With that, showing our heels to the Place de la Bastille, we took the route to the female workers' colony, established beyond the Place du Trône.

On the way, going along the Faubourg Saint-Antoine, I noticed a drinking-fountain at every street corner. They were all encumbered by early-rising Rachels drawing the day's water.

At an intersection, ten omnibuses harnessed to vigorous whinnying horses were crossing paths avoiding one another and pursuing one another competitively. On top were blouses and smocks, inside, dresses of coarse cloth, and no one else.

In response to my bewilderment, my companion told me that between two o'clock in the morning and two in the afternoon, when workers of both sexes went to work and returned home, all the omnibuses in Paris took passengers at the reduced price of five centimes per seat, that there was no distinction between the inside and the top deck, no ostracism against packages and tools, but the same routes, the same service and the same rights of connection as during the day— which was a great relief for the artisans, their domiciles always being a long way from the city center, and also for old people and children, and that advantage was taken to collect the family's provisions and in order to carry work back and forth from the shops.

A few paces further on, outbursts of voices attracted our attention. We advanced. Female workers, with a few males, were forming a circle round a young man, a young woman and an organ. All three could be heard loud and clear, blending their voices or alternating them, according to how best to set the scene for the poem they were enacting. The joyful crowd knew the words by heart, and joined in enthusiastically.

We remained silent, our ears and souls paused. Alas, why were there only six acts! Their titles were: *The Baptism in the Worker's Home; The Departure for the Flag; The Honor of the Workshop (A Song of Victory); A Sister's Marriage; The Convalescent Child—a Mother's Joy*; and *A Good Boss's Funeral*.

Surprisingly enough, the words were touching and cheer-ful, always simple and poetic. The music was lively or plain-tive, appropriate to the theme. Everything was suggestive of a poet and musician of genius.

When the concert was over, the singer made a tour of the circle, offering, for a price of fifteen centimes, a rather stout volume, well-printed and well-bound, bearing the title *The Popular Parisian Almanac*. It included the six songs, with the music, and many other things. One was offered to me too; I accepted, but tremulously, with a kind of shame. The price seemed derisory to me compared with the value of the book.

"You're throwing propriety to the winds, aren't you?"

"Yes."

"Well, this is the key to the enigma. The city of Paris publishes *The Popular Parisian Almanac* itself. The text is confided to writers of a proven and popular talent. It appears on the first of January every year. This is the version that ex-pires today—that's why you're the only one to have bought it, as all the songs are firmly engraved in the memory of the crowd. In addition to what we've just heard, and a calendar, it summarizes, clearly and methodically, all the documents use-ful to a Parisian worker, in his professional labor, his educa-tion and that of his family, the differences between artisans and employers—in sum, all the circumstances most commonly encountered in the life of a workshop. It also contains an an-notated list of charitable organizations, public and private, where a family can receive help and advice in moments of trial. Finally, there are a few well-written anecdotes and sto-ries of courage and probity carried out the previous year with-in the working class, which are the parchments of nobility of the people of Paris."

"Very good. But that doesn't tell me the source of those delightful songs, whose tunes are so pure in style.

"I can't say everything at once. Every year, the Prefect of the Seine offers the subjects half a dozen popular songs, cheer-ful, religious, heroic, dolorous or consoling, but always moral, not so much in the words but in the ideas and their coloration, always appropriate and always designed to interest the people of Paris. The poetry is put out to competition, and then the music. The victors in the contest receive, for the six songs, music and poetry, a dozen lovely gold medals, expressly struck, bearing their names. You would not believe how competitively those recompenses are disputed, modest as they are."

"In truth, the idea is admirable—and, which does no harm, inexpensive. But tell me, what is that woman selling, over there in that glazed stall. One could swear that she's giving away her merchandise free, so eagerly are people pressing around her."

"That's the *Parisian Weekly Bulletin.* It costs five centimes. This week's issue has just appeared, and, as you can see, all hands are reaching out to obtain one. It's the same idea again, following its path. The collection includes longer stories, varied, instructive, attractive and, above all, very morally uplifting. Elevated morality is the nub of the matter. You read them at your ease, and you see good and wise advice taking as much care to disguise themselves as vice and sedition once did. The unsuspecting readers, abused by the seduction of style and form, by the emotion of what they call romance, are improved without wanting to be, and, which is the apogee of success, without being aware of it. The city publishes the bulletin itself. The articles, amply remunerated, are the work of the best litterateurs in France."

What an explosion of joy! What a racket!

At the door of a tavern, a number of women are clapping their hands, stamping their feet and manifesting a thousand other signs of approval at a large white poster, still damp, invading the exterior of the shop. At a signal from one of them, the tumult dies down, and silence falls. The orator in a headscarf reads aloud, while laughing:

"*Tavern-keepers have no legal right to demand from drinkers the price of the beverages consumed. If they start any argument with then, they will be arrested for disturbing the peace.*"

"That's new!"

"No, it's an old measure against drunkenness found in a corner of the imperial printing shop. It dates from the time of Henri IV. The bill-poster had forgotten to stick it up for two hundred and sixty years."

We come to a church. To go in, parade a glance rapidly around and come out again is more rapidly done than written. We have noticed numerous heads piously bowed over joined hands.

"Look where these ingenious levers of moralization end up," I said. "The people commence their day with a prayer."

"Yes, and as you see, the solicitude of the administration follows them all the way into church. This one, although in a poor parish, has a parquet floor and is heated. There is no longer a barrier marking the enclosure reserved for the opulent, no more chairs upholstered in red, blue or green velvet, denouncing a privilege or a favor where none has any reason to be, wounding the dignity of the people and diminishing the church to a place almost always vacant. Equality in the republic of wicker chairs. The most noble is the one that prayer has most worn away.

While speaking and making these observations we had arrived at the Place du Trône. On two marble columns we read the inscription: *St. Antoine Workers' Colony*.

IV. Popular Progress Continued

Between the Place du Trône and the citadel of Vincennes, to the right and left of the road, a pretty hamlet stands, recently born, very airy and fitted out, as busy and breathless as the inside of a bee-hive. That is the St. Antoine Workers' Colony. All the houses have façades—I almost said faces—that are welcoming and varied, with a certain resemblance, like members of a family. On the ground floor are unostentatious shops, on each floor the lodging of workers, consisting of an entrance, two rooms with fireplaces, and a little kitchen with a stove. In the common courtyard there is fresh air and drinkable water.

The colony is divided into two halves, with the road to Vincennes in the middle. In the center of the first we find a square, with shade and a pond; it is ornamented at its interior angles by four sculpted groups representing four Frenchmen dear to the multitude, memories of miseries relieved:

Parmentier,[47] his face radiant, is showing peasants a potato that he has just picked. Other root vegetables lie at his feet. The peasants, bowing down, amazed, are admiring the ground and the happy agronomist by turns.

Jacquard[48] is having a female worker from Lyon try out her mew métier, with a pert little apprentice by her side.

St. Vincent de Paul[49] is bending down to pick up a poor naked child abandoned at the foot of a boundary-stone, who is reaching out her arms toward him in order to receive an open apron.

And the Abbé de l'Épée[50] is conversing, by means of his fingers, with a deaf-mute worker. A child is following their actions with his gaze, curious to learn.

"This square," says my companion, "is more particularly frequented by men. The young people there, going back in-

---

[47] Antoine-Augustin Parmentier (1737-1813) was an enthusiastic promoter of the potato as a source of nutrition; thanks to his efforts, the Paris Faculty of Medicine declared potatoes edible in 1772, but it was not until the late 1780s that large-scale cultivation began in the region—too late to assist in countering the famines that precipitated the Revolution.

[48] The programmable loom designed by Joseph-Marie Charles, nicknamed Jacquard (1752-1834) was first exhibited in 1801, but its use only became widespread after 1815.

[49] Vincent de Paul (1581-1660) founded organizations for assisting the poor that are still active.

[50] Charles-Michel de l'Épée (1712-1789) was a philanthropist and educational pioneer who developed the first programs to teach sign language.

side, have just been devoting themselves to games appropriate to the development of vigor and skill, such as gymnastics, shooting with rifles or bows, or handball. The fee charged is insignificant. It's the voluntary hardening of the soldier.

"The four exterior faces are, as you can see, four large buildings.

"Firstly, there is a theater in a simple style. Seats there are sold cheap. Only moral and patriotic plays are performed there. It also opens its doors, on occasion, to concerts and all kinds of popular ceremonies.

"Secondly, a covered market. Staple foods are sold there, without haggling, at reduced prices. Inside there are vast food shops.

"The third building contains the medical offices, the pharmacy, and a group of Sister of Charity uniquely devoted to the needy. It is from there that help emerges when people fall ill at home, or are injured, and when women are in child-birth and nursing their babies.

"In the fourth edifice several useful establishments are brought together, including a pawnshop truly worthy of the name of *mont-de-piété*, the interest on advances, whatever guise they take, never rising above three per cent, and a li-brary, heated and well-supplied, which hosts readings during the day and in the evening and where the printing of profes-sional and attractive books is authorized. In all the rooms there are educative lecturers, experiments and instruments."

"Before going any further," I said, "tell me by what mag-ic this laborious hive was made to spring from the ground."

"The magic is quite simply the law of expropriation for public utility, but enlarged. I shall talk about it again soon. With that law in hand, the vast terrains necessary for its crea-tion were expropriated *en bloc* in exactly a week. Then, what you call a laborious hive was marked out with the aid of sur-veying-staff, as one does for an English garden. The city of Paris took for its lot the streets, squares, gardens and public establishments. All the rest were bravely put up for sale at auction, with low reserves, in small fractions, with the unique condition of building houses there within a year, on prescribed plans, invariable for the façades as for the internal dispositions.

"That resale covered the sale price, nothing more, but that had been anticipated. One does not speculate when doing good."

"I imagine that a maximum rent was agreed for each dwelling."

"Not at all. The particular furnishing of the lodgings, the physiognomy of the popular milieu and its destination scarcely admitted any other inhabitants than working men, so that an affluence of white posters established moderate monthly rents of its own accord.

"That was already a great success, undoubtedly, but success has its obligations; it was necessary to aliment the colony cheaply. Listen to what the city of Paris did. Storage skips were suspended in the marketplace for use as granaries. Mountains of provisions were stored there, collected everywhere is propitious times for ready cash. There is flour, potatoes, fresh and dried vegetables, butter, eggs, cheeses, salt and pickles. The flour is delivered to the colony's bakers and the surplus sold in the market, at a price that sometimes falls below, but with an injunction to conform to it, a fixed tariff.

"I forgot to say that a recent decree has reduced the outflow of those precious foodstuffs, prohibiting their sale, in future, to be devoured by factories.

"Every year, industry used to crush, to meet its needs, thousands upon thousands of cartloads of cheese, potatoes, soya beans, haricot beans, peas and lentils; it consumed thousands of baskets of fresh eggs. What is that, if not the bread of the people? It was understood that the first step to take was to enter into life cheaply was not to destroy the harvests of God. Whatever enables human to live is sacred.

"To begin with, a few great ladies, strangers to the colony, were not ashamed to send their servants to the market to buy provisions, but that was soon put in order by a prohibition of selling to the same person on a single day goods worth more than a determined price. A firm line was taken and the scandal vanished.

"The rest is explained in the same fashion; the games in the square, set up by the city of Paris, were yielded to a farmer, with orders not to demand any more than a tokenistic retribution. The pharmacy store is provisioned on a large scale; the medicaments are disturbed at a low price to those who can pay, or given away to others. It is the same for the physicians; they receive a complementary salary from the administration.

"With regard to physicians, a great innovation is commencing to take root—I mean the abandonment of the hospital system. Indigents go into them without confidence, or any expectation of a cure, with an emphatic reluctance. *Poor devils as we are*, they say, *the doors frown at us when we go in, and we smile when we take our leave of them. Alive, we train the doctors to save their opulent clients; dead, we become their professors of anatomy.* An atrocious, criminal prejudice soiled with ingratitude, but a real, active prejudice.

"What could be done?

"The administration has taken a valiant initiative. Today, with regard to people afflicted with chronic or incurable conditions, the invalids are cared for under their own roof in their familiar bed, under supervision, with the aid of their relatives. From that measure, public assistance receives two benefits: palpable economies in a heavy budget, and a harvest of recoveries and blessings."

V. Popular Progress Continued

From one half of the colony we passed to the other. There too we found a square similar to the first, but adopted for preference by women.

Four groups decorate it; they represent French heroines, with slightly theatrical poses and settings calculated to appeal to the eyes and mind alike.

There is Sainte Geneviève, the patron saint of Paris, on the bank of the Seine, distributing to blockaded and storing provisions a convoy of food that she has brought herself, at the risk of her life, from Corbeil and Mélun.

There is Jeanne d'Arc, the little shepherdess, sitting on a mound, surrounded by her flock. Floating above a tree, an angel is offering her a sword with one hand and pointing the way to Paris with the other. He seems to be saying to the historic walls: 'I am the Archangel Michael; I have come to command you, on behalf of the Lord, to go into France, to help the Dauphin, in order that, through you, he will recover his kingdom, and you will take him to be crowned in Reims.' She, trembling and transported, is extending her arms toward the celestial apparition.

There is Louise Bergame, the daughter of the valet pursued during the Terror for having assisted his master's flight. The scene is nocturnal. At the first sound, Louise has dressed in haste in her father's livery. She has opened the door and presents herself to the police, who, taken in, arrest her. At her feet are her robe and bonnet behind her, Bergame, whom she has hidden carefully, asleep on a chair. There is a lamp on the table.[51]

Finally, there are two women bearing arms; one of them is also holding a small child. A Spanish soldier, gripped by admiration, is presenting arms to them respectfully.

That group immediately puts me in mind of a touching story I read in the work of an old chronicler. In the time of Charles V, some French town in Flanders having been besieged and captured, the furious enemy not wanting to grant any other capitulation except that the gentlewomen could come out, on foot, with their honor safe and the precious things they could carry. The old author adds that throughout Flanders that act of heroism is recalled every year by the general ringing of bells, that the anniversary is known as Ladies'

---

[51] This anecdote appears to be original to the present story, unless the name is misrendered.

Eve, and that on that day husbands must do their wives' bidding, with an exemplary docility.

Beneath each group is inscribed, briefly, the story illustrated.

Four buildings accompany the exterior façades of that second garden.

Firstly, there is a church.

"You can see that the edifice is vast, is it not? Well, on Sundays and Feast Days, there is no room inside. That is because on those days, the most celebrated preachers compete for the honor of going up into the pulpit. Make no mistake, one comes here to conquer one's blazon of Christian eloquence. The workers flood in, initially attracted by the charm of the speech, and then nailed to their chairs and softened by touching advice."

Opposite is the building of refuges and schools.

On one side, the public baths and washrooms.

On the other side, the fourth edifice, bears on its fronton the inscription: *Women's Syndicate*.

"That astonishes you, I see, and I'll take the lead. Under a regime where so much has been done for those who suffer, the question of women was bound to arise, to be studied and resolved. It was—but believe me, it wasn't easy. For a long time it was whispered that misery, which speaks in the shadows to the ears of the daughters of the people, does not give them good advice; that a working woman cannot, if her work is not protected, provide for her needs and keep herself pure; and that in the final analysis her honor is that of her father, her mother and her family, for which society answers. But bah! There is no urgency—no strike of women, not one secret club, not the slightest '93; and yet honesty tells us that the more a creature is gentle, trusting and unarmed, the more it is necessary to look after its rights. Finally, what was said clandestinely came to be voiced aloud. Then, people set bravely to work; a system of protection—no, I mean a system if distributive justice—was organized on behalf of women, summarized in measures of which I shall briefly sketch a few:

"The admission of women, and only women, to the employments reserved for them by nature. Of their own accord they went into workshops, storehouses and shops dealing with some branch of female attire an ornamentation, and the preparation and selling of food—everywhere, in fact, where neither physical vigor nor mental toil was required. Console yourself then, my friend, for no longer seeing, in shops of caprice, demure paws laying out before your wife and daughter, silk, lace and perfumes for them to ogle. On the other hand, you will no longer see, in sordid factories, feeble creatures bent over hard labor which is the natural lot of men.

"The modification of work in prisons, sweatshops and convents, in such a manner that it never contrived to provide dishonest competition, thus coming to assail the seamstress in her honest, often charged with a far greater burden than she was able to bear.

"Prescriptions and encouragements tending to provide during unemployment, and to maintain salaries in equilibrium with the needs of the day.

"The gratuitous return to her province of any woman requesting it, when deprived of the means of self-sufficiency in Paris.

"It was necessary, above all, to supervise those new-born rights, to prevent them being stifled in their cradle. For that, the Women's Syndicate was devised. A sentinel of the privileges of the weak, it mounted good guard around them, defending them against the poaching of the strong, drawing up legal evidence of faults and denouncing them to the authority, which intervened forcibly.

"Justice to whomever merits it; our Parisiennes have been sublime in feminine devotion and patriotism. If one of their boutiques allowed itself to be invaded by men, it became a leper-colony. People prudently passed it by on the other side of the street, in order to avoid the contagion of its display. Any merchandise usually associated with women that was suspected of virile origin remained unsold.

"There was, however, one moment of hesitation, the only one. When it was a question of opening bedroom doors to midwives, bourgeois women were in no hurry to dismiss doctors. The example then descended from the greatest ladies in Paris. It needed no more. From that day on the midwives were furious; it did not take long for it to be proven that they were as adept as their male colleagues, that skill substituted for force, and all was said."

I was assured that there would soon be a meeting of husbands in the great hall of the Women's Syndicate, and that the women would be voted the recommended hand-kisses, but I dare not affirm the fact.

"Look over there .You can see, can't you, those swarms of women, busy whispering in that enclosure. One might almost think that one were listening to a pack of hunting-dogs murmuring."

"What you call an enclosure is the portion of the square devoted, without mixture, to women, just as certain railways compartments are on railway trains. They are gathering this morning to vote on a prize of three thousand francs that the city of Paris grants every year, on the first of January to the woman, married or widowed who has reaped the votes of her companions. On July the first it will be the turn of the young women. Otherwise, there is no program or condition for election. The electors are the sole judges of merit and, what is more, of the kind of merit to be lauded. The prize is awarded by the president of the Syndicate, in the Great Hall, in the presence of the maire and priest. If the young woman who obtains the favor of the urn in July gets married in the course of the year, the city takes charge of the wedding gala.

"A similar ceremony, renewed twice yearly, takes place in every Mairie in a district, as in the colony. Even better—a fortunate contagion of good—on a large number of workshops, the chiefs of industry have installed urns at their own expense on behalf of the women they employ."

"In truth, you amaze me."

197

"Well, before surrendering to your amazement, know too that every female worker who marries, maiden or widow, receives on her wedding day a capital of five hundred francs drawn on the State's income. There is only one condition: that she be French and Parisienne; or, to replace that latter title, that she has won the right of that city by ten years of uninterrupted labor and domicile in Paris."

"What! It suffices for a Parisienne to take a husband to become entitled to draw upon the public purse!"

"It's ruination, isn't it? Well, my friend, on that point, take stock of the State's balance-sheets, leaving aside, if you wish, the moral balance-sheet, and you'll see that it's a usurer's deal. The calculation is simple. The exposure of foundlings is much rarer since this institution. Now, the five-hundred-franc dowry of each bride, invested with half-yearly dividends, would be a long way from ever reaching the level of the millions that it costs the State to shelter those poor bastards, replaced today by legitimate, pampered, caressed children brought up under their parents' roof. Believe me, in the final account, expenditure of that nature always enriches a State."

VI. Popular Progress Continued

Nine o'clock chimed. Hunger set to work. I proposed to my indefatigable companion that we should pursue our popular studies over the morning meal.

A kind of restaurant came along in a timely fashion, if it is permissible to attach that name to the simple refectories distributed about the colony. The waitress, the table, the cloth, the cutlery and crockery are all appetizingly clean. We sit down, and the conversation continues apace, without our missing a bite.

"Don't think, my friend, that the district you've just visited is the only one of its kind. There are many of them around Paris, but this is the most complete. Don't think, either, that everything is soothing relief for the masses that have taken refuge here, like those in a temple who have a right to sanctuary. Not in the least. What you see you will find again, grouped around the Mairie, in every district. Paris is overflowing with privileges for the people. There does not exist, so far as I know, any public establishment that is unique, without a tributary.

"In the theaters—and I don't except any—places are reserved for them, seats that are comfortable, clean, and, to sum it up in one word, honorable. The prices are modest. They routinely make up a quarter of the audience. It is forbidden to book them in advance; they wait, without overmuch impatience, for the doors to open, under the illuminated galleries, sheltered from bad weather. One no longer takes one's ticket and one's head-cold to the same box-office window.

"In great national ceremonies, in the bosom of the solemnities of science, the arts and politics, the people have their bench of honor, the stalls that await them. Nothing is complete without them. As you can well imagine, a good guard is mounted around their reserved areas, otherwise there would be brisk, quiet invasions, by virtue of the maneuvers of office workers.

"On the railways, their compartments are in every respect similar to those of opulence, almost of luxury—which is replaced by an exquisite cleanliness. Hot water bottles in December, blinds in July, cushions in all seasons. The prices are very moderate. There is better still: tickets for the suburban lines, already lowered during the week, cost even less on Sundays and feast days: a fortunate and moral innovation that gives the artisan, at a stroke, a kind thought and the facility to go on excursions on those days, with his wife on his arm and his children holding his hand.

"On those days, too, in all the workplaces in the State and the city of Paris, the workman plays the bourgeois. For him, it is the seventh day of Genesis. In spite of that, if he has not missed the summons during the week, he receives his wage not for six days but for seven. Between us, that's only just; admit that he would only be getting the right to repose in jest if it were not combined with the money to nourish himself.

"Let us proclaim it loudly, to the glory of Parisians: that evangelical example has been as contagious, and as rapid in its contagion, as that of the midwives. In the major administrations, in factories and department stores, all the way to the doorstep of the corner shop, everyone has bravely acclaimed the Christian precept. On feast days, the workshop falls silent and shop windows are shuttered. It's necessary to confess that on the way there, rebellious displays—and I mean the most flourishing in Paris—have been seen to collapse, never to rise again, under Parisian malediction; but in sum, the holy day of Sunday has remained victorious. Monday is in flight. What Paris wants, God wants."

"Let me come back momentarily to the theaters, the railways, the omnibuses. How are the liberalities imposed on their treasuries financed?"

"From the authority's usual funds, of course: additions to lines, prolongations of privileges, revisions of tariffs, sometimes even annual indemnities. All that were seen previously were subsidies profitable to the wealthy classes; it's only just that the multitude should have its own."

"Wait, look through the windows. What are those two men doing, standing on the sidewalk, one passing out colored pieces of paper and the other counting out silver coins—that postman and that artisan?"

"Those pieces of paper are postal bearer bonds—a recent progress—for a hundred francs or less, valid for three months at most and yielding no interest. One can find them at any post office, and, as you can see, in the postman's box. There's no more expeditious means of transferring small capital sums either between quarters in Paris or between Paris and the provinces. If a worker wants to share his salary with his absent mother he no longer waste three hours of his day—what am I saying?—his entire day. Out there, the good woman is no longer forced to drag herself to the next town to beg for the assistance of two local witnesses because she cannot sign her name—and all to receive a few francs. No, no one would believe that today, if the poor old woman were in bed, incapable of going out, she only had two courses of action: submit to the expense of a procuration passed before a notary or to abandon her son's pious aid to the State."

"It would be better, it seems to me, to issue banknotes of less than a hundred francs."

"They would be in round figures: five francs, ten, twenty and fifty. The postal orders represent, with the aid of additional coupons, the exact sum requested. They would not, moreover, be delivered gratuitously. Would you like to know what a new idea is worth. Listen at the door of the people. Well, the grateful crowd call the postman their 'little banker.'"

VII. Popular Progress Concluded

"These aged relatives you mention, these honorary artisans, are worthy of interest. Have they at least found their place in the midst of so many ameliorations?"

"I'll tell you what I know. The sovereign has founded a shelter for them in Vincennes. The old veterans of the workshop are cordially welcome there; they enter it with joyful hearts. But the doors there cannot open as easily as at the Hôtel des Invalides, for cannons have long silences, while the battle against poverty knows no armistice. It recommences every morning at daybreak. For that reason, a new idea has been born, which, while the working man prepares a future of ease for his family by means of labor, will give satisfaction—at least, one hopes so—to his duties toward his aged relatives. Listen carefully.

"The administration of the Public Assistance, with the aid of the law of expropriation, bought, four kilometers from Paris, the area known as Long-Boyau, a green oasis extending to either side of the railway line to Lyon from Maison-Alfort to Villeneuve-Saint-Georges, where it reaches the Seine. Once having become its owner, its first concern was to build a railway station in the center and to divide the domain up into small parcels, with skillfully-drawn avenues to serve each plot. After that it delivered the whole to the Credit Bank of France with the following instructions:

"Every Parisian worker will be free to have designs on a six-hundred-meter plot of land and to do with it was he likes, on promising to pay once a week, on Sunday, a centime for each two meters of land, for a period of five years—which would make, for the six hundred meters, three francs a week, twelve a month, 156 a year and, in total, 780 francs for the five years.

"That weekly payment of three francs will comprise both the price of purchase and the interest. Acquitted week by week, with no lacuna, it will confer, at the end of five years, the investiture of the plot of land. If the acquirer cannot keep up the payments he will still have the choice either of allowing the plot to be sold at his own risk, with a simplified and economical procedure, accepting the loss or profiting for any surplus, or of abandoning the property to the Credit Bank without any chance of gain, in return for the sum he has contributed thus far, without interest.

"For the worker, therefore, even if he falls into difficulties, it will be a means of saving, a kind of piggy-bank.

"He will, in addition, have the right, by adding a second payment of three francs a week, to demand, when the time comes, the construction on his land of a solid house containing two rooms to the ground floor, two on the first floor, a small cellar and a loft.

"All that has been done, and this is what has resulted from it:

"The area of Long-Boyau has been resold in parcels, and further villages have been marked out on the same basis. The least well-off artisans have made the purchase, first of the land, which they have cultivated for five years, and then of the house. The most robust or the most artful have bought the land and the house simultaneously and have acquitted themselves at the end of five years, by paying six francs instead of three per week."

"Thus far I don't see where the relatives come into it."

"We're getting there. The worker has taken his aged father and mother there. They have cultivated the small domain, guarded and maintained the house. The small income, doubtless very modest, is sufficient for them to live—one needs so little when one has one's own harvest, and that little is so good! Believe me, the privilege of domestic production is easily accommodated in the neighborhood of want. It is a burden, but one has the strength to bear it. They get by there. Then again, the children send small sums from time to time; they come on Sundays, conveyed cheaply by the railway, and those worthy people have the pride, when they embrace their parents, of treading upon their own land, the dream and chimera of their whole lives. They feel that they are proprietors, attached to the land, the heritage of their labor, the horizon of their small family, and hence to the nation, to the order, and to the sovereign, which have given them so much enjoyment."

"Very good, but what deal has the Credit Bank done with the Public Assistance?"

"I don't know, but the contract wasn't difficult. In sum, the land can now be resold on a basis of one franc thirty a meter, interests included. I'll wager that there's a profit on the acquisition *en bloc*.

"No one is permitted to obtain these advantages if he is not French and Parisian, or, if not Paris born, he does not count ten years of continuous residence and labor in Paris."

"Why is that?"

"Can't you see that without that rule, all France would descend on Paris? In any case, establishments of that sort are beginning to spread through the provinces."

Our frugal meal was finished, and our purses had only been lightened by a few coins. A mystery, in the epoch in which we're living, but a mystery explained by the moderate rent paid by our restaurateur and the ease with which he obtains provisions.

We quit the Saint-Antoine colony, only encountering in our passage smiling faces, and very happy ourselves with all that we had seen.

VIII. Material Progress

"Let us now consider physical progress, and know first that the most splendid and fecund of all is the removal of the Canal Saint-Martin and the railways, great and small, all the way to the gates of the city."

"No more canal or railways in Paris! People don't miss them?"

"Miss what? The canal? I won't talk about all the harm it did to Paris—forgotten and forgiven. But tell me what services it has ever rendered? Opened to navigation in 1822, it was already flagrantly unnecessary a few years later—which is to say, when the railways came to gravitate around us. No more reason for being then, but it existed, and was allowed to exist, that's all. In any case, it isn't entirely dead; it flows underground, reduced to the modest role of a large cast iron tunnel, alimenting the houses and drinking-fountains of the surrounding area.

"The circular railway of Auteuil? It no longer did any more, in favor of circulation, than a simple omnibus. The new one, about which I'll tell you shortly, is much more important.

"The lines to the suburbs, the provinces, and beyond the frontiers? Their bourgeois stations, planted in the entrails of the city, certainly offered, by virtue of that circumstance, a few advantages for the comings and goings of businessmen, always in a hurry: short distance economies, it's true, but economies that were dearly bought.

"Look, in order to judge the matter better, place yourself in a balloon, above Paris, and look around. You'll see, in the confines of the city, an edge skirted by four lines: the first is an interior boulevard, the second the fortifications, the third and extramural railways line and the fourth another boulevard. The three thoroughfares and the rampart run in parallel, and thus make a circular tour of Paris. It is to that rim, that set of circular routes, that the railways and highways heading for the metropolis come to connect; it's there, instead of gates, the monuments of stations are planted. Everything is therefore linked, like the strands of a web, and the suburbs too are admirably served.

"Now look down into the interior of the city. You will see rich avenues unfurling over the effaced lines of the railways and the canal, full of sunlight and pedestrians.

"Believe me, it is at present that Paris is truly Paris, the city *par excellence*. On the first of January 1860, at the blast of a whistle, the old enclosure flew away, like a backdrop in the Opéra. Very good—but the furrows of the railways and the muddy ditch of the canal still remained, along with other enclosures forgotten by the demolishers, inside which there was nothing but walls and solitude, mud and rags. Paris has swept away those barrages and all that filth; it has entered everywhere, has spread everywhere, from the center to the circumference. Today its level rises limpidly to the rim of the vase."

"All right, I yield to your lyricism. But what an expense for the city and the State!"

"Bah! You ought to say what profits! Listen. The State, in accord with the Parisian municipal authorities, has conceded to companies the right to take over and parcel out the land occupied in Paris by the railways and the canal, on condition that the acquirers cover it, within an agreed interval, with buildings constructed following an overall plan, and that they build new extramural stations with monumental proportions and elegance. The sale of the land was fruitful—so fruitful that the State and the municipality, for the contingent of advantages they had reserved, found their coffers filling up with banknotes, and the capital being adorned by opulent constructions.

"Apart from those bold reforms you will see many other ameliorations while floating at the height of your balloon. Paris is transfigured, my dear, and if you ask me how that gigantic work was accomplished, I will reply that the services were accepted of a powerful enchantress and numerous small genies, her children.

"The enchantress, you already know, is the new law of public expropriation. Paris is the jewel-case of France, the gateau-city, the fishing-hook-city. It has been said that it merits being a exception, that all in all, it is alone, and ought to have its own law, the law of a father and mother toward an only daughter; that it is useful for the outlying districts if the center is splendid, splendor there being, inversely to the common principle its necessity. Having understood that thought, houses and land were expropriated not only for streets and squares but for great popular foundations like the Saint-Antoine Colony, and also for conceptions of wholeness, grandeur and brilliance."

"One can go a long way with those three words."

"Don't interrupt, I beg you. The protective measures of old are still there, maintaining a good guard, and, in addition, the commission of artists that I mentioned is of a nature to reassure Parisians. I'll go on.

"One bourgeois does not want his hillock leveled, another refuses to fill in his cellar, a third leaves a visible terrain in the state of a rubbish-dump. If the matter is of interest to the municipality, the hillock, the cellar and the rubbish-dump fall into the hands of the city, after a decree, and investigation of public interest, judgment, the fixation of compensation, etc.

"Another innovation: it's no longer necessary that the indemnity be paid out before taking possession. Part is paid in cash; the city pays the remainder over time."

"But..."

"I can guess your objection. The law determined that payment, in matters of public utility, would be in advance. Well, my friend, that statute no longer exists. A great pity, in truth, for Parisians! Their wealth is estimated on a broad footing; they have confidence in the city. In any case, as I've told you, it's a matter of a spoiled only daughter, and the State has paternally returned caution to her clothing allowance.

"Thanks to these facilities, our lord mayor, always devoured by the fever of beautiful things, has been able to lead from the front, with loose reins, large-scale works, some of rigorous utility, others decorative, on either side of the river. He has done it, unusually, without adding anything, or very little, to the charges of the municipal budget."

"Unusual, indeed."

"And yet, quite real, as you'll understand. The city, as far as is possible, does nothing by itself; that's its law. Thus, in every deal, it substitutes companies for itself, to which it transmits its engagements, only remaining involved to supervise and extract its share of the profit, and to reassure, by its guarantee, the evicted proprietors.

"So much for the law of expropriation and its consequences. As for the other means put to work, I'll cite you a few, in summary.

"Fuming factory chimneys have been swept out of Paris, without mercy, as one frees a drawing-room painted with frescos from a smoking hearth. It is forbidden to establish new factories, even if they do not produce smoke. The existing ones are maintained precariously, in return for a gradual indemnity until the epoch of their retreat.

"Terrain ceded by the city must be covered with buildings within a given time, and under the prescribed conditions.

"Finally, the most precious complement of the preceding institutions, is that of a committee of artists—true artists— charged with studying and supervising the execution of the thoroughfares, squares and monuments. It is composed of all the greatest geniuses of France and abroad, genius being cosmopolitan. Its mission is to bring expatriated beauty back to Paris. In some instances it acts by itself, in others it opens competitions. Nothing is free from its control. If a proprietor wants to build, he submits his plans to it. It can veto either the dispositions of the edifice, in the interests of hygiene, or the external appearance, or its points of contact and harmony with neighboring edifices. Where public works are concerned it signs its works magisterially on stone as the poet does in vellum, because it hopes, like him, for immortality."

"Well, I can see that Parisians have abdicated all their rights."

"Their rights to what? Paris is not only for Parisians; it belongs, does honor and brings profit to all. Absorb that thought. After all, if it is a tyranny, the tyranny is elegant, artistic and fertile. The Parisians find it good to allow themselves to be embellished and enriched, without protesting too much."

"You haven't noticed that your enthusiastic chatter has brought us back to our point of departure, the Place de la Bastille."

"I know—it was deliberate. Now look at the square; I permit you to do so. What a harmonious distribution, what a brilliant meeting of brought thoroughfares! To judge it well, let's place ourselves in the center facing the Seine.

"Behind us is the Boulevard Beaumarchais, in front of us the Boulevard d'Italie, the old Arsenal station. You can see it over there crossing the river over the new Pont d'Austerlitz, connecting the Route d'Italie, which is regenerates in passing, to the Boulevard de l'Hôpital, thus connecting by a single magisterial thoroughfare the Bastille and the Porte d'Italie.

"To our right is the old Rue Saint-Antoine; to the side, the new Avenue de l'Arsenal, which has punctured the overly peaceful quarter of Sully.

"To our left is the great Boulevard de Lyon, usurping the course of the former railway, the Faubourg Saint-Antoine and, finally, the Avenue Richard-Lenoir, a cheerful thoroughfare that now traverses the entirety of Paris and is prolonged as far as Pantin, in the place where that obscure, filthy serpent known as the Canal Saint-Martin once crawled and drooled.

"Could one not say that all the sumptuous ameliorations that I sketched just now meet at this point?"

IX. Material Progress Continued

"You will now see file before your eyes a host of examples of petty, familiar, everyday progress. Individually, they are trivial, but collectively, they make up a whole. Let's go along the Boulevard Beaumarchais.

"At intervals of distance, you'll notice these slim and elegant bronze columns; they're new candelabras whose light is artfully put to profit: at the summit, a gas-lamp, above it, a large clock-face, luminous by night, striking four times an hour; to either side of it a barometer and a thermometer. Lower down, large display panels for posters in white, blue, pink and green, all tastefully disposed.

"You're looking at me; this is the thinking: the municipal authority has appointed itself the general farmer of Parisian bill-posting—both farmer and proprietor—and it earns good money thereby, while morality does not lose by it. No more of those filthy advertisements that made women and children lower their eyes, no more pell-mell inscriptions ruining the cleanliness of our streets. A Parisian wall, no matter where, if it is not carved from stone, must be painted in oils. A fence that encloses a plot of land or a property under construction is made of flat planks carefully juxtaposed, covered with oil-based paint. A façade, whether it is called the Rue Mouffetard or the Faubourg Saint-Honoré, is neat and fresh. That is wanted, and it is enforced, and that is what has given Paris the festival air of wealth that delights the eyes.

"Here and there, police-cicerones are on sentry duty, informing foreigners in French, English and German.

"Around us, everything is neat, cheerful and uniform: the tables in front of the lemonade-sellers, the awnings, the chairs, the displays, and even the hand-carts of the street-traders-in a word, everything that has the right, granted by the Prefect, to be stationed or to circulate along the sidewalk and paved areas. Look at these small circular redoubts, so useful for passers-by. For the sake of greater decency and sanitation, the daylight comes to them from above, accompanied by forceful ventilation. They're closed in all directions and equipped with doors that close of their own accord. A particular sign outside indicates which station is occupied; it's the occupant himself who posts that indication, without being aware of it, by means of a mechanism placed beneath his feet."

At that moment a group of people blocked out way. They were clustered around a wooden carriage stopped by a policeman, who was arguing with the driver.

"You're looking at some poor devil caught in default. A legal document is being drawn up. Paris is provisioned and cleaned during the night and morning, until midday. When noon chimes, the carts of suppliers of food, services and materials, and those of cleaners, no longer dare show themselves. Look—the agent is pointing at the public clock; it shows fifteen minutes past noon; the poor fellow is lowering his head.

"Examine that vehicle. It's neatly painted and maintained; it's the model prescribed for heavy transport—and what an ingenious disposition! It serves itself as a balance to measure the weight and volume of the merchandise it carries. The operation can be carried out easily, anywhere. Can you see? The policeman is bringing the mechanism into play, and the cart is telling him whether the weight or the volume is incorrect.

"The authority has extended that honest system to its ultimate limits. Every jar, bottle or cask, and every item of merchandise, no matter what, is stamped, no matter how difficult it might be, with a device indicating its capacity, its weight and its dimensions, and in order that nothing escape its control, the stamp is subject to a fiscal duty."

The scene involving the policeman and the carters was unfolding between the Place Saint Martin and the Place Saint-Denis. I noticed, to my surprise, that the two gates had disappeared.

"You're looking for the two monuments that were erected here and there aren't you? What do you expect, my dear? Those two glories of Louis XIV have been moved. They haven't been lost; they can still be admired at the summits of the Faubourgs Saint-Martin and Saint-Denis."

"It's a great pity, in truth, to have perched the radiant face of the sun and the handsome Hercules felling people with his club so high. They're so ingenious—and most of all, so naïve!"

"Personally, I think it's well done. The hero was planted there, blocking the traffic, no doubt in order to be better admired; there were two centuries of that. Meanwhile, the neighboring ground swelled up, year by year, in accordance with the eternal law of cities; imperceptible, successive, silent deposits were superimposed. The two giants, incapable of rising up, saw their heels, then their feet, buried alive; then two damp craters were hollowed out around them. Finally, uniquely in order to conserve those stones and foundations, it became necessary to cut to the quick, through the heart of the boulevards, a road in the fashion of a ditch, between two masonry escarpments—a ugly and unhealthy affair. Once the two gates had gone, the two squares were simply raised to the height of the neighboring levels; now one can circulate there dry-footed; the sunlight penetrates them—the true sunlight—and there's no longer any danger of breaking one's neck there.

"Don't believe, please, that these two isolated points are alone in benefiting from the clearance; its benefits extend by degrees, all the way to the Bastille. Once, no feminine costume dared to venture here. It was—no pun intended—the Pillars of Hercules of elegant society. To any stroller coming from the direction of the Madeleine, they cried from afar: "Halt there!"—and people stopped, meekly, and turned back. Today they're no long here, thank God. Everything is forgotten and forgiven. The boulevards beyond, like those within, share the same prosperity, because they share the same splendor. Sometimes, trivial things lead to great ones.

"Since we're on the subject of public squares, the time has come to tell you about the system adopted by the committee of artists for the ornamentation of the most celebrated. Those which bear the cachet of an epoch or a reign of the

211

monarchy are enriched with statues appropriate to the situation. Thus, Napoléon I, on his colossal pedestal in the Place Vendôme, Louis XIII in the Place Royale, Louis XIV in the Place des Victoires, and good old Henri IV at the top of the Pont Neuf, now live in company with the warriors, ministers, scientists and artists that made their reigns illustrious. The square has been restored in the styles of those epochs. At the feet of those men of bronze and marble one reads brief captions reminding the people of the services they rendered to France.

X. Material Progress Continued

"Our beautiful city, thus adorned, but tastefully adorned, was enthusiastic to receive, at least once a year, her sisters the provinces, in order to show them her costume and its jewels. She asked for her festival and obtained it, as was only just, since the most obscure hamlet has one. The fifteenth of August, already dear by virtue of the touching memories of the faith, became the festival of Paris, the sovereign and all France.

"It lasts from the Assumption to the second Sunday thereafter, so it can never extend longer than a fortnight, but the only days truly celebrated in a popular fashion—I mean, illustrated by lanterns open air games and fireworks—are the fifteenth of August and the two following Sundays.

"High society willingly stood aside from those kinds of enjoyments; they were not required, said its members, and there was nothing for them there. It was a lacuna in their prejudice. Provision was made for them by composing a program of entertainments familiar to all classes of society. Even the mind is tempted by good fortunes that are not found in any other epoch. Thus, they mingle, albeit in an orderly fashion:

"Horse races in the Bois de Boulogne and Vincennes, with prizes for the winners;

"Premieres of first-rate lyric and dramatic works;

"Symphonies by the Societé du Conservatoire, with the collaboration of the choral societies of Paris and the départements;

"Attractive exhibitions of useful and agreeable arts;

"Academic and political ostentations;

"Shooting ranges for firearms and bows, organized in all the quarters of Paris, with recompenses and distinctions appropriate to stimulate competition;

"Simulated battles on the Champ-de-Mars;

"Vast open circuses in the Bois de Boulogne and Vincennes, for scenic exercises in equitation;

"Balls in the administrative palaces and under marquees;

"Scrutiny for prizes accorded to women in all the quarters; the distribution of the prizes; the marriages of young women endowed by the city;

"The inauguration of great national enterprises, etc;

"Add pleasure trains spreading through Paris like a spring tide;

"All of it composes a varied, lively and national picture. One finds there, alongside the hubbub of the people, the delicate intoxications of which men of the world and thinkers are the gourmets.

XI. Material Progress Concluded

"The best guarantee of calm for a capital is the wise administration of the Head of State. You know that, and you also know that today, more than in any other epoch, we have it. At any rate, the government has judged it appropriate, and no one takes it ill, to place the metropolis out of range of any explosion or attack. To do that, it has devised an ingenious telegraph network, which can be summarized thus: Electric wires profoundly buried underground, defying any destructive hand, linking together, among others, the Ministries of the Interior and War, the houses of the Prefects of the Seine and the Police, and the principal military posts in Paris. Hence they can all, in unison, receive orders from the sovereign in his study.

"Protective forces are, therefore, scattered throughout Paris, and, at a given moment, combined in the hand of the authority."

"I admire that combination; it's truly fortunate and reassuring. But you have better things than that to tell me, have you not? Everyone is at the limit of astonishment when they talk about electricity, the invisible child of magic. You could tell me that the Institut exchanges dispatches with the angels on high, or with the fallen angels down below, and I swear that I'd take you at your word. Come on, where are we up to? What are the latest results that have been observed?"

"Oh, you want results? Well, so be it—you shall have them, my dear. I kept silent in that matter, curious as I was to show you Paris in its most luminous facets, but finally, since you want it, here it is..."

"How you catch fire!"

"Transport yourself in thought, in order to spare your legs and mine, to the heart of the Faubourg Saint-Honoré, a little above the Église Saint-Philippe du Roule. You'll find two buildings in front of you. One of them, a vast building with a severe physiognomy, encloses a hospice of the Quatre-Vingts. The other, which one might take for the Florentine abode of Lorenzo the Magnificent, of the Medicis, is a madhouse, neither more nor less.

"Push the door of the former and you will find yourself in the heart of the republic of the quasi-blind: men, women, children, old people, the rich and the poor mingling pell-mell, all making impotent efforts to hold on to a little of the light that still reaches them. Now ask the attendant on duty to introduce you into the palace next door; go into its rooms decorated with frescos and you will see people there well-dressed, holding their heads high and speaking loudly, but struck by idiocy at the age when reason is ordinarily in full flowers."

"God forgive me, that's the preface of a fantastic novel."

"I'm getting to the facts. Light springing from electricity served, first of all, to illuminate the subterranean galleries of mines; the day after, public square and streets; the day after that, factories, workshops, department stores, theaters, barracks; the day after that, domestic interiors. In the presence of that radiant enemy, the eyes initially stood firm, but dazzlement followed by degrees, ephemeral at first, then periodic, and, in the final count, obstinate. That was the first result."

"I understand—but what about the madness of the great lords?"

"Our bigwigs of finance, industry and business thought it good, since the opportunity was offered, to steal a march of Mother Nature—who, let it be said in passing, had treated them meanly, in enclosing them between oceans and mountains. They told themselves that those shackles, acceptable at the most for matter, were unworthy of their genius; that they ought to be able to go around the globe in thought, while remaining at repose."

"Now it's a lecture in philosophy."

"No, the game would be too beautiful. I'll finish. For that, each of them had attached in his study, at a corner of his desk, the electrical wires that attached his coffers to our colonies in Africa, Asia and America. Comfortably seated at his table, he chatted by means of his fingers with the distant correspondents at his counters strewn over the Earth's surface. One told him, at ten o'clock in the morning, about the wreck of a millionaire ship, lost with all hands and cargo, in the seas of Oceania; another, and five past ten, about the sudden collapse of the most solid company in the Americas; a third, at ten past ten, about the radiant entry into the port of Marseille of a ship laden with everything harvested in the vicinity of San Francisco—all one after another. Those poor heads, robust as they were, buckled, as the shoulders of a Hercules of the marketplace would if he loaded them with ten sacks of wheat instead of one. Hence the second result. So you want more."

"Thank you—that's heart-rending.

"Don't despair too quickly. In the chapters of the intellectual and moral, Paris has great compensations to offer you.

Come this way; consoling pictures await you on the banks of the Seine."

"Go on—I'll follow you."

XII. Moral Progress

"Why have you brought me here, to the main courtyard of the Palais de Justice? I've been familiar with this monument of Old Paris, the ancient residence of our kings, for a long time."

"Leave the edifice to one side; it's not that with which I want to occupy you, but the beneficent innovations to which it gives shelter. Hold on, there's no need to go any further; let's approach these two Messieurs coming down the step, smiling at one another affectionately."

"They're certainly not antagonists."

"We'll see—ask them yourself."

"You seem happy, Messieurs," I said to them. "If it's not an indiscretion, be so kind as to allow us to share your joy, which is overflowing, and tell us the reason for it."

"No indiscretion, Monsieur; to satisfy your kind curiosity is a pleasure for us. We're brothers, heirs of two estates separates by a paltry dividing wall. When I say brothers, we have only been that for a quarter of an hour. To list all the follies that that devil disguises as old stonework put into our heads would be impossible. We've been fighting for thirty years, Monsieur—thirty years! And we'd still be fighting now if this palace, the arena of our hatreds, hadn't opened its adjustment chambers to us.

"I can see in your eyes that you don't understand. I'll explain it to you.

"When a difficulty arises—and know that the current proceedings certainly belong to the category of difficulties arisen—it is sorted out in the study or before the tribunal of a justice of the peace. There's no innovation in that, except that the two contestants are obliged to meet face to face. If the difference is not ironed out or, as a last resort, judged, it goes into

216

the Palais de Justice, but only by the door to the adjustment chambers.

"Each of those chambers is made up of a president and two assessors. The adversaries appear there in person, without citation, on a simple letter from the president. They each explain their case, with the aid of their advocates; the advocates plumb the legal questions, bringing to light each individual's rights; then the session is adjourned. In the second session, a plan of adjustment prepared by the judges is waiting for them. It is discussed, amended, and, if possible, signed during the same session. All that happened quietly, in private, behind closed doors. The contract is signed by the advocates, and the solicitors; the president adds the final signature."

"It seems to me that the person who raises the difficulty has no great interest in appearing."

"If he abstains from coming, not supporting his claim, he places himself in the wrong and it is rejected. If it is the other who defaults, he condemns himself by his refusal to defend himself, and loses his case."

"What if one of the adversaries is absent through illness?"

"There's an answer for everything; he's granted a delay before presenting himself, or one of the magistrates is delegated to go to him, with the adverse party. In brief, the adjustment judge has full powers to make peace. He acts as the father of a family would act when constituted as an arbiter between his two children.

"Believe me. Monsieur, it's less difficult than one might think for men of authority and good will, calm and enlightened, to reconcile two adversaries. For us, it required a quarter of an hour, no more."

"Yes, a quarter of an hour—but preceded by thirty years, if my memory serves me right. After thirty years and a quarter of an hour of quibbling, one has run out of summonses, recourses, appeals, etc."

"Perhaps not, Monsieur, but in any case, I'm glad that a time has come when the law has said its last word. Two adversaries put in accord by an immutable verdict, doubtless good but not accepted, are still enemies, as before. War has ceased, but the hatred survives. Far from that, in signing an adjustment, people smile at one another, esteem one another, begin loving one another again in new circumstances. So much time has been wasted! That's the difference. Do you understand?"

"Perfectly."

That said, the two brotherly friends, after a cordial salute, went down the staircase arm in arm.

"Those Messieurs lost me on the way, in their explanations, but you can substitute for them. Tell me, if two adversaries answer all the summonses, but in the end they resist the logic and appeasement of their solicitors, their advocates and the pontiffs of adjustment, what happens then?"

"The affair wins its right of entry into the litigious court, and follows its course in the first, second, and sometimes the third instance.

"What? In the third instance?"

"Of course. It goes without saying that our magistracy is out of the affair, in what will follow: impeccable probity, long experience and objectivity are its familiar environment. It isn't a matter of that now.

"That reserve made, let's debate, if you wish.

"In principle and in logic, so far as I know, only inferior and superior tribunals exist, If one assumes, among the magistrates of appeal, more enlightenment and more aptitude for judgment than those of the first instance, the latter are unnecessary. What is the man who loses in the first instance but has the upper hand in the appeal the victor? It's a contingency. He would be vanquished if the court and the tribunal had exchanged magistrates. Of two battles, he has lost the first and won the second. I cannot see there, in good conscience, anything but a man half-vanquished and half-victorious. If two champions have wounded one another, one triumph each; they wait for the deciding pass of arms, to settle matters, that's all. Can anyone tell me why, of two judges having two different opinions, the one who speaks last is fatally the oracle of the truth?"

"Remember that the case going as far as the court of appeal has been investigated and studied with care, that it has emerged from the first ordeal filtered, purified and distilled, having become transparent. Remember, too, that the judges of the second degree are more numerous than those of the first."

"Permit me, my dear fellow...on the one hand, I say loudly that the same study and the same care presides over the first judgment. On the other hand, if the second tribunal presents, by virtue of its composition, more guarantees than the first, why not go to it directly? On that count, it would almost be to admit that those vanquished in the first battle would be naïve if they did abstained from throwing down a second gauntlet.

"In the new system, the three degrees of instance are on the same level. Error being the eternal rock on which the human mind runs aground, it requires two similar decisions on two different levels to cement an immutable verdict; if they are produced successively, all is said. Alternatively, if each of the adversaries has one decision his favor, it is the scrutiny of the third degree that decides. Of course, no one is obliged to exhaust that triple jurisdiction.

"Adjustment never surrenders. It lies in wait for the adversaries even in the bosom of the litigious courtrooms. At every step one takes, one has to take it into account. Thus, one cannot pass from one jurisdiction to the other without presenting oneself again and in person in its study, whether victor or vanquished."

"Tell me, then: such a system, if I'm not mistaken, places the advocates in a permanent state of conflict, between their wishes and the will of the legislator."

"Not at all. Everything has been anticipated, and everyone finds satisfaction in the adjustment. The advocates are better paid for a peace treaty than winning a battle. Apart from that, when the tribunals shut their doors, honorific recompenses are accorded to the magistrates of all ranks, including advo-

cates and solicitors, who achieve the greatest number of rec-
onciliations in a year.

"Let us hasten to say, because it's an essential point, that
the addition of a third jurisdiction has not inflated costs, by
virtue of the economy and simplification of procedure. There
again, the advocates lose nothing; their honoraria no longer
have, as a counterweight in the balance, the volume of the
dossier, but the significance of the affair and the results obtained.

XIII. Moral Progress Continued

"You've seen adjustment sitting, under the judge's toga,
in our civil tribunals; I'm going to show you, standing between society and the guilty party, other adversaries, holding
one hand out to one and one to the other, obtaining, for their
reconciliation, indulgence and pardon.

"When a poor fellow falls, by virtue of a first stumble,
into the hands of the law, whether it is a matter if a misde-
meanor or something more serious, he appears before the tribunal of pardon. The case is heard behind closed doors. If the
guilty party confesses, if the damage he has done to another
party is repaired, if the judges, having become family counselors, recognize in his tears and in the intervention and solidari-
ty of relatives and friends sufficient guarantees for the future,
he can be absolved. Furthermore, the tribunal of pardon only
answers to itself; its prudence and its soul are its code. Everything that happens there remains buried there.

"What about society?"

"Well, what about it? Do you believe, in conscience, that
a young man, a child, confused by his first false step, weeping
before his family, before the judge, who opens his arms to
him, is a very redoubtable enemy? Locking him up, as was
done before, was done in order to correct him, it was said.
Leave him there for three years, three months, or three days, if
you wish; then wait for him on the threshold and see whether
he has been corrected. Instead of a fever of childhood, light

and ephemeral, you will see him come back among us impregnated with the moral plague that reigns permanently in prisons, like typhus on the edges of a marsh. I need only take for a witness the nickname given to prison by its regular guests: college. Tell me, the college of what? Of French? Of morality? Of religion? No. Of argot, of theft, of murder—yes. He goes in trembling, his expression humiliated; he comes out with a firm tread, holding his head high.

"By contrast, pardon is expiation by speech, without jail, and hence without contagion. The sin is forgotten by all, except the one granted mercy. He has sworn to become better, and he does. Instead of the furtive eye of a policeman, his family watches over him, honest protection at which he does not blush.

"Go interrogate the Prefect of Police; he will tell you that his disarmed justice does more than the brigades for the security of Paris.

"And besides, Christianity, the religion of our land, recommends the forgetfulness of injury and pardon. 'Let him who is pure cast the first stone.' That precept has remained a prisoner in the holy book for a long time. It was the prerogative of the State to bring it out, to spread it by example. The kindly face of Christ radiates in the law court, above the head of the judge."

"If he is really there, he must be pleased!"

"No oath is demanded from one who is granted mercy. Well, one sees those poor, bewildered, sobbing creatures raise their hands toward God, who looks them in the face, and take him as their witness for the promise they make.

"That isn't all; after the pardon, the indulgence.

"When the time for punishment arrives, for misdemeanors or crimes, a new scale of penalties is applied, elongated at the bottom by several rungs. One begins with a reprimand; it is pronounced in open court, with the doors open, but without any other publicity. Afterwards, and by gradations, come corporal and pecuniary punishments, as before, but in more clement measures."

221

"I doubt that a reprimand ever serves as Medusa's head for a bandit."

"There are no bandits among those who trip up. One is not born a bandit, as one might come into the world missing and arm or crippled. In sum, what is society doing? It is calling to its aid the conscience of its enemy, his good instincts, his dignity, for there is all that is yesterday's guilty party. Yes, I contend, a reprimand is a punishment for a man who still feels, just as a crown of laurels was once a triumph. I will go further, and say that one punishes with two whips: rehabilitation and lashes; but one only corrects by means of the first; with the second, one extracts vengeance. A tip of the hat addressed, in the right time and place, to someone who does not merit it, does more to moralize than scorn or anger.

"Let's get back to punishments; they are scales with just measure; the only difference is that the point of departure is situated lower down. Three months and six months of simple captivity are, in my eyes, equal to three years and six years of convict labor. Hard labor for life, or relapse, is a ring stuffed with poison for Mithridates. The conscience of the one, like the stomach of the other, has been hardened, that's all. And then, human life is so short, so full of punishments of every sort—as witness poverty."

"In truth, my dear, I'm saturated with philosophy and progress. Five o'clock! And I've been admiring since five in the morning! An entire circuit of the clock-face in the contemplation of marvels, in truth, is too much."

"One more step. I've reserved, for the final scene, the sight of the most beautiful place on earth, and the most blessed creation of heaven. It's at the top of the Champs-Élysées. Come on, follow me; this will be our final stage."

I resume marching, relaxed and mobile, as if borne up by such beautiful words.

On the threshold of the Palais de Justice, my companion, pointing a finger at the Tribunal of Commerce, tells me that after thirty years of irreproachable work, in the shop, the factory or the fallow field, after investigation, scrutiny, the homologation of the consular tribunal, etc., one can be elevated to the rank of honorary merchant, industrialist or agriculturalist; that the dignity in question is conferred by a decree of the Head of State, on the recommendation of the corporation to which the candidate belongs; and that a decoration denounced to everyone the respects of those men nobly aged by labor.

On the way, in the Place de la Madeleine, he shows me the edifice that has replaced the old Bibliothéque de l'Arsenal, exiled to the Sully quarter, where it no longer has any guests but its books. He tells me that all the libraries in Paris receive workers between nine and five o'clock, and after dinner, between seven and nine o'clock; that the catalogues of each of them, printed and published, ordered by subject and alphabetical order, are put at the disposal of the public; that in addition, erudite men are permanently stationed there, in shifts, forming a second repertoire, but a repertoire that thinks and reasons, easier to interrogate.

Not far from there he points out to me, in passing, the new auction house—an establishment regenerated and reconstituted on an entirely new basis, he tells me, very useful to the opulent classes and more useful still to honest households of artisans.

Finally, we reach the foot of the Place d'Étoile; it is the land of Canaan, praise God!

XIV. Moral Progress Concluded

"Confess that this plateau has not stolen the name of Place de l'Étoile."

Twelve avenues, broad and rectilinear, converge at the center like twelve luminous spokes escaping from a planet; between those spokes, majestic town houses; in the middle, at the place of the star, the superhuman monument that the entire world has come to salute.

"My friend, you've wasted your rhetoric. I've seen all this before my departure from Paris."

223

"No, you're mistaken. The Arc de Triomphe was not yet surmounted by that colossal golden ball, the image of the terrestrial globe, on which one sees engraved our legions and our cannons, and our fleets navigating in Europe, Africa and Asia. Those circular houses, of a very different aspect, sober and sinewy, as heavy as anything great, only existed then in a sketchy state; nor are you familiar with those four groups.

"Learn that Parisians have paid homage to Napoléons in two city squares: in the Place de l'Étoile to Napoléon I, in the Place du Trône to Napoléon III. Out there, as here, a military monument testifies to the prodigies of valor accomplished under the two reigns. Here and out there, four bronze groups, each of several individuals, give life, by means of ingenious and touching allegories, to the principal civil and charitable institutions that recommend both emperors to the love of the nation. They are:

"In the Place du Trône:

"The Credit Bank of France;

"The extension of the limits of Paris and the Transformation of the capital;

"The Societies of Mutual Aid and the Treasury for Retreats in old age;

"The principal charitable establishments created for the relief of the masses, such as the Shelter of Vincennes, the Society of Mothers, the Prince Imperial's Orphanage and the Society for the Abolition of Child Labor.

"In this square:

"The Civil Code and the Université de France;

"The Concordat signed between the First Consul and Pope Pius VII, the signal for the reopening of the churches;

"The Imperial Order of the Légion d'Honneur;

"The Bank of France.

"Each pedestal bears a caption with the date of the foundation. The block representing Paris mentions the great works accomplished under Napoléon III."

"These additions are beautiful, I agree, and completely worthy of the location, which has no equal anywhere, but it's seven o'clock, and, without reproach, I'm collapsing with fatigue and hunger."

"That isn't the only reason I've dragged you here. Look in this direction, listen to me for five minutes, and then tell me whether you still regret our forced stage, and waiting for our dinner."

And he pointed a finger at one of the circular buildings. The setting sun illuminated the fronton of the edifice. There I read the following words, inscribed in golden letters on a white marble backcloth, and framed by a fiery aureole:

Parliament of Peace

"It's here," he told me, "that the great assizes of Europe are held, composed of the great nations. Each one sends two or three delegates; all of them defend the rights of their country, but only one of them cast a ballot. To the ball deposited in the urn by each people a number is attached a number of votes equivalent to its relative importance in the European league.

"The court pronounces as an arbiter as often as possible, and if not, as a supreme court, on the following questions:

"The Nationalities of peoples;

"Differences between a nation and its sovereign;

"Reparations for international insults, violations of treaties, territorial borders, usurpations; and, in sum, any difficulties emerging between brother peoples;

"Excessive extensions of dominations or influences susceptible of threatening the balance of European power;

"Defense, either of all Europe against anyone, or of one of its people against the aggression of a foreign nation within the league;

"Finally, the treatment of black people, piracy, tyranny, and all questions of elevated humanity and general interest.

"For the sake of greater clarity, it is a family league, appeasing by conciliation or cutting short by means of the sword when necessary, any quarrel:

"Between a people and its sovereign;

225

"Between two peoples.

"Between the league and outsiders.

"A vote once passed—but only after deliberations, offers of arbitration and indefatigable efforts of adjustment—is an immutable oracle. Its execution becomes the act of an executive power resident on the head of one of the sovereigns elected by the league. The common forces at his disposal form the total of contingents furnished by each people, in proportion to its size.

"Thus far, let us say hastily, the solutions have been peaceful; the executive power has not taken up arms.

"It is the Head of State who nominates our three representatives. He has the right to recall them. They are replaced or reappointed every three years.

"That is not all. In addition to its great debates, the parliament has scheduled for discussion an ensemble of questions that, at first glance, seem to have nothing to do with peace. They do not, it is true, have the pretention of constraining peoples to lay down their arms, but, believe me, they will work usefully to that result, by establishing between them gently, without their being aware of it, habits of commerce and amity. These are the principal ones:

"The adoption of a common language, a language that will be taught in the public schools of all States, but only, of course, after the study of the national language;

"A uniform system of postal tariffs;

"Identical regulations and prices for the great European railways, for passengers as well as merchandise;

"General reciprocity in the regime of passports and protective measures for foreigners;

"A single money everywhere; identity of values, titles and modules; one of the faces European, the other national;

"The same system of weights and measures."

"All that is truly great, to the point of the sublime, almost the divine."

"That right. Also, I believe that, without an inspiration from on high, it would not be given to anyone, I don't say to take a great enterprise to its conclusion, but to attempt it. Furthermore, Providence had silently prepared everything:

"The massacre between the two Americas, the disorder in world commerce, the distress in the bosom of the working masses;

"Engines of destruction refined to the point that war has become truly impossible;

"The new world rearing up, ready, once its family affairs are regulated, to hurl itself upon the old.

As you can see, the terrain was good, and the idea, having fallen, could not refuse to germinate.

"As for the fruits, they have surpassed all expectation.

"Mass disarmament, by order of the Parliament of Peace, had pushed Europe into unexplored paths. To speak only of France, her position is such, at present, that she has been able to devote herself, with full hands, to agriculture, the arts, commerce, industry and the ever-gaping needs of multitudes. I say devote herself, but as one devotes the month of November, sack in hand, to newly plowed furrows. It is at such a point, I tell you, that already, in the great book of public debt, one things after another is being crossed off; there are some who say that our century will see the volume close of its own accord, having become unnecessary."

"What! No more public debt!"

"Perhaps…one day...

"But an even more interesting consequence, if that is possible, of the new state of things, is that peoples have been able to come into such close accord, by themselves, on conditions of labor and competition between nations. They have been able to establish an understanding, no longer here and there but everywhere: an understanding equitable and protective for the consumer, the manufacturer and the worker, making law for all. That question, you know, is life or death for the masses and..."

XV. Anticipated Denouement

"Well, indefatigable sleeper, have you quite finished snoring? You quit my company in Lyon, when the train pulled away, and here we are in Paris."

"What! Are we pulling into the new station?"

"What new station?"

"You know very well, outside the walls of Paris, at the gate."

"No, we're at the Gare de Lyon, in Paris, on the Boulevard Mazas. Come on, you're still asleep. Wake up!"

"Oh, my friend, what a beautiful dream I've had!"

"I congratulate you for it. After all, you haven't wasted your time, since you've consecrated it to repose."

"Yes, perhaps I haven't wasted my time, even in dreaming. Oh, if I were sure of it, I'd soon go to sleep again!"

Victor Hugo: *The Future*

From the Introduction to the Paris-Guide
(1867)

In the twentieth century, there will be an extraordinary nation. That nation will be great, which will not prevent it from being free. It will be illustrious, rich, intellectual, peaceful, and cordial to the rest of humanity. It will have the gentle gravity of an elder. It will be astonishing in the glory of its conical projectiles, and it will have some difficulty in determining the difference between the general of an army and a butcher; the red of the one will not seem very distinct from the red of the other. A battle between Italians and Germans, between Englishmen and Russians, between Prussians and Frenchmen, will appear to it as a battle between Picards and Burgundians appear to us. It will consider the spillage of human blood as futile. It will only experience a mediocre admiration of a large number of men killed.

The shrug of the shoulders that we give with regard to the Inquisition, it will give with regard to war. It will look at the battlefield of Sadowa with the expression with which we look at the quemadero of Seville. It will consider as stupid the oscillation of victory that invariable ends in funeral returns to equilibrium, and Austerlitz always balanced by Waterloo.

It will have almost the same respect for "authority" as we have for orthodoxy; a lawsuit against the press will seem to it as a trial for heresy seems to us; it will consider vindictiveness against writers as just as we consider vindictiveness against astronomers, and without comparing Béranger closely with Galileo, it will no more be able to understand Béranger in a cell than Galileo in prison. *E pur si muovo*, far from being its fear, will be its joy.

It will have the supreme justice of bounty. It will be modest and indignant before barbarians. The vision of a raised scaffold will be an affront to it. In that nation, punishment will soften and decrease in increasing education like ice in the rising sun. Circulation will be preferred to stagnation. People will no longer be prevented from passing. Frontier rivers will be succeeded by arterial rivers. Cutting a bridge will be as impossible as cutting off a head.

Gunpowder will be drilling powder; saltpeter, the present utility of which is piercing breasts, will have the function of piercing mountains. The advantages of the cylindrical bullet over the round bullet, and the flint over the fuse, of the percussion-cap over the flint, and the hammer over the percussion-cap, will be incomprehensible. Marvelous culverins thirteen feet long in hooped steel, able to fire either hollow or full bullets, will leave people cold. There will be no gratitude for the Chassepot surpassing the Dreyse or the Bonnin surpassing the Chassepot.[52] That in the nineteenth century, the continent, for the advantage of destroying a town, Sebastopol, sacrificed the population of a capital, seven hundred and eighty-five thousand men, will seem glorious, but singular.

That nation will esteem a tunnel under the Alps more than the Armstrong cartridge. It will push ignorance to the point of not knowing that in 1866 a cannon weighing twenty-three tons was fabricated, named Big Will. Other beauties and magnificences of the time will be lost; for example, those people will no longer see budgets, such as that of present-day France, which makes a pyramid of gold every year ten feet square at the base and thirty feet high. A poor little island like Jersey will think twice before indulging, as it did on the sixth

---

[52] The Chassepot was the standard French military rifle in 1867. Dreyse was a prominent German arms manufacturer earlier in the century whose name survived his death (in that same year) as a brand. "Bonnin" is probably a misrendering of "Browning" but appears to be common to all the printed versions of the article.

of August 1866 the whim of hanging a man whose gibbet cost two thousand eight hundred francs. There will be no more luxury expenditures of that sort.

That nation will have for legislation a facsimile bearing as close a resemblance as possible to natural law. Under the influence of that dynamic nation, the incommensurable fallow lands of America, Asia, Africa and Australia will be offered to civilizing emigration; the eight hundred thousand cattle annually burned for the hides in South America will be eaten; it will reason that, if there are cattle on one side of the Atlantic, there are hungry mouths on the other.

Under its impulsion, the long trail of the wretched will magnificently invade the rich and fat unknown solitudes. People will go to California or Tasmania not for gold, today's coarse and deceptive bait, but for the land; the starveling and the barefoot vagabond, those dolorous and venerable brothers of our myopic splendors and egotistical prosperities will have, in spite of Malthus, their table served under the same sun; humanity will swarm outside of the cemetery, become narrow, and cover the continents with its hives. The probable solutions of problems that are ripening, heavier-than-air and directed flight, the sky populated by aerial vessels, will aid these fecund dispersions and pour life everywhere over that vast ant-hive of laborers.

The globe will be the house of humankind, and nothing of it will be wasted; the Corrientes, for example, that gigantic natural hydraulic apparatus, that venous network of rivers and streams, that prodigious ready-made irrigation system, traversed today by swimming bison and ferrying dead trees, will bear and nourish a hundred cities; whoever desires it will have on virgin soil a roof, a field, wellbeing and wealth, on the sole condition of enlarging throughout the earth the idea of fatherland, and considering himself a citizen and laborer of the world; with the result that property, that great human right, that supreme liberty, that mastery of mind over matter, that sovereignty of humanity forbidden to beasts, far from being suppressed, will be democratized and universalized.

231

There will be no more ligatures, no tool-gates on bridges, nor customs-barriers at city-gates and State frontiers, nor isthmuses between oceans, nor prejudices in souls. Initiatives alert and questing will make the same sound of wings as bees. The power-house nation from which movement will radiate over all the continents will be among other societies what a model farm is among smallholdings. It will be more than a nation, it will be civilization; it will be better than civilization, it will be a family.

Unity of language, unity of money, unity of measurement; unity of meridian; unity of legal code; fiduciary circulation to its highest degree; paper money ensuring that any rentier has twenty francs in his pocket; a incalculable added value resulting from the absolution of parasitisms; no more idleness of arms bearing arms; the gigantic expense of sentry-boxes suppressed; the four millions per year that permanent armies cost left in the pockets of citizens; the four million young workers honorably annulled by the uniform restored to commerce, agriculture and industry; iron disappearing everywhere in the form of blades and chains and reforged in the form of plows; peace, the goddess with eight breasts, majestically seated in the midst of men; no exploitation, whether of the small by the great, or the great by the small; and everywhere the dignity and the utility of each sensed by all; the idea of domesticity purged of the idea of servitude; equality emerging ready-constructed from gratuitous and obligatory education; gutters replaced by drainage, punishment by education; prison transformed into school; ignorance, which is the supreme indigence, abolished; a man who cannot read as rare as one born blind; *le jus contra legem*[53] understood; politics absorbed by science, the simplification of antagonisms producing the simplification of events themselves; the artificial aspect of events eliminated; for law, the incontestable, for the unique senate, the Institut.

---

[53] Law (in the sense of right) against the law (in the sense of legislation).

Government restricted to that considerable vigilance, highways, which has two necessities, circulation and security, the State only ever intervening to offer patronage and purification gratuitously. Competition on absolutely equal terms, in the presence of the type marking the minimal standard of progress. No impediment anywhere, the norm everywhere, College normal, the factory normal, the warehouse normal, the shop normal, the farm normal, the theater normal, publicity normal, alongside liberty. The liberty of the human heart respected by the same title as the liberty of the human mind, love being as sacred as thought. A vast march forward of the crowd Idea led by the spirit Legion.

Circulation multiplied tenfold having the result of production and consumption multiplied a hundredfold; the miracle of the multiplication of bread become reality; watercourses dammed, preventing floods and poisonings, which will produce life at a lower cost; industry engendering industry, arms calling to arms, work done ramifying in innumerable works to do, a perpetual recommencement emerging from perpetual achievement, and, everywhere, at every hour, under the fecund ax of progress, the admirable rebirth of the heads of the holy hydra of labor.

For war, competition; for the mob, intelligences toward the dawn; impatience for good scolding slowness and timidity; all other angers vanished; a people excavating the flanks of night and operating, to the profit of the human race, an immense extraction of light; that is what the nation will be.

That nation will have Paris for its capital, and will not be called France; it will be called Europe. It will call itself the Europe of the twentieth century, and in the following centuries, further transfigured, it will be called Humanity.

Humanity, the definitive nation, is at present only glimpsed by thinkers, those contemplators of penumbras; that what the nineteenth century is witnessing is the formation of Europe.

A majestic vision: there is in the embryogeny of peoples, as in that of individual beings, a sublime moment of transpar-

233

ency. The mystery consents to allow itself to be seen. At the moment where we are, an august gestation is visible in the womb of civilization. Europe, united, is germinating there. A people, which will be France sublimated, is in the process of being born. The profound ovary of fecund progress bears the future, in that form henceforth distinct. That nation to come is palpitating in the Europe of the present like the winged being in the reptilian larva. In the next century, it will deploy its two wings, one made of liberty, the other of will.

The fraternal continent, such is the future. If everyone plays his part, that immense happiness is inevitable.

Before having its people, Europe has its city. If that people does not yet exist, the capital already exists. That seems a prodigy; it is a law. The fetus of nations proceeds in the same way as the human fetus, and the mysterious construction of the embryo, simultaneously vegetation and life, always commences with the head.

Gustave Marx: *Love A Thousand Years Hence*
(1873)

One

It is generally unknown that for centuries, the Great Kabbalah, or Occult Science, is the only science that has rendered great services to humankind.

It is by virtue of that science that humans learned about writing, numbers, astronomy, the compass, gunpowder, printing, magnetism, the telegraph and the steam engine. The art of healing owes its best and simplest prescriptions to it. Philosophy and politics owe everything to it. Strangely enough, it is from a race scorned by the vulgar that all these treasures of science, religion and human knowledge have emerged.

It is generally by rabbis replete with years and knowledge that the great physicians, celebrated monks and illustrious philosophers who have traversed the centuries have been initiated—after long and dangerous proofs—into the revelation of some progress, of some mystery that brought innumerable changes and advantages to nations. It is to the Kabbalah that secrets societies are owed, and it is to the Kabbalah that, after centuries of service, the three great divine words were brought to light.

What were Moses, Solomon, Plato, Mohammed, Gutenberg, Luther and Franklin? Great and august initiates!

The author of these few lines is one of the most infimal among the infimal initiates and the publication of these pages will close the doors of the temple to him forever, for he belongs to the impatient, and is committing a great sacrilege by revealing what ought not to be revealed. But what does it matter? He is one of those who desires enlightenment for everyone and not for a few rare privileged individuals, and if he must pay with is life for his indiscretion, he will die without dread, for he is merely relieving his conscience.

Two

In my capacity as an initiate, I received, two days ago, a letter from my brother Mardochée, and it is that letter I want to communicate to you, because he who has the truth in his hand ought to open it.

Before then, however, I ought to tell you, my friends, who Mardochée is.

Mardochée was born on 22 March 1852. He is the unique heir of Rabbi L. Scheloumé of Iffendorf, a small village in our dear Alsace.

The old Rabbi is of the holy tribe of Levi.

He married six times; he married, by turns, the five sisters of his first wife, and, as if the finger of God had struck him, he could not conserve one of them.

He had eleven sons. He lost them all successively. His children bore the names of the first eleven sons of the patriarch.

The final words of the sixth wife, Refk Sephora, were: "The child who will be born, and whom I shall not see, should not be called Benjamin; it is necessary to name him Mardochée, and he will live."

Rabbi L. Scheloumé, who as a zealous believer in the Kabbalah, said: "What must be, will be," and he did not murmur against the Eternal, who took his last wife from him.

But he consecrated his son, as the nasir Samson had once been consecrated.

Before publishing his letter, I ought to tell you that it was during the war of 1870 that I knew Mardochée.

A native of Nancy, I belonged to the *garde mobile* of the Meurthe, Mardochée to that of the Haut-Rhin.

Both wounded and taken prisoner, confined in a village in Silesia, our characters gelled during the long hours of captivity, and after a few proofs, Mardochée instructed me in the

Kabbalah, which is the unique language of the Children of God and the friends of humankind.

The letter came to me from New York.

The old Rabbi and his son, having been unable to opt for Germany, had departed for America, without abandoning all hope of return.

Three

New York, 25 March 1886[54]

My only friend,

It is under the influence of the most vivid joy that I address these few lines to you; I know that everything fortunate that happens to you rejoices your heart, so I am in a hurry to make you party to my felicity.

It is nothing but a dream, my dear friend, but a dream so beautiful that I cannot forget it, and will never forget it as long as I live.

In confiding it to you, I am proud of it, and if I did not have such a great respect for the Kabbalah I think it would be good to make it known to our fellows. This is the dream:

For a month, my father had been pensive; in the evening, he looked at me in a strange way, but with increasing affection. He prayed with an even greater ardor, perhaps, than usual. He sometimes shut himself up in our oratory for hours on end. A week ago, he came to me and said:

"Mardochée, the great day is approaching, that of your dear birth, and also that of the death of your poor mother. Tomorrow, you will fast with me, and in the evening"—and in saying these words, his gaze and his voice had a supernatural quality—"my son, you will drink the water that will enable you to see ten centuries: the marvelous water that I have prepared for you since the day of your birth; the water that the

---

[54] This date is inconsistent with the others given in the text, and was presumably altered in the reprinted version of the story without the others being altered to match.

237

great prophets Isaiah and Jeremiah drank, and which only one person may drink every hundred years.

"Your heart will not weaken at the last moment, because, you know, the one who drinks the water and who has committed a single sin against God or men dies instantly, and I would not like to be your murderer. Is our soul pure?"

"Yes, Father," I replied, simply.

The next day, my father and I fasted; in the evening, my father accompanied me to the little room where I slept; he poured me a few drops of a green liquid whose taste was unfamiliar to me, but which had an extremely sweet flavor.

Scarcely had I taken that beverage than my head became heavy, my eyes closed and I went quietly to sleep, my hands in those of my revered father.

This is what I dreamed.

Four

I was in Paris in the Champs-Élysées, but that promenade had been subjected to extraordinary changes. I found myself a short distance away from the Place de la Concorde, where, like the enigma of the Pharaohs, the needle of granite ornamented with its hieroglyphs still stood; but the Palais des Députés bore little resemblance to the one that I had known.

In its place, a superb temple rose up, of gigantic proportions, surmounted by five magnificent domes, whose base was formed by thousands of columns of porphyry, marble and gold.

Colossal statues crowned the edifice. On its fronton was inscribed: *Temple of Concord.*

I perceived a great number of devotees dressed in bright costumes, holding crowns of laurels and enormous bouquets of roses in their hands.

The wind brought me a faint echo of delightful melodies coming from two sumptuous kiosks placed to either side of the façade of the temple, where two orchestras of a hundred musicians in satin, silk and velvet uniforms were located.

The Champs-Élysées resembled an immense forest sculpted by skillful sylviculturalists.

Somber groves of centenarian chestnut-trees could be seen there, into which the sun never penetrated, and which rendered an inexpressible coolness.

On all sides, trees of the most bizarre forms rose up, forming various and charming tableaux in which all the shades of green were fused, against the azure of the sky.

Numerous birds with multicolored plumage and delightful songs were flying through the air.

Fountains rose up at the corners of all the pathways.

A thick and velvety lawn was resplendent with myriads of buttercups and large daisies, extending as far as the eye could see, inviting repose.

Silvery sand was spread in the spacious pathways, where brilliant carriages were transporting the excursionists.

In the large avenues, the trees were linked together by garlands of honeysuckle, which hid the branches hung with chandeliers, and when the lights came on in the evening, as if at a stroke of a magic wand, the lighting must have been magical.

Villas, chalets and kiosks hidden behind hedges of laurel, lilac and virgin vines were visible in all directions.

The Champs-Élysées had become a veritable paradise.

Five

I was sitting on a bench.

A stranger stopped in front of me, who said to me: "Young man, you've come from far away, very far away; you seem surprised by all this magnificence of nature."

"Indeed," I replied.

"I have been charged with serving as your guide. Take my arm, and I will bring you up to date with matters that might interest you."

"But who gave you to suppose…?"

"You shall know that in due course, Mardochée," he told me, smiling. And exclaimed: "Oh, young man, the centuries have moved on since the year of grace 1873"—and he smiled ironically as he pronounced those words—"for it is now the twenty-second of May 2873, and you have slept for a thousand years in drinking the holy liquor."

"That's true," I said, without reflection.

"Yes, Mardochée," he went on, gravely, "ten centuries have gone by, and in those ten centuries, everything has changed—everything!"

And he drew me away, walking rapidly. Then he cried, enthusiastically: "Holy and great Kabbalah, it is to you that all this felicity is due!" And he traced feverishly, with his cane, in the white sand of the pathway, an alpha, the first letter of the sacred alphabet, which darted blue flames and vanished into the air.

Six

"But where shall I begin, and, moreover, import chrono-logical order into my story?" he said, suddenly. "Mardochée, I have been sent to inform you as to the march of those ten centuries; lend me an attentive ear, and through the events, recognize the face of the Eternal who presides over all the actions of humankind.

"I shall initiate you into all the progress accomplished in those ten centuries, and you shall see how everything down here holds together and is connected.

"One of the greatest inventions that transformed the globe was certainly that of human wings."

"Human wings!" I exclaimed.

"Oh, don't be astonished, my dear child, for you will learn of things far more marvelous in due course.

"It was, I believe on the ninth of September 1954 that the celebrated Dumont Dartois revealed his first wings.

"Like all elite minds, Dartois had only had, in the course of his existence, one single dream, one single hope and one single goal.

"He wanted to steer balloons.

"He sank a considerable fortune into fruitless attempts.

"Day and night, he dreamed and forged aerial vessels, balloons with fins, flying houses, aerostats with propellers. He had renounced amour, friendship, everything; he lived alone with his books of geometry and his mathematical instruments.

"A hundred times he thought he had succeeded, but, a new Icarus, he fell back to earth, broken, for want of the lever, the breath, that gives life to the machine, and which every inventor seeks.

"Often, he wanted to kill himself, but what retained him to existence was is eternal hope, and his work.

"During his last experiments, he took refuge in the country on the solitary banks of the Marne, at Petit-Bry; and here in the company of his forge and his alembics, he passed in the locale for a veritable alchemist, for he had veiled the search for his terrible unknown.

Seven

"One evening, he received an anonymous letter in which someone said to him: 'Dumont, tomorrow at dawn go to the temple in the Rue Notre-Dame de Nazareth, and see.'

"Dreamers, scientists and poets are great believers.

"The next day, he went to the temple, at the early hour when the ten primary faithful were reciting the daily prayer for the dead, and after the audition of the Kaddish, a mendicant curbed by old age approached him. Dumont gave him a large offering.

"'Thank you, Master,' said the mendicant. 'For your alms, hear this: I know the language of the birds. The other day, an indiscreet swallow said to me: *How ignorant humans are! They believe that we can fly. Birds do not fly; they swim in the air.*'

"Dumont shook the old man's hand and said to him: 'Who are you, illustrious envoy of Adonai?'

"'My name is Rabbi Akiva ben Gombel. I have followed your ambitious work for a long time; but do you believe that it would be a good thing if humans could traverse the skies, as they cleave the ocean, where they once discovered a new world?'

"'I believe that the greater humans are, the more they will recognize their pettiness before the works of Providence,'

"'Alas,' said the old rabbi, 'humans are very ingrate; however, the hour has sounded, you work shall see the light of day, but always remember the Eternal, for the one who invokes his name will never be forgotten, and the work of his hand will succeed.'

"And the old man disappeared.

Eight

"Dumont returned in haste to his dwelling, and resumed work furiously. He sensed something divine within him, driving him to his endeavor.

"The needle that he held seemed to him to be animated and guided him through the cloth that had been so rude before. For an hour he worked; his arms were exhausted—but the wings were made.

"He only had a little gutta-percha and a few centimeters of cardboard, but the work seemed alive; throughout the labor, the sacred breath was recognizable. Dumont waited feverishly for the arrival of night. I have said that he had retired to a solitary street, the Rue de la Marne, in Petit-Bry.

"At ten o'clock, he opened his window, and, with an anxious and tremulous heart, he put on the wings.

"Scarcely had he fitted them to his shoulders than he felt himself rising up and launched into the immensity. He only pronounced one name: *Miriam*; and he flew, like a giant bird, through the air.

Nine

"It required a few minutes to tame the work of his hands, but he had soon mastered it, and he spend the whole night soaring through the atmosphere, sometimes rising up like an arrow to infinite heights with frightful rapidity, sometimes describing curves, traversing vast forests, surprising frightened birds in their nests, whose song fell silent at his approach. The miracle had happened! Henceforth, humans had wings! The inventor went home—but he was no longer the same man; he was transformed, and the gleam of success gave his gaze a splendid radiance.

"The next day, he went to the Marais, to one of the small manufacturers with which Paris is overflowing.

"Paris always contains within its walls a host of outsiders, in the arts, in commerce and in industry.

"The most curious are the outsiders of industry: the Parisian manufacturers of articles.

"Who knows what miracles of genius and patience are given birth every day between the Porte Saint-Denis and the Porte Saint-Martin, what curious poverties and what incredible fortunes can be discovered among these Bohemians of industry.

"More than one has gone without food in order to procure, in the Sentier quarter, the piece of muslin with which he is going to create myriads of artificial flowers that will inform astonished generations as to whether the weather is propitious to go to Saint-Cloud, or whether Saint-Medard is worthy of faith.

"More than one has deposited his last mattress with a complaisant pawnbroker to buy a few sheets of gilded paper with which, thanks to a bizarre procedure, our artist will throw a new article into the arena, which, for a week—no more and no less—will cause a resounding sensation, will be in all hands, will depart for all lands, and after having inundated the world, will disappear from consumption and will be extinguished as if it had never existed.

243

"It was to one of those skillful workers that Dartois went.

"'Here is a model,' he said. 'I need a thousand of them by this evening.'

"'Wow! Fins!' said the artiste. 'Are you going to populate aquaria with rubber fish. It's an idea. I can do that.'

"'I want a thousand objects similar to this specimen; I'll pay what's necessary, and there'll probably be a larger order in three days...'

"Pardon me, Monseigneur," said the smiling artist, "can you clarify the order?"

"'Here's a thousand francs,' said Dartois, handing him a banknote.

"'That's too much,' replied the artiste, bowing, 'but I never turn down money, so I'll make you two thousand of your swimmers, and if you desire, they'll say *Papa* and *Mama*.'

"Our inventor could not help smiling, and he left.

Ten

"The next day, Dartois, accompanied by a workman, went to the Thiers barracks, which were situated in the Place du Château-d'Eau.

"A colossal statue had been erected in that square to the Liberator of the territory.

"With the years, the glory of the illustrious citizen had increased further and public gratitude had given him a splendid monument. The statue was in white marble. The great man was standing, with one hand resting on the lion of Belfort.[55]

---

[55] The Lion of Belfort is a huge sculpture by Fréderic Bartholdi—the sculptor of the Statue of Liberty—made to commemorate the dogged French resistance during the siege of Belfort by the Prussians between December 1870 to February 1871. It was not completed until 1880, so this inclusion suggests a latter date of first publication than 1873; smaller replicas were

"An immense genius with deployed wings was crowning the Statesman with golden laurels. The railings that surrounded the monument were literally covered with immortelles.

"Dartois went past the statue and into the barracks.

"Introduced to the colonel, whose office was situated on the first floor, Dartois tried to explain his discovery to him briefly.

"The other initially took him for a madman. Confronted by his hesitation, Dartois put on his wings and, the window being open, launched forth into the courtyard, which he circled for a few minutes, to the amazement of the colonel, the officers and the soldiers who ran to all the windows to see the flying man.

"Dartois, having rejoined the colonel, told him that he had brought a thousand more sets of wings with him, with which he wanted to pay homage to his regiment.

"The colonel, radiant, had the call to the flag sounded. In an instant, all the men were assembled in the courtyard.

"Dartois fitted each man with his wings personally, informing them in a loud voice, as if he were a drill instructor, of his new theory.

"When he thought the instruction complete, the regiment having been divided in platoons, sections and companies, a new command was heard for the first time: 'Forward flight!'

"And the entire regiment, rifled shouldered and kitbags on the back, sappers, drummers, band and canteen workers to the fore, took off into the air.

Eleven

"The band was playing the eternal and heroic *Marseillaise*.

"In two files, the regiment went to take up a position on the boulevard facing the barracks.

---

made for various locations including the Place Denfert-Rochereau in Paris.

"The crowd, the Parisian crowd—which is to say, an enormous, bewildered, unconscious crowd growing by the second; a variegated, crazy and shrill crowd—surrounded the soldiers, touching their wings.

"The word spread that those military men had emerged from their barracks like a flock of wild birds, and the crowd was breathless and feverish in the expectation of something great.

"People were already shouting: 'Hurrah for the line!' and they had not seen anything yet.

"Suddenly, a drum-roll caused all noise to die down in the vast square, and to the precipitate sound of the charge, the regiment, with Dartois and the colonel at the head, rose into the air, to cries a thousand times repeated of 'Long live Republic!' and 'Long live Progress!'

"The spectacle, moreover, was magnificent.

"In a few seconds, the military men traversed the boulevard to go and alight in front of the Chambre des Députés, at the end of the Pont de la Concorde.

Twelve

"But the crowd had followed, and even preceded, the soldiers.

"The people of Paris, impressionable to excess, could not see the phenomenon of winged men without an extraordinary emotion.

"People went from door to door, proclaiming the new miracle.

"The shops closed all over the city. Only the cafes and the taverns stayed open, crowded with curiosity-seekers.

"The députés and the ministers were in the Place de la Concorde.

"The President of the Republic himself, hastily alerted, arrived to compliment Dartois, and, with an accolade, pinned the medal on him that he had so nobly earned.

"Carried in triumph by the people, Dartois was escorted back to his little house in Petit-Bry.

"That day, the Marne, furrowed by boats, was reminiscent of the grand canal in Venice.

"Paris, decked with flags, illuminated as if for a fête, was intoxicated and enchanted.

"As there is always a spot on the sun, however, in the midst of the concert of felicitations that the press and the telegraph were expanding through the world, a petty so-called orthodox newspaper leaked a bittersweet article in which it predicted some great misfortune for the nation because of that new progress provoked by Lucifer.

"Dartois was offered a million for his invention. Like all great men, Dartois was scornful of money, and refused, but he obtained from the government an undertaking that a hundred thousand sets of wings per month would be put within range of the public.

"That discovery brought large number of people to Paris from all over the globe, running to acquire wings. But Dartois had no rest, until the day when he could accomplish his great idea: that of undertaking a voyage to the Moon."

"To the Moon!" I could not help exclaiming. "That's impossible!"

"Nothing is impossible with the aid of God, Mardochée, but let's not anticipate events. At any rate, Dartois died six months after his invention. Everyone has his task down here; he had done enough for humankind; it was someone else who had the honor of making the first journey to the Moon."

I looked at my cicerone with an interrogative expression.

"I can see in your gaze that you want to make an experiment with human wings; nothing is simpler, for I always carry several pairs with me.

"Since the inventor Dartois they have made immense progress; as you will see, they are, above all, not cumbersome.

He undid the buttons of his shirt-cuffs, which opened up in the form of a fan. He pinned those improvised wings to my shoulders. From a little gold-mesh purse he took out an exactly similar pair, and pinned them to himself. After a slight effort, I felt myself rising gently into the air.

"Where do you want to go, Mardochée?" he asked me.

"To Iffendorf, in Alsace," I replied.

He looked at the little compass mounted in his ring and replied: "That's fine."

As we were at an altitude of about twelve hundred meters, I felt a sharp pain in my temples and ears, as if my blood, violently compressed, were about to break through the arteries to escape.

I said to my guide: "I'm doomed."

Smiling, however, he made me breathe from a little bottle, which immediately restored me completely.

"It's the liquor of life, and when they breathe it the devotees of the Kabbalah say the following prayer: '*Baruch atah Adonai merayai amaisim.*' Be praised, Eternal, who revives the dead!"

Scarcely ten minutes had gone by when we arrived, with no other difficulty than that slight indisposition, quickly calmed.

Thirteen

I had difficult recognizing my poor birthplace. It was entirely transformed; it was a true city—but for the child, the cradle always has certain ineffaceable signs, and I could not help shedding a few tears in front of the place where the modest school had once stood in which I learned to read.

It was certainly unrecognizable, but I found profoundly incrusted, on a stone bench that time had cracked and covered with moss, the debris of a multiplication table that I had made myself when I as teaching my fellow pupils calculus.

I headed thereafter for the little cemetery, where I had a great deal of difficulty finding the graves of my family. I saw my own crypt and that of my children, and after having paused for a while before the tombs of my relatives I said to my guide: "Once there were three separate cemeteries: that of the

Catholics, that of the Protestants and that of the Jews. To-day..."

"I know," he said, smiling. "Once, there were three religions in Iffendorf, and there were thirty thousand of them on Earth."

"Well?"

"Today, there is only one," he said, gravely. "Yes, Mardochée, men are all brothers now, and not only the people of our planet, but those of the Moon, Jupiter, Saturn and billions of stars. Races and colors differ, but the human heart is the same everywhere. The great fusion is accomplished, there is no longer more than one religion in the universe; the reign of Unity, so often announced and predicted, has arrived."

And in the tone of an ancient prophet, he cried: "*Shema Yisrael Adonai eloheinu, Adonai Ehad!*"[56]

Listen, Israel, the Eternal is our God, the Eternal is One.

Fourteen

"But then," I said, as if impelled by a secret instinct, "there is no more than one sole language, one sole people, one sole flag, and it was merely a deceptive illusion when I saw written in our beautiful French on the walls of my old city: *Liberté, Egalité, Fraternité, Unité!*

"Yes, dear child, you saw correctly," he said, embracing me effusively. "It is glorious France, it is your holy fatherland, that has been chosen to be at the head of nations, because she has always been the most noble and the most magnanimous, because she has always shed without regret, and with joy, the purest of her blood for the great cause of humanity. She has marched at the forefront of progress, at the head; she has placed her liberal flag everywhere—everywhere; here, look!"

He suddenly took me by the arm; we launched into the air, and he showed me, one by one, Vienna, Constantinople,

---

[56] The opening of a verse from the Torah corresponding to the Biblical *Deuteronomy* 6:4.

Moscow, Saint Petersburg, Stockholm, The Hague, Berlin, Rome, Madrid, Lisbon and London; and in all the capitals, on all the palaces, on all the domes and monuments, I saw, delightedly, the glorious tricolor flag fluttering.

"What a triumph!" I exclaimed.

"It certainly is—but it was not by means of tears and blood, but by fraternity alone that it was acquired. But is it not time for you to recover a little strength?"

Fifteen

I had forgotten hunger, but I sat down with pleasure at an elegantly-set table in a courtyard planted with trees, into which we had just penetrated.

My guide told me that we were in Nice. The weather was superb and the orange-trees in the courtyard embalmed that simple dwelling, in the best taste, with their perfumes.

A young woman served us a modest cheese soup, macaroni, a chicken and a salad, all washed down with an exquisite wine.

We chatted while eating, but from time to time I darted an anxious glance at a dog that was a short distance away from us and which did not seem to me to be very friendly.

"It's a wolf," my guide told me.

"A wolf!"

"Have no fear, there are no more dangerous or wild animals. Come here, Lupus."

And Master Lupus advanced awkwardly, as a wolf might advance who wants to be gracious, and licked his hands.

My guide then continued: "Thus far I've only talked about human wings, but progress never arrives alone. Some time afterwards, toward the end of the twentieth century, a Russian Orthodox priest made an exceedingly useful discovery, that of Petrifying Water.

"What is Petrifying Water?"

"That's the name that was given to the discovery that transformed the Russian people, who had lived until then in servitude and misery, into property owners.

Sixteen

"The priest had remarked in the countryside in the vicinity of Odessa that the water of a small pond situated a quarter of a league from his parish sometimes became very dense, especially after stormy weather. He had the idea of spreading gravel there.

"One tempestuous day, while the thunder was rumbling and everyone in the village was involving all the saints of holy Russia, he went on his own to the edge of the pond, armed with a long iron crowbar, and feverishly stirred the gravel that he had thrown into the dormant water. He pronounced cabalistic words, and felt the water and the gravel gradually forming a paste that hardened under the iron.

"When the storm ceased the pond no longer existed; in its place there was a small quarry of gray stone, easy to carve, appropriate for sculpture and excellent for construction.

"The good priest, who did not have a storm to hand every day, but who understood all the resources of electricity marvelously, did not make anyone else party to his discovery at first, but he went a league further on, to another pond, which he similarly filled with gravel. He launched electric currents through the layers, and after a certain labor, he obtained the stone again.

"Soon, the discovery was propagated, and when, with the water and grains of sand, people were able to create stone, huts, shelters and houses rose up everywhere.

Seventeen

"That was a great source of union between people, for it is necessary not to hide the fact that the major source of dis-

251

cord and hated between them, for a long time, had been the question of rent.

"From the day when everyone could easily become a property-owner, life really became cheap.

"I forgot to tell you that in that epoch, an Arab shepherd found that everywhere, even in the most arid deserts, one could cause a spring to well up by means of a magnetized iron bar perforated in a certain fashion.

"Progress succeeded progress as if by enchantment. An Italian discovered a method..."

"Of singing?"

"Better than that, Mardochée, of reading and calculating, which could be learned in an hour."

"And writing?"

"Writing took longer; it required two days because of the different kinds of strokes."[57]

"That's strange."

"Schools sprang up in every village and education gained a marvelous impetus.

"Like a river too long dammed, which broke its dykes, there was a sudden rush, a delirium.

"There were cheap reprints of all the classics and all the books of science; literature and the truth ere laced within the range of the people. Shakespeare, Byron, Schiller, Hugo, Sand, Balzac, Musset and Gautier were in the hands of working people, who devoured their works with delight.

"Paper was, moreover, very common and printing much cheaper since a grandson of Laligant of Maresquel[58] had started making paper with grass and leaves."

---

[57] *Pleins et déliés*, here translated weakly as "different kinds of strokes" is a common French phrase, originally referring to emphatic and delicate operations in calligraphy, it acquired a number of metaphorical meanings, which have a vague correlation with the uses in English of such pairings as "ups and downs" and "fast and loose," but which do not lend themselves readily to substitution.

"With grass!"

"Yes, Mardochée, with the least of vegetables, and America was exporting paper at one franc per hundred kilos.

"But what about the fuel, the coal to power the machines?"

"They could be powered by water, but electricity rendered even greater services. With fifty centimes' worth of electricity, a machine functioned for a week. Enormous vessels were constructed, and railways trains took on large quantities of wagons."

"But what about accidents?"

"They were no longer to be feared, thanks to a brake-mechanism invented by a Bosnian. Every train had a wagon at the head and the tail fitted with a brake with which the train could be halted instantly, and if encounters took place in thick fog, there was no more than a sight friction that no one except the mechanics perceived. But it's nearly one o'clock; what it we were to leave this place?" my guide added.

I made as if to pay.

"Don't do that," said my cicerone, who approached our host.

The latter came to shake our hands, and offered us cigars that had a delicious perfume.

"What is this bizarre hotel, then?" I exclaimed.

"There are no more hotels, Mardochée. All the houses on the globe are open to travelers; everyone receives the same welcome everywhere."

"What a century!" I cried. "Why hasn't it always been thus?"

---

[58] The family firm of Laligant et Guyot set up an important paper-making factory in the town of Maresquel—already well known for that kind of manufacturing—in 1859; by the 1870s, thanks to its automation, it was the most important supplier of paper to newspapers in France.

"Because people were poor and ignorant before. Now that they're educated, and comfortable, there are only men as God created them, humane, good and sociable."

Eighteen

"But there no poor people any longer, you say?"

"Eh? How could there still be any? Not only are there no more poor people, there are no more laborious classes. There are no longer any workers, domestics, slaves or wage-earners."

"There are no longer any rich people or aristocrats, then?"

"What would be the point? Everyone is rich, everyone is noble. There is no longer anything but people who hold one another in esteem, who are equal and who are happy."

"What a dream!"

"But it's the reality, and it had to arrive in the fullness of time by virtue of the sequence of progressive improvements that removed the links, day by day, from the chain of human misery."

"Where are we going?" I said to my companion, for we had bid farewell to our host and had taken to the air again.

"We can returning to Paris if you like, and I'll show you the Capital of the world."

Nineteen

And my guide continued his narration.

"To follow approximately the order of the successive progress brought by the last ten centuries, I should tell you that, from the day when education was generalized and popularized new ideas sprang forth from the most obscure lairs that were easy to realize: utopia one day, routine the next.

"A large number of periodicals were created: scientific periodicals, humorous periodicals, popular newspapers, always at very low prices.

"The people were educated, and wanted more and more education.

"The primitive instruments of labor were improved very rapidly, and arms were folded before the marvelous engines that were constructed to replace them.

"Compositing machines were invented that could print a poster or a newspaper automatically in less time than it took to correct the proofs, but they could not be printed fast enough for the mass of readers.

Twenty

A tailor devised a machine that could produce a hundred overcoats, two hundred pairs of trousers or five hundred waistcoats in an hour.

"A carpenter designed a plane that replaced mechanical saws.

"A baker constructed an oven in which a thousand loaves were cooked in five minutes.

"A painter replaced window-glass with colored transparent paper that did not cut the fingers when it broke.

"Dirigible balloons were made that could carry a hundred passengers.

"Fires were extinguished with a chemical compound.

"Bridges were built over the ocean and across all the seas.

"An Englishman imitated all wines and liqueurs with a few drops of essence.

"A coal-merchant found diamond in a piece of coke.

"A simple confectioner was able to mimic all the precious stones.

"The heart of Africa was penetrated, where no traveler had ever set foot. Forests were found there populated by a highly intelligent species of apes, which, transplanted to every country, replaced humans in all domestic labor.

"Even agriculture, before the voyage to Ceres that I shall tell you about shortly, had made extraordinary progress; agricultural implements, plows and seed-planters, were all powered by electricity; the price of food diminished, and as all the peasants profited from it, there was no more competition, and life no longer cost anything.

"Photography had taken giant strides. It had completely dethroned painting.

"By means of the new methods, people succeeded in immediately depicting forest scenes and entire cities in five minutes, and the walls of the most modest habitations were ornamented with them.

"Soon, people only worked in order to distract themselves. Shops and restaurants opened in which everything was provided gratuitously. One only had to present oneself to take advantage of them. Theaters put on performances for nothing. Newspapers followed suit, and an advertisement taking up the entire fourth page of every newspaper only cost two francs fifty a month.

"Mail was replaced by the telegraph and the telephone, each of which were placed in every town, in every house and on every floor, and eventually, thanks to cables connecting the planets, one could communicate very rapidly with any point whatsoever, from one globe to another.

Twenty-One

"One rather curious thing happened in the year 2250. There was a great exhibition in the Champ-de-Mars in Paris.

"The exhibition opened on the first of May.

"At eight o'clock in the morning the Champ-de-Mars was bare, devoid of constructions and machines; by midday five hundred thousand people of all nations were strolling in magnificent galleries. Everything was functioning; all the industries of the globe were represented there.

"Splendid cafés were open.

"There was a marvelous botanic garden: a superb collection of all the plants, all the birds and insects of all lands.

"Every visitor received a free guide-book to the exhibition, which was printed in front of them, and which included portraits of all the exhibitors.

"On display at the exhibition were music boxes that could replace entire orchestras, umbrella-hats, sleigh-shoes and the famous night-lights that procured the most magical dreams that anyone could desire.

Twenty-Two

"But here we are back in Paris. Let's sit down outside this café and I'll tell you in a few words about human excursions to other planets.

"About a hundred years after the invention of human wings, when all the scientists on Earth had gathered in Paris for a choral festival, it was decided to attempt an expedition to the Moon, all the more so because, for some time, notable changes had been observed in the physiognomy of that planet.

"In certain parts, in the middle of the night, the Moon took on a vivid red coloration; some astronomers even claimed that it was on fire.

"An assembly was thus formed, numbering two thousand, the majority consisting of the greatest scientists of the epoch. They did not take any weapons, but cargoes of jewels and precious fabrics to offer to the inhabitants they hoped to encounter. In addition, they were furnished with an enormous quantity of brass wire, which they were to unroll as they rose into the sky, in such a way as to create a telegraphic cable.

"The weather was magnificent, and the voyage very pleasant; the travelers wore furs in order to traverse the cold currents, but they scarcely perceived any change in temperature because, as they approached the moon, they felt a gentle heat produced by its luminous rays.

Twenty-Three

"The voyage lasted two days because of the delay caused by the extension of the cable.

"Finally, they arrived.

"Would you believe it, Mardochée? They were awaited with impatience, and the red flames perceived on Earth were produced by the burning of vast forests, which the Lunatics had set ablaze in order to signal to the inhabitants of Earth.

"A population of extraordinary mildness was found on the Moon. The Lunatics were very learned, almost all astronomers, and very well versed in calculation. For a long time they had been fabricating optical instruments of an extraordinary powers and precision. They spent their lives gazing at other planets, principally Earth.

"First of all, they had seen human wings functioning. They were very jealous of them, but had been unable to imitate them in spite of all their efforts.

"They had hoped to see a few Terrans disembarking on their world some day.

"The sciences and arts on the Moon were at almost the same point as on Earth; they copied our progress from afar.

"But they were much more gentle and benevolent than Terrans, and had only formed a single family for a long time.

"In matters of religious belief they had retained the Old Testament but practiced the sound and fraternal maxims of the Gospel.

Twenty-Four

"The cable having succeeded perfectly, a dispatch was sent to Earth to announce the success of the voyage and, at the same time, to order the wings that the Lunatics were impatient to acquire.

"The Moon resembled the Earth very closely. It had mountains, lakes and rivers, as down here.

"The Lunatics made a gift to the Terrans of a turquoise that had the quality of taming the most ferocious animals and rendering them as meek as sheep.

"The next day, a second caravan arrived from Earth; it brought a cargo of wings, which were received with enthusiasm, and the Lunatics prepared to make a voyage to the planet Mercury, which was immediately accomplished.

Twenty-Five

Mercury had been chosen because the Lunatics had observed that among the Mercurians there were no cripples, nor hunchbacks, nor any other infirm individuals, as there were among them and among Terrans.

"The reception was extremely cordial.

"They quickly learned the cause of the perfection of the race of the inhabitants of Mercury. They were admitted to the study of medicine from the most tender infancy, and had discovered secrets that cured paralytics, relieved hunchbacks and enabled the lame to walk straight. There were no invalids among them.

"Cuts, falls and wounds were healed as if by enchantment.

"Headaches, toothache and stomach aches were unknown, and the Terrans were very glad to get to know those curious Aesculapians.

A large number of Mercurians received wings, and joined in with the expedition that was made to Saturn.

Twenty-Six

"On that planet there were many other marvels. It was inhabited by an eccentric population that was nourished entirely by bread, and which, with the aid of a certain liquor, had found the means of prolonging existence and no longer aging after thirty years.

"No one among them was unhappy. No more wrinkles, no more white hair, no more false teeth, no more old age, no more annoyances.

"An eternal youth reigned throughout that fortunate planet, which chagrins and anxieties never penetrated.

"They too had seen our wings, but they were not jealous of them.

"They had no envy at all of mortals, having made a pact against death.

"On the arrival of the strangers, they welcomed them fraternally, and informed them of the means to remain immortal, like them.

Twenty-Seven

"The scientists of Earth were going from one surprise to another, and from one marvel to another. They decided to go to Jupiter. On that planet, they found a population even more amiable than those they had found elsewhere.

"The inhabitants of Jupiter, too, brought their tribute to science and progress.

"They had found the means of improving their senses. Thanks to a soap manufactured with the juice of certain plants, which they dissolved in marble vats, they took marvelous baths, on emerging from which the body had obtained extraordinary qualities, which were truly magical. The ears could hear at a distance of a hundred leagues. The eyes could see to infinity. The nose had an extraordinary sense of smell. The hands could break the hardest iron like glass.

"One could go without sleep for a fortnight without experiencing the slightest fatigue.

"And what was most advantageous of all was that one was endowed with a second sight so powerful that the most secret thoughts were instantaneously divined.

They exchanged their soap for human wings and became very good friends with the travelers from other planets.

Twenty-Eight

"As you can see, Mardochée, every planet brought humankind a new marvel. The invention of wings was about to change the world, for everyone was to profit from the benefits brought by virtue of voyages.

"From planet to planet the electric cables were extended. Inhabitants of Earth were arriving all the time, attracted by curious dispatches.

"On Earth, there were continual celebrations and rejoicing. People embraced in the street, congratulating one another; everyone was crazy.

Twenty-Nine

"On the planet Ceres, to which the caravan went, it found the magnificent vegetal growth, the miraculous land, on which everything grew without cultivation. Flowers, fruits, trees, plants, cereals and vegetables, everything that provides shade, all the verdure that delights the gaze, all the woods that shelter the joyful concerts of birds, all the perfumes and all the charms of nature were created instantaneously, and on Ceres, there was no fatigue or labor; the soil smiled at everyone; it was the good mother with fecund breasts, to which the universe went for nourishment and rejoicing.

Thirty

"But the most curious planet of all, and certainly the most appreciated, was Venus.

"One did not find there astronomers, nor physicians, nor fertile soil, nor marvelous soap; everywhere, one found nothing but flowers. Venus was an immense garden filled with birds with melodious songs and insects with ravishing wings; no snow, rain or fog ever penetrated that planet. One saw nothing but rose-bushes, clumps of myrtle and oranges.

"One breathed the sweetest perfume there, and the travelers, hastening from other planets, did not know what to attribute the disturbance by which they were surprised when they set foot on Venus.

"They were on an enchanted and enchanting planet. Venus seemed to be uninhabited. In fact, it was, but the flowers that grew on the branches of the rose-bushes, the myrtles and the orange-trees were seductive sirens that had all the charms, all the seduction, all the grace and all the voluptuousness of womankind.

"They were created purely for amour, they only lived in order to be loved.

"They had ravishing voices, celestial eyes and divine bodies.

"But everything that is intoxicating is ephemeral.

"They only lived for the day when the mouth animated them with a kiss, and when the amour that one experienced for them weakened, they immediately lost their perfume and their color, and their beautiful, melancholy, languid heads suddenly wilted on their beautiful stems, and never recovered.

"To love and to die, such was the fate of the flowers of Venus.

Thirty-One

"The voyage to the planets had lasted six days.

"On returning to Earth, the scientists perceived that many changes had been accomplished in their mores. What was the point, with the new discoveries, of the barriers that separated nations? What was the significance of names, ranks and titles? Even the kings understood and the final congress was held in Paris.

"France was adopted as the Fatherland, for the unique worship of the Supreme Being, and the Musée de Cluny received in deposit, along with the scepters and crowns of empires and monarchies, all the coins, all the banknotes, al the title-deeds, share certificates, bonds and incomes that interest and cupidity had created.

"There were no more stock exchanges, or barracks, or palaces; nor were there any more prisons, hospitals or cemeteries.

"And now, if you would care to cast an eye over Paris…look!

Thirty-Two

"Paris extends, to the north, as far as Amiens; to the south, as far as Fontainebleau; to the east, as far as Meaux; to the west, as far as Chartres. Great cities are the same everywhere.

"They have let out their belts; the world has become the abode of pleasures and joy.

"Everywhere you see boulevards bordered by fruit trees, fountains, cascades, and flowers in every widow.

"Velocipedes with two, four or six wheels, boats, balloons and omnibuses of all sorts are stationed everywhere.

"Every house is a palace containing all the luxuries and comforts of existence. There are no more stairways, no more steps to climb; convenient elevators exist everywhere. In the evening, electric beams of all colors illuminate the cities, where musicians of every land often wander.

"That is the approximate aspect of big cities.

"Newspapers continue to appear, but are given away free.

"The newspapers report news of all the planets.

"Have I told you that there are no more soldiers, or bailiffs, or concierges? That salespeople and waiters have been replaced by elegant and obliging apes?

Everything everywhere is free.

Equality reigns over the entire Earth, and with the most perfect happiness.

Thirty-Three

"There are no more atheists.

"From time to time, some dreamer thinks of denying the existence of God. He is sent to travel on the other planets, and when he has contemplated everything, admired everything, and visited all the works of the Creator, if he is still in doubt, he is transported for five years to some inhabited star and his wings are taken away; after a short while, cured, he asks to come back among human beings.

Thirty-Four

"The science of the Kabbalah has made immense progress.

"People no longer have any great difficulty with its language, once so challenging, and there is no ten-year-old child who does not know the parable of Jehovah, or How Humans Came to Speak, which was once not taught until the age of thirty...."

I expressed to my guide the desire to know that parable.

Smiling, he said to me: "You shall see where humans came from, and I shall tell it to you gladly; you will be able to judge the progress accomplished through the ages."

Thirty-Five

How Humans Came to Speak: A Cabalistic Tale

At the commencement of the world, a very long time before the deluge, the children of Adam lived like brutes in the forests and the fields, in the midst of other animals, which they resembled in the their passions. That lasted for a long time.

A few groups emerged from that human rabble and sensed that there was something superhuman in creation.

Was it the sun? Was it the sky? No matter; they believed in a species of divinity and, involuntarily, they rendered it a kind of homage.

But in that very distant epoch, humans did not speak.

They had neither the hiss of the serpent, nor the roar of the lion, nor the bellowing of bulls. They made guttural sounds, sometimes profound and sometimes shrill. Tears, screams and smiles were their most eloquent languages.

One man among the new believers was cruelly tested by God.

He adored his father, his mother, his wife and his children, and all of them, in turn, betrayed him and deceived him. He had a thirst for honors and glory, and in that epoch, already, there was a certain rivalry, a certain pride, and he was dishonored publicly for a crime he had not committed.

Throughout his misfortunes, through all his disasters, that man never murmured against fate. So God sent an angel to him, who told him: "The name of the creator of all things is Ieoua—Jehovah. I am telling you that because you have been great in all ordeals; but anyone who pronounces that name will perish."

From that moment on, the man's heart became even more noble and he marched through life smiling. Other men, jealous of him, said to themselves in their mute language: "He knows something that we do not know; he must reveal it to us, or we will kill him."

They took possession of him and, under torture, he confessed that he knew the name of the Supreme Being, but that he was not permitted to reveal it to other humans.

Instead of showing him mercy, they lit a pyre to which they had attached him, and the flames were soon licking at the martyr's limbs.

For a long time he suffered in silence, but twisted and broken, half-consumed, when his soul flew away toward his creator he uttered, in his supreme suffering:

"Ieoua! Ieoua!"

When that name resounded for the first time on Earth, a great miracle was accomplished. The man who was burning emerged safe and sound from the furnace and the torturers fell, struck down, at his feet.

But he asked for mercy for them, and God granted that their lives would be spared this time. And in the name of Ieoua, the human who, until then, had had no knowledge of vowels, learned to know them, and speech was given to humankind. But in order not to invoke in vain the name of the Lord, they changed the order of the vowels, and instead of Ieoua they classified them a e i o u.

My guide stopped speaking, and as I raised my eyes, I saw him grow in size and disappear into the clouds.

Thirty-Six

I woke up.

My father, who was praying next to my bed, shed abundant tears of joy on learning from my mouth all that I have just written to you.

He embraced me tenderly and said: "Mardochée, it is necessary to write your dream."

And that is why, my dear friend, I have sent you this long letter, authorizing you to publish it in France, to which we shall soon return. It is too cold here for us; there is only one sun, and it is that of our dear France; there is only one Fatherland, that of liberty.

And now, dear readers, that you know the voyage of my friend Mardochée through the planets, can you guess the one that I would like to inhabit if it were necessary for me to quit the Earth?

It is, however, not very difficult, and I would like each of you to make a brief stay there, if not in reality, at least in dream.

Is not dreaming, for human beings, half of happiness?

SF & FANTASY

Adolphe Alhaiza. *Cybele*

Alphonse Allais. *The Adventures of Captain Cap*

Henri Allorge. *The Great Cataclysm*

Guy d'Armen. *Doc Ardan: The City of Gold and Lepers*

G.-J. Arnaud. *The Ice Company*

André Arnyvelde. *The Ark; The Mutilated Bacchus*

Charles Asselineau. *The Double Life*

Henri Austruy. *The Eupantophone; The Olotelepan; The Petitpaon Era*

Barillet-Lagargousse. *The Final War*

Cyprien Bérard. *The Vampire Lord Ruthwen*

S. Henry Berthoud. *Martyrs of Science*

Aloysius Bertrand. *Gaspard de la Nuit*

Richard Bessière. *The Gardens of the Apocalypse; The Masters of Silence*

Albert Bleunard. *Ever Smaller*

Félix Bodin. *The Novel of the Future*

Louis Boussenard. *Monsieur Synthesis*

Alphonse Brown. *City of Glass; The Conquest of the Air*

Émile Calvet. *In a Thousand Years*

André Caroff. *The Terror of Madame Atomos; Miss Atomos; The Return of Madame Atomos; The Mistake of Madame Atomos; The Monsters of Madame Atomos; The Revenge of Madame Atomos; The Resurrection of Madame Atomos; The Mark of Madame Atomos; The Spheres of Madame Atomos; The Wrath of Madame Atomos* (w/M. & Sylvie Stéphan)

Félicien Champsaur. *The Human Arrow; Ouha, King of the Apes; Pharaoh's Wife; Homo-Deus; Nora, The Ape-Woman*

Didier de Chousy. *Ignis*

Jules Clarétie. *Obsession*

Michel Corday. *The Eternal Flame*

André Couvreur. *The Necessary Evil; Caresco, Superman; The Exploits of Professor Tornada* (3 vols.)

Camille Debans. *The Misfortunes of John Bull*

Captain Danrit. *Undersea Odyssey*

C. I. Defontenay. *Star (Psi Cassiopeia)*

Charles Derennes. *The People of the Pole*

Chevalier de Béthune. *The World of Mercury*
Georges Dodds (anthologist). *The Missing Link*
Charles Dodeman. *The Silent Bomb*
Harry Dickson. *The Heir of Dracula; Harry Dickson vs. The Spider*
Jules Dornay. *Lord Ruthven Begins*
Alfred Driou. *The Adventures of a Parisian Aeronaut*
Sâr Dubnotal *vs. Jack the Ripper*
Odette Dulac. *The War of the Sexes*
Alexandre Dumas. *The Return of Lord Ruthven*
Renée Dunan. *Baal; The Ultimate Pleasure*
J.-C. Dunyach. *The Night Orchid; The Thieves of Silence*
Henri Duvernois. *The Man Who Found Himself*
Achille Eyraud. *Voyage to Venus*
Henri Falk. *The Age of Lead*
Paul Féval. *Anne of the Isles; Knightshade; Revenants; Vampire City; The Vampire Countess; The Wandering Jew's Daughter*
Paul Féval, *fils. Felifax, the Tiger-Man*
Charles de Fieux. *Lamékis*
Louis Forest. *Someone is Stealing Children in Paris*
Arnould Galopin. *Doctor Omega; Doctor Omega and the Shadowmen* (anthology)
Judith Gautier. *Isoline and the Serpent-Flower*
H. Gayar. *The Marvelous Adventures of Serge Myrandhal on Mars*
G.L. Gick. *Harry Dickson and the Werewolf of Rutherford Grange*
Delphine de Girardin. *Balzac's Cane*
Léon Gozlan. *The Vampire of the Val-de-Grâce*
Jules Gros. *The Fossil Man*
Edmond Haraucourt. *Illusions of Immortality; Daah, the First Human*
Nathalie Henneberg. *The Green Gods*
Eugène Hennebert. *The Enchanted City*
Jules Hoche. *The Maker of Men and His Formula*
V. Hugo, P. Foucher & P. Meurice. *The Hunchback of Notre-Dame*
Romain d'Huissier. *Hexagon: Dark Matter*
Jules Janin. *The Magnetized Corpse*
Michel Jeury. *Chronolysis*
Gustave Kahn. *The Tale of Gold and Silence*
Gérard Klein. *The Mote in Time's Eye*
Fernand Kolney. *Love in 5000 Years*
Paul Lacroix. *Danse Macabre*
Louis-Guillaume de La Follie. *The Unpretentious Philosopher*

Jean de La Hire. *Enter the Nyctalope; The Nyctalope on Mars; The Nyctalope vs. Lucifer; The Nyctalope Steps In; Night of the Nyctalope; Return of the Nyctalope; The Fiery Wheel*

Etienne-Léon de Lamothe-Langon. *The Virgin Vampire*

André Laurie. *Spiridon*

Gabriel de Lautrec. *The Vengeance of the Oval Portrait*

Alain le Drimeur. *The Future City*

Georges Le Faure & Henri de Graffigny. *The Extraordinary Adventures of a Russian Scientist Across the Solar System* (2 vols.)

Gustave Le Rouge. *The Mysterious Doctor Cornelius* (3 vols.); *The Vampires of Mars; The Dominion of the World* (w/Gustave Guitton) (4 vols.)

Jules Lermina. *Mysteryville; Panic in Paris; To-Ho and the Gold Destroyers; The Secret of Zippelius; The Battle of Strasbourg*

André Lichtenberger. *The Centaurs; The Children of the Crab*

Maurice Limat. *Mephista*

Listonai. *The Philosophical Voyager*

Jean-Marc & Randy Lofficier. *Edgar Allan Poe on Mars; The Katrina Protocol; Pacifica; Robonocchio; Return of the Nyctalope;* (anthologists) *Tales of the Shadowmen 1-11; The Vampire Almanac* (2 vols.)

Xavier Mauméjean. *The League of Heroes*

Joseph Méry. *The Tower of Destiny*

Hippolyte Mettais. *The Year 5865; Paris Before the Deluge*

Louise Michel. *The Human Microbes; The New World*

Tony Moilin. *Paris in the Year 2000*

José Moselli. *Illa's End*

John-Antoine Nau. *Enemy Force*

Marie Nizet. *Captain Vampire*

C. Nodier, A. Beraud & Toussaint-Merle. *Frankenstein*

Henri de Parville. *An Inhabitant of the Planet Mars*

Gaston de Pawlowski. *Journey to the Land of the 4th Dimension*

Georges Pellerin. *The World in 2000 Years*

Ernest Pérochon. *The Frenetic People*

Pierre Pelot. *The Child Who Walked on the Sky*

J. Polidori, C. Nodier, E. Scribe. *Lord Ruthven the Vampire*

P.-A. Ponson du Terrail. *The Vampire and the Devil's Son; The Immortal Woman*

Georges Price. *The Missing Men of the Sirius*

Edgar Quinet. *Ahasuerus; The Enchanter Merlin*

Henri de Régnier. *A Surfeit of Mirrors*

Maurice Renard. *The Blue Peril; Doctor Lerne; The Doctored Man; A Man Among the Microbes; The Master of Light*

Jean Richepin. *The Wing; The Crazy Corner*

Albert Robida. *The Adventures of Saturnin Farandoul; The Clock of the Centuries; Chalet in the Sky; The Electric Life; The Engineer Von Satanas*

J.-H. Rosny Aîné. *Helgvor of the Blue River; The Givreuse Enigma; The Mysterious Force; The Navigators of Space; Vamireh; The World of the Variants; The Young Vampire*

Marcel Rouff. *Journey to the Inverted World*

Léonie Rouzade. *The World Turned Upside Down*

Han Ryner. *The Superhumans; The Human Ant*

Pierre de Selenes: *An Unknown World*

Angelo de Sorr. *The Vampires of London*

Brian Stableford. *The New Faust at the Tragicomique;The Empire of the Necromancers (The Shadow of Frankenstein; Frankenstein and the Vampire Countess; Frankenstein in London); Sherlock Holmes & The Vampires of Eternity; The Stones of Camelot; The Wayward Muse.* (anthologist) *News from the Moon; The Germans on Venus; The Supreme Progress; The World Above the World; Nemoville; Investigations of the Future; The Conqueror of Death; The Revolt of the Machines; The Man With the Blue Face*

Jacques Spitz. *The Eye of Purgatory*

Kurt Steiner. *Ortog*

Eugène Thébault. *Radio-Terror*

C.-F. Tiphaigne de La Roche. *Amilec*

Simon Tyssot de Patot. *The Strange Voyages of Jacques Massé and Pierre de Mésange*

Louis Ulbach. *Prince Bonifacio*

Théo Varlet. *The Golden Rock. The Xenobiotic Invasion; The Castaways of Eros; Timeslip Troopers* (w/André Blandin); *The Martian Epic* (w/Octave Joncquel)

Pierre Véron. *The Merchants of Health*

Paul Vibert. *The Mysterious Fluid*

Villiers de l'Isle-Adam. *The Scaffold; The Vampire Soul*

Gaston de Wailly. *The Murderer of the World*

Philippe Ward. *Artahe ; The Song of Montségur* (w/Sylvie Miller) *Manhattan Ghost* (w/Mickael Laguerre)

Victor Margueritte. *The Bacheloress; The Companion; The Couple*

MYSTERIES & THRILLERS

M. Allain & P. Souvestre. *The Daughter of Fantômas*
A. Anicet-Bourgeois, Lucien Dabril. *Rocambole*
A. Bernède. *Belphegor*; *Judex* (w/Louis Feuillade); *The Return of Judex* (w/Louis Feuillade); *The Shadow of Judex*
A. Bisson & G. Livet. *Nick Carter vs. Fantômas*
V. Darlay & H. de Gorsse. *Arsène Lupin vs. Sherlock Holmes: The Stage Play*
Séamas Duffy. *Sherlock Holmes in Paris*
Paul Féval. *Gentlemen of the Night; John Devil; The Black Coats ('Salem Street; The Invisible Weapon; The Parisian Jungle; The Companions of the Treasure; Heart of Steel; The Cadet Gang; The Sword-Swallower)*
Émile Gaboriau. *Monsieur Lecoq*
Goron & Émile Gautier. *Spawn of the Penitentiary*
Paul d'Ivoi. *Around the World on Five Sous* (w/Henri Chabrillat)
Rick Lai. *Shadows of the Opera: Retribution in Blood; Sisters of the Shadows: The Curse of Cagliostro*
Steve Leadley. *Sherlock Holmes: The Circle of Blood*
Maurice Leblanc. *Arsène Lupin vs. Countess Cagliostro; Arsène Lupin vs. Sherlock Holmes (The Blonde Phantom; The Hollow Needle); The Many Faces of Arsène Lupin; The Island of the Thirty Coffin; 813*
Gaston Leroux. *Chéri-Bibi; The Phantom of the Opera; Rouletabille & the Mystery of the Yellow Room; Rouletabille at Krupp's*
Richard Marsh. *The Complete Adventures of Judith Lee*
William Patrick Maynard. *The Terror of Fu Manchu; The Destiny of Fu Manchu*
Frank J. Morlok. *Sherlock Holmes: The Grand Horizontals; Sherlock Holmes vs Jack the Ripper*
Jean Petithuguenin. *The Adventures of Ethel King*
Antonin Reschal. *The Adventures of Miss Boston*
Frank Schildiner. *The Quest of Frankenstein*
P. de Wattyne & Y. Walter. *Sherlock Holmes vs. Fantômas*
David White. *Fantômas in America*
Pierre Yrondy. *The Adventures of Thérèse Arnaud*